NEWHAM LIBRARIES

D0190041

SAVAGE ISLAND

For my Uncle Denis, who always bought the best books.

STRIPES PUBLISHING
An imprint of the Little Tiger Group
1 Coda Studios, 189 Munster Road,
London SW6 6AW

www.littletiger.co.uk

A paperback original
First published in Great Britain in 2018
Text copyright © Bryony Pearce, 2018
Cover copyright © Stripes Publishing Ltd, 2018
Mountain illustration © Shutterstock/PNE
Circle illustration © Shutterstock/Hakki Arslan
Map illustration © Artful Doodlers, 2018

ISBN: 978-1-84715-827-7

The right of Bryony Pearce to be identified as the author
of this work has been asserted by her in accordance with
the Copyright, Designs and Patents Act, 1988.

All rights reserved.

A CIP catalogue record for this book is available
from the British Library.

This book is sold subject to the condition that it shall not, by
way of trade or otherwise, be lent, resold, hired out, or otherwise
circulated without the publisher's prior consent in any form of
binding or cover other than that in which it is published and
without a similar condition, including this condition, being
imposed upon the subsequent purchaser.

Printed and bound in the UK.

10 9 8 7 6 5 4 3 2 1

SAVAGE ISLAND

BRYONY PEARCE

RED EYE

Prologue

"What would you do with a million pounds?"

There was something important behind Lizzie's question; I could tell by the way she kept twisting her short dark hair into knots as she showed us into her room. She was a ball of condensed energy, all excitement.

"You bring us up here for a quiz, Lizzie?" Grady asked as he dumped himself on to a beanbag. His knees almost hit his ears and he grinned. Grady could be a bit odd, but his smile was infectious and Lizzie grinned back.

I leaned my skateboard against the doorway, took a Coke from the six-pack Grady handed me from his bag and passed the rest around. Carmen had already made herself at home and was lying on the bed. She downed half of her can before Lizzie opened hers. My brother, Will, eyed his before taking it, as if wondering what Grady would want from him later if he accepted.

Lizzie was still running her fingers through her pixie-cut. I remembered the row three years earlier when she first wanted the style. Her mum had forbidden it, so Lizzie had hacked off her long plaits with nail scissors.

"I thought we were heading into town?" I said.

"I need to show you something first. Take a seat – it'll take a while to load." She switched on her computer, but remained standing.

As the monitor flickered into life, I looked around her room. The last time I'd been in here, the walls had been pastel pink and we'd spent whole days playing *Legend of Zelda* on her Wii. Now the walls were a light blue-grey, the posters had morphed from Justin Bieber into Nina Simone, and there was a pile of climbing gear in one corner. But it was the same desk; I ran my finger over our initials carved into the right-hand side and smiled. The bed was the same too: plain white ironwork, decorated with home-made paper birds and butterflies wired on to the joins. I sank my feet into the rug, remembering the feel of the wool on my stomach, the controller in my hand and Lizzie beside me.

"What happened to your mum's 'no boys' rule?" Will slid into the chair by the desk. The way his hair was always hanging over his eyes drove me insane, but girls liked it, apparently.

"Seeing as I'll be at uni in a few months, Mum got reasonable." Lizzie didn't take her eyes off the screen.

"I'm *so* glad it's summer. I mean, those exams nearly killed me!" Grady took a sip of his Coke and sighed. "Hey, have you heard about the Coca-Cola conspiracy?" He didn't wait for an answer. "Did you know that Coke is the main cause of the US obesity epidemic? These cans contain, like, over forty milligrams of sodium. That makes you even thirstier, so you drink more. It's why there's so much sugar in it – to hide the salt."

I pointed at the Coke. "So, you don't want it?"

"It's all about making informed choices, Ben. I can have a glass of water after." Grady burped.

Carmen laughed. "You *are* funny, Grady."

Will looked sideways at Carmen, then away.

"OK, ready!" Lizzie turned her monitor so the rest of us could view the display and pointed to a spinning logo. "Check this out."

3

GOLD
FOUNDATION

Carmen rubbed absentmindedly at the blue kestrel tattooed on the inside of her wrist. "What's the Gold Foundation?"

"It's run by Marcus Gold," Grady jumped in. "The multibillionaire. He owns half of Silicon Valley, runs all those charities, has that airline – Goldstar." He took a deep breath and carried on. "He's rumoured to be part of Yale's Skull and Bones society. He's definitely a Freemason and probably one of the guys behind 9/11, he—"

"The only people behind 9/11 were the terrorists." Lizzie frowned at him.

Grady sighed. "If you'd ever read the information I send you—"

I kicked his beanbag. "We're never going to take anything written by David Icke seriously, Grady. He thought he was the Son of God. Give it up."

"Guys." Lizzie grabbed her mouse and scrolled down the page. "Look!"

IRON TEEN

Are you the best? Are you driven to succeed?
Are you in top physical shape?
Will you be between sixteen and twenty years old on 15th August 2018?
Can you get a team of five together?
Do you want to win £1 million ... each?

Under-eighteens need permission from a parent or guardian to apply.

Grady rolled off his beanbag and moved closer to the screen. "A million pounds *each*!"

"That's what it says." Lizzie nodded excitedly.

Will frowned. "Why is Gold offering so much money?"

"He's a philanthropist," Lizzie said. Grady snorted loudly but she ignored him. "See here, it says he wants to give bright, proactive teens a push in life. The winners get investment advice to help them make the best of their prize money."

"Well … we don't have to *take* the advice," Grady said thoughtfully. "There's a lot I could do with a million pounds."

Carmen began to skim read the text. "It says we have to fill in a load of assessment forms."

"But what's the competition?" Will put his hands behind his head. "What do we have to do?"

"The teams that pass the assessment stage go into a lottery. Ten teams get chosen and they're flown out to a remote island owned by Gold, where there'll be tests of endurance and intelligence." Lizzie could barely suppress her excitement. "It sounds like orienteering and puzzle-solving along with a bit of geocaching, rock climbing … that kind of thing."

"That sounds great!" I looked at my brother. I hadn't come up with anything to occupy us over the summer. "We'd enter even without the prize money. Right, Will?"

Will shrugged.

"There's nothing in here we can't do." Lizzie bounced on her toes. "We've got Grady's gaming skills for puzzle-solving. Will was the best orienteer when we did Duke of Edinburgh and we all know his brain is a miracle. You can fix practically anything, Ben – and Car, you were brilliant when Noah broke his leg last year. If we pass the assessment and get through the lottery, we could totally win this." Lizzie looked at Carmen. "What do you think?"

"I don't know, *chica*." Carmen avoided her gaze. "I'd have to take time off work. I told the salon I could work full-time, starting next week."

"You enjoyed Duke of Edinburgh."

"I liked helping at the animal shelter. But when I agreed to do DofE you promised that we'd have a *fun* summer. This does not sound like fun."

"A million pounds, Car." Will brushed his hair out of his eyes. "It would pay for vet school."

"That was a secret." She glared at him. "A stupid dream."

"You never told me that's what you wanted to do!" Lizzie adjusted her glasses and sat next to her. "You have to come with us. You'd be a fantastic vet!" She smiled. "We can't do it without you."

"Fine." Carmen threw up her hands. "I can always get another floor-sweeping job if I lose this one."

"What about you, Grady?" Lizzie asked.

He grinned. "I'm in if you guys are."

We'd only let Grady join our Duke of Edinburgh squad after Noah's accident left us a man down and his dad put him forward but, despite his oddities, I was glad we had. Grady never went anywhere without his 'bag of tricks' – he took that old scout motto *Be prepared* to heart. Also, Will seemed to like him, which was a definite plus.

"We're entering then?" I looked around.

"This is going to be *amazing*, you guys." Lizzie leaped up and clicked on the link to download the entry forms.

My phone blinked and vibrated. "Will, Mum's calling."

"She's calling *you*." Will didn't even look up.

I left my drink and went out to the landing. There was no telling what mood she'd be in. I took a deep breath, let the phone ring for as long as I dared and then accepted the call.

"Where are you?" she snapped.

"Hi, Mum. We're at Lizzie's."

"Will's with you?"

"Where else?"

"Don't take that tone with me." I could picture

her sitting on the chair in the hall, her pale brown fringe hanging over her face. Her hair was just like Will's – mine was ginger, like Dad's. "Are you watching him?"

"He's almost seventeen, Mum."

"You know how delicate he is."

My jaw tightened. "Yes, I'm watching him."

"You have to *be there* for him, Ben."

"Yes, Mum."

"He was the worst affected when your father left."

"I know, Mum."

Her tone changed. "You'd better not be eating anything over there. I've got your dinner on."

"Yes, Mum. I mean, no, we're not eating."

Will and I were only allowed what Mum put on the table. This month we were doing the Atkins diet. I never thought I'd miss carrots and I'd kill for a plate of chips.

"Just like your father! You make promises then you go and do whatever you want." She was working herself up; probably standing now, pacing.

"I'm sorry."

I held the phone away from my ear as she began to yell at me. "… your responsibility … don't you go thinking you're too good…"

I waited until she calmed down, then said, "Everything's fine here, Mum, honestly. We'll be back for dinner."

"Promise?"

"Why don't you make a cup of tea and relax?"

"That's a good idea, Ben." Her voice softened and I sighed. I couldn't figure out if she'd worry more when we left home or less. She was the one who had let Will do his exams a couple of years early and apply to Oxford. She wanted to be able to brag about her genius son.

I took a deep breath. "I'll see you later, OK?"

Will looked up as I walked back in. "The usual?"

I tossed the phone on to the bed. "The usual."

The forms had to be filled in by hand and posted, so Lizzie had printed them out. The others had already started. Carmen hummed tunelessly until Lizzie reached over and switched on her old record player. Nina Simone's deep voice filled the room.

"Are you sure your mum will let you come, Will?" Lizzie asked. Her fingers had gone back to her hair, worrying. I wanted to hold her hand to calm her; I gripped my pen tighter.

"She'll be fine with it," Will said.

I snorted. "She won't be 'fine with it'. But Will should be able to talk her round. It would be easier if we could tell the local paper we were applying – she'd love that. But the prize money should go a long way towards persuading her."

"I don't understand this dumb confidentiality clause – why can't we tell the papers?" Grady frowned. "It seems suspicious to me. If this was all above board, it would be *everywhere*."

"It's on the *Internet*, Grady." Lizzie tapped her pencil impatiently. "It *is* everywhere."

"It's not a bad thing," I said. "The fewer people who know about the competition, the more chance we have of getting through."

"Anyway," Carmen added, "do you really want to be in the papers saying, 'We're entering this competition'? If we lose, everyone will know. If we win, we'll be hounded for the money – it happened to my Uncle Javi."

"You have a millionaire uncle?" I asked.

Carmen let out a laugh. "*Chico!* No! He won a year's supply of ham. All he had, day and night, were calls from people wanting free ham." She

11

rolled off the bed. "I don't know my blood type. I need to call Mami. Can I use someone's phone?"

"Out of credit again?" Lizzie tossed hers over.

Carmen caught Lizzie's phone. "Always." She danced into the hall and down the stairs. "*Buenos días*, Mrs Bellamy. You look lovely today!"

I started my own form while Carmen was out of the room, looking up only when she jumped back on to the bed saying, "I am O negative, by the way."

"That's unusual, isn't it?" Lizzie frowned.

"I am Spanish, remember!" Carmen said, as if that explained it.

"Actually," Grady said, "it means you're descended from the Nephilim … or aliens. Opinion is divided on which it is. I'll send you a link."

Carmen grinned.

"Ben, have you got to part two?" Lizzie asked me. "These questions are nuts – listen to this. *Success is based on survival of the fittest; I don't care about the losers.*"

I turned over my page. "I'm not there yet…"

"What are we meant to answer though? I mean, what do they want us to say? Look at these." She shoved her form at me.

12

Choose the answer that most strongly reflects your opinion about each of the following statements. Please answer honestly.	Strongly disagree	Slightly disagree	Neutral	Slightly agree	Strongly agree
Success is based on survival of the fittest; I don't care about the losers.					
I find myself in the same kinds of trouble, time after time.					
For me, what's right is whatever I can get away with.					
In today's world, I feel justified in doing anything I can get away with to succeed.					
I am often bored.					
Before I do anything, I carefully consider the possible consequences.					

I pointed to the question at the bottom of the page. "That's easy – we've got to strongly agree, right? Show that we're going to think things through, not rush into dangerous situations."

"Carmen would have to lie, then." Lizzie ducked as Carmen threw a pillow at her head. "Seriously though – I don't know what they *want*." She looked

13

at Will. "What do you think? Should we tell the truth?"

Will folded his arms. "You're asking me if I think you should manipulate the system?" He showed his Will-grin; a semi-scathing twist of the mouth.

I looked at my form. "You're really OK with cheating, Lizzie?"

"For a million pounds, are you kidding?" she cried.

I shook my head. "There are two *hundred* questions here. It's designed to trip us up. And you don't know what they're looking for – I think we need to answer honestly."

Will nodded. "Ben's right."

"*You* want to be honest?" Lizzie's eyes were round. "*You* – Will Harper?" She turned to Carmen, who flicked her pink-tipped dark hair over one shoulder. "Carmen?"

"It'll be easier to do it as myself, *chica*. More fun."

"I agree." Grady tossed his pen in the air but dropped the catch.

"Of course you do," Lizzie muttered. "Fine. But I'm going to blame you guys if we get rejected before we even reach the lottery."

14

IRON TEEN

1. Congratulations, Elizabeth Bellamy, Torben Harper, William Harper, Grady Jackson and Carmen Holguín. You have been selected to take part in this year's three-day Gold Foundation Iron Teen contest.

2. Please be at Bristol Airport, at 10 a.m. on 17th August, wearing the identification badges included in this pack.

3. Your flight will be direct to the Shetland Islands on a private Goldstar plane, GF124.

4. Make sure you are carrying everything you need. There will be no opportunity to make purchases once you have boarded.

5. Late arrivals will not be permitted to board.

6. Arrival at the airstrip on Fetlar will be at 12.30 p.m. The other teams will have arrived ahead of you. You will be guided from the plane to the crossing, but will be expected to go alone to Aikenhead.

7. Aikenhead is a private island owned by Marcus Gold. There are a great many caves on the island and the wildlife predominantly consists of sheep,

seals and seabirds, including puffins. You will find no information about Aikenhead on Google. Please use the information in your pack to educate yourselves on the island. A data sheet on the local flora and fauna as well as a detailed Gold Foundation survey map, which will be used for reference henceforth, are included.

8. When you reach Aikenhead, proceed to grid reference 53.10:-04.21 where you will find the first checkpoint on the course. There you will find a box containing coordinates for the next checkpoint.

9. Each checkpoint includes a locked box. Your team leader, Elizabeth Bellamy, will need to record your arrival by pressing her thumb on the scanner on the box, which will enable you to open it. Inside is a geocache box. You will need to take the contents of the geocache box and replace them with something of equal or greater value at each checkpoint.

10. The winner will be the team that brings all the geocaches to the final checkpoint within the shortest amount of time.

GOLDPRINT

Elizabeth Bellamy, as you are team leader, the Gold Foundation will require a copy of your thumbprint. Please download the following app: GoldPrint on to a device running iOS 8.0 or later. Press your right thumb on the scanner, follow the instructions and press SUBMIT. Your team will not be permitted to take part in the competition without submission of the print.

GOLD
FOUNDATION

Flora and Fauna of Aikenhead by D. Hodgekiss, by permission of the Gold Foundation

The last ice sheet left Aikenhead around 10,000 years ago, leaving behind a bare landscape of rock, broken stone, gravel, sand and mud. This was then colonized by a scrub of willow, hazel, rowan, poplar and birch. Climatic deterioration during the Bronze Age, around 4,000 years ago, left open, peat-covered moorland and grassland with virtually no tree cover. In recent years, small areas of rowan and birch have been planted by the Gold Foundation in an attempt to 'reinvigorate' the island's ecosystem.

North Atlantic gales sweep across Aikenhead, with gusts of over 173mph. Erosion by the sea has created the cliffs, caves, rock arches and geos (inlets). The North Atlantic Drift brings relatively warm waters moving past Aikenhead from the south. This current is rich in plankton, which pass the islands in a constant stream, supporting a great range of marine wildlife. Over eighteen species of cetaceans have been identified in Shetland waters. The most common around Aikenhead are killer whales, white-beaked dolphins, white-sided dolphins and Risso's dolphins. Minke whales can also be spotted. Seals (grey and common) are frequent visitors. In the autumn, grey seals give birth to their pups in Aikenhead's sea caves. Grey seals have elongated noses and are heavily built, particularly the males, which are 210cm long and weigh 230kg. Common seals are smaller – the males are between 140cm and 190cm long, and have softer, more doglike heads. Otters can also be seen, particularly in bays with streams flowing into them.

The sea cliffs of Aikenhead are 130m high and are home to over 70,000 nesting seabirds. Gannets are common from April to September – a spectacular sight as they dive into the sea from heights of 30m in pursuit of mackerel and other fish. Also breeding on the cliffs from May to September are fulmars, kittiwakes, shags, black guillemots and gulls. There is a thriving colony of puffins.

On the moors above the cliffs, you will find great skuas or 'bonxies', as they are known in Shetland. Walk with caution – these aggressive seabirds will attack intruders in breeding areas. Red-throated divers also breed on freshwater lochs, giving a distinctive high-pitched, wailing *Ya-roo, ya-roo, ya-roo* call.

Plants are small and ground-hugging. Dwarf willow grows in relative abundance. Much of Aikenhead is covered in moorland – a peaty layer on which grow coarse grasses, sedges like cotton grass (bog cotton), heather, orchids and bog asphodel. In sandy soils derived from glacial deposits, heather and grasses grow, as do some rarities such as moonwort, orchids (frog and fragrant), mountain everlasting and fairy flax. Wildflower meadows can also be found.

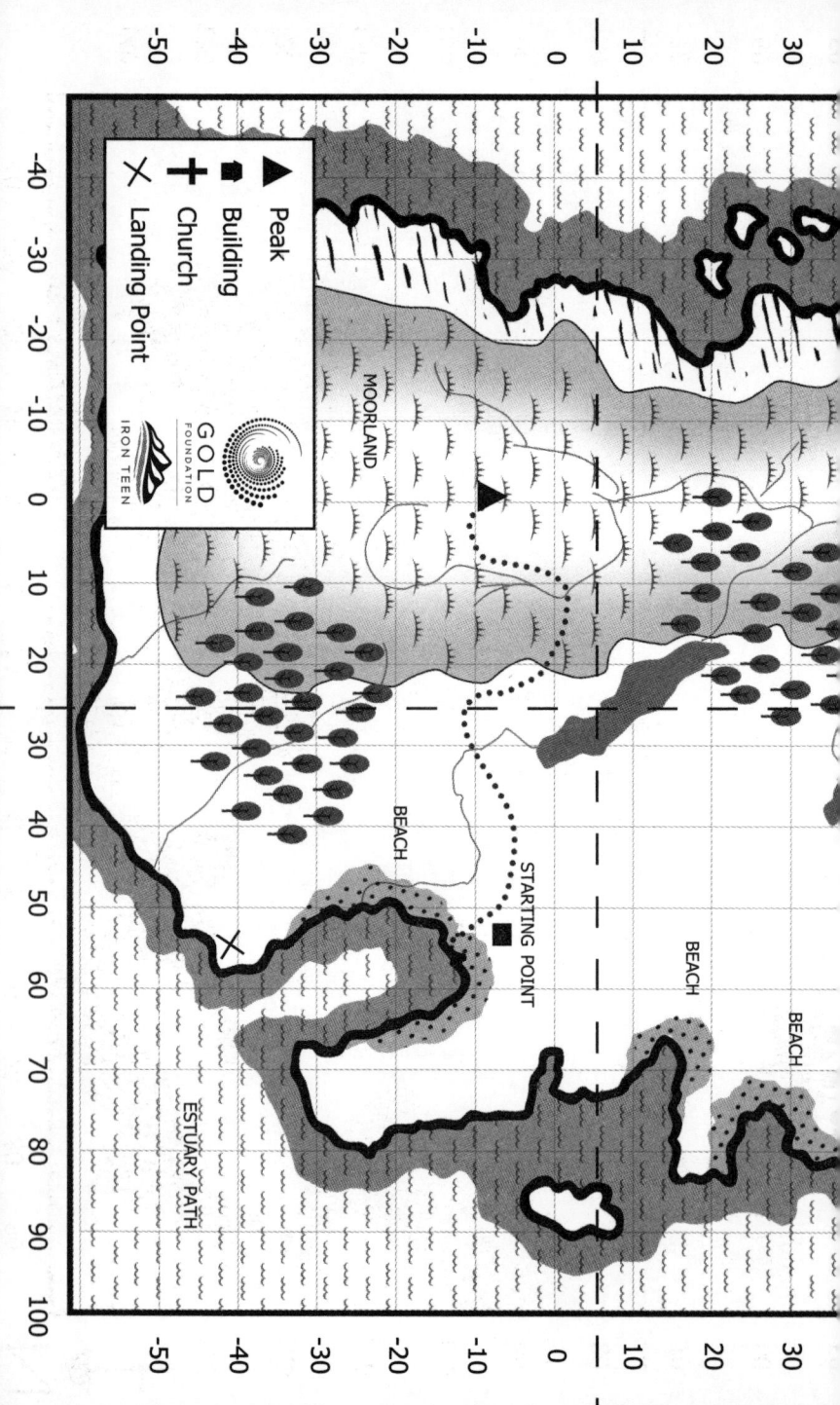

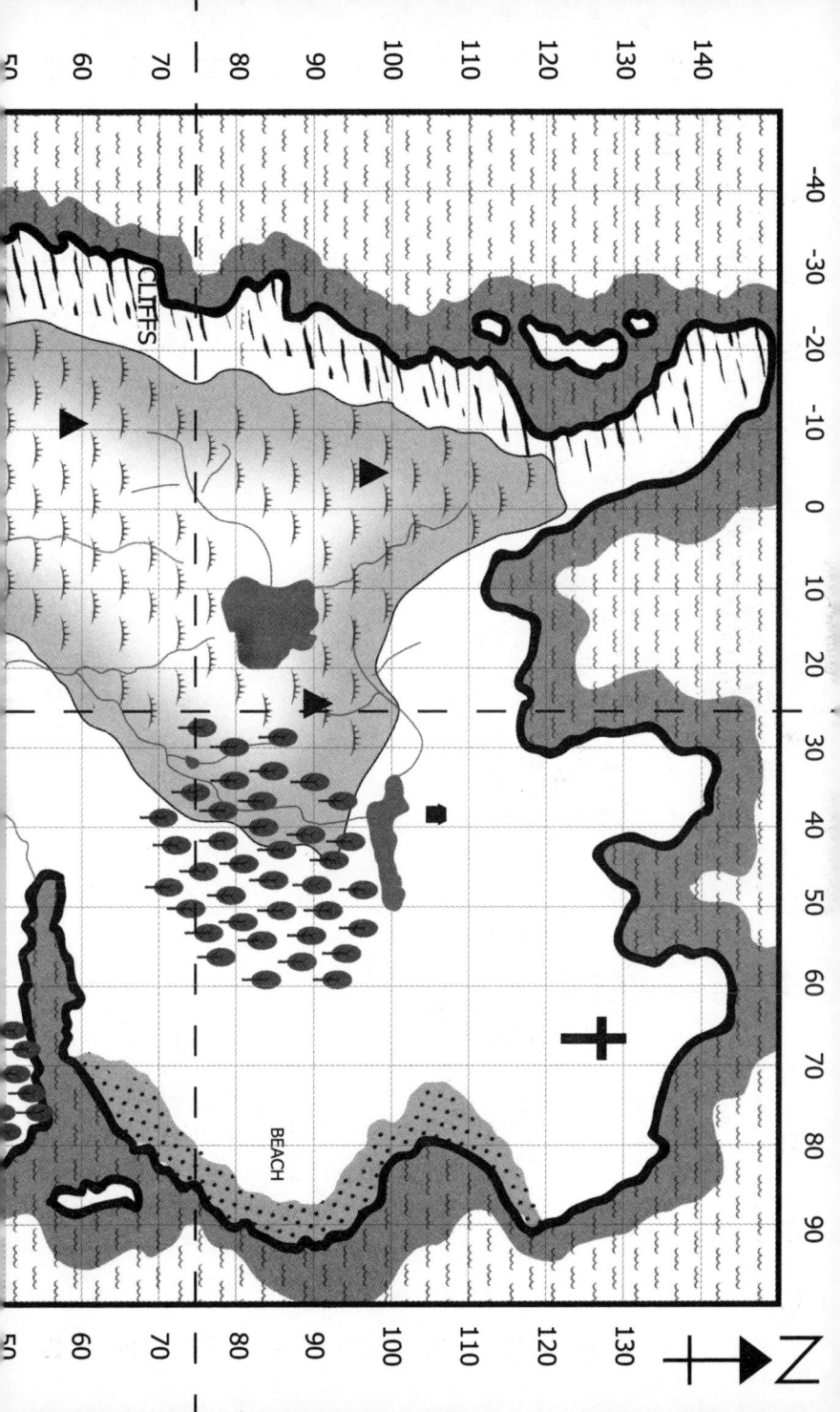

Chapter One

When we arrived at the crossing the tide was so far out that we could see nothing but miles of damp sand. Aikenhead itself was invisible behind solid grey mist.

"Watch your footing, girlie." The old man wearing the Gold Foundation jacket stood by the phone box, his thinning hair shifting in the breeze. "Those rocks are still wet."

Carmen hid a grin but allowed him to hold her hand and guide her down to the crossing.

It was a kind of narrow road that was elevated above the level of the surrounding sand. A series of buoys marked the edge of it.

"Now, remember," he said, "stick to Gold's crossing. It's strong enough for a ten-tonne lorry, so you'll be fine, but it ain't safe to leave it. Mind — an hour and a half an' that tide comes back in. This whole area'll be underwater and there're strong currents and a helluva rip tide. You gotta be on Aikenhead by half two."

"I'll set an alarm to remind us when we've half an hour left." Will revealed the smartwatch Mum had bought him before we left. I had Grandad's old army watch, which worked fine.

"Ain't gonna be none of that there Wi-Fi on Aikenhead, young man. None of yer *Angry Birds*." The old man made air-quote with gnarled fingers, looking at Will's wrist.

"We'll be fine, thanks." Lizzie said quickly. "Will, don't rely on the alarm. Keep a close eye on the time for us too, please." She turned back to the old man. "Are we the final group to arrive?"

"Aye. The last team left an hour ago. You'd better get moving. Don't forget those currents."

"We won't. See you in a few days. Thanks for the help." Carmen waved and she and Lizzie set off.

Will and Grady followed close behind.

After a couple of hundred metres, I looked back. The fog was sliding over the town and the red phone box had already vanished.

"So the crossing is only raised every three days?" I stamped and my boots made a hollow sound.

Although there was a thick layer of sand beneath our feet, the road was solid.

Lizzie shrugged. "Guess he doesn't want uninvited guests on his private island."

"But why every three days?" Grady mused.

"I expect that's when he has deliveries," Will said. "The airstrip isn't open the whole time either."

"He doesn't live on the island, Will." Grady frowned. "He has houses all over the world."

"Well, someone must be there." Carmen shook her hair into the wind. "Why have a private island if no one's going to be there?"

Buoys appeared just ahead of us one by one as we hiked through the haze. Invisible gulls cried overhead and the far distant trombone of whale song made us freeze and listen with our hearts in our mouths.

Finally, a shaft of sunlight cleared the mist and Aikenhead shimmered into reality. Its slate cliffs were thick with pale-coloured birds and, for the first time, we could see the strip of beach at the other side of the crossing.

"So, what will you all do with the prize money?" Lizzie asked.

"You know what *I'll* do." Carmen strode round a rock that had been deposited on the crossing. "Put myself through vet school, set up my own practice." Her eyes went dreamy. "Specialize in horses."

"What about you, Will?" Lizzie tilted her head. "What'll you do?"

"Start my own business." He adjusted his rucksack. "App design, consultancy, something like that."

Lizzie dropped back to walk beside me. "What about you, Ben?"

My eyes slid away. "Haven't thought about it."

"Liar." Lizzie nudged me. "You must have."

I shook my head. "What are your plans?"

"Pay off my parents' mortgage and cover my uni fees so Dad can retire. Buy a house. Come on, Ben, you must have a wish list."

"*I'd* invest the money," Grady called. "Eventually I'll be able to ... uncover some real truths." Grady's breath got shorter as he spoke. "Then I'd set up my ... magazine. I've figured it all ... out. It's gonna be called ... *The Con: Conspiracies You Can Believe*."

I stared. "What've you got in that bag, Grady? It must weigh a ton!" He wasn't that unfit, so I couldn't see why else he'd be struggling.

"Oh … you know me." Grady waved his hand.

"But we agreed what we were all bringing." Light glinted from Lizzie's glasses and nose ring. "We wrote a list."

"I didn't want to … forget something … important." Grady ducked his head and shifted his bag, which clanked like an old car.

I shook my head and looked at Lizzie. She shrugged and we walked on.

"I'd give my money to Will, for his business," I said finally, my voice so low only she could hear. "He's the brains of the operation, after all. I'm just the brawn."

"You're not *just* the brawn." Lizzie frowned. "Since when have you started saying that?"

"I am though. Come on, Will's not even seventeen and he's going to uni."

"So are you. You're doing engineering!"

I cleared my throat. "I … I turned the place down. Mum wants me to get a job in Oxford – to keep an eye on Will."

Lizzie stumbled to a halt. "But … what about our plans? We were going to be close. Oxford's nowhere near Swansea!"

I flushed. "I can still come and see you. Look, it'll be fine. I've found a place offering apprenticeships for mechanics, so I'll be earning right away."

"But … that's not what you wanted. What about being able to work all over the world? You were going to build better buildings, disaster-proof schools—"

"Lizzie, please. This is something I've got to do. And Mum's buying me a car. I'll be able to drive us places."

"I don't care about that." She looked away. "But I guess it's your life."

I gripped the straps of my rucksack. "Don't be like that."

"I never understood the hold your mum's got on you." She lowered her voice to a whisper. "You don't have to do your dad's job for ever. Don't you want to see who you can be when you're not looking after your brother?"

I didn't reply. What could I say to that?

"I've got the place." I skidded into the kitchen. "Mum, I got in!"

Mum was standing at the sink, scrubbing with single-minded focus. She didn't reply.

I got a tea towel from the drawer and began to dry the pan on the draining board, careful not to leave streaks.

Once she had removed her gloves and set them down, I said it again. "I got in."

"In?"

"To Cardiff, to do civil engineering." I put the tea towel into the washing machine, closed the door and buffed my prints off the handle with my sleeve.

Mum cleared her throat and straightened a placemat. "What about Will?"

"Will?" I frowned. "He already got his results. He's going to Oxford, like you wanted."

"Yes." Mum wiped an invisible stain on the table.

"And I'm going to Cardiff."

Something wasn't right. Hadn't I earned a smile? I sat in the chair opposite her and gnawed at my thumbnail. "You'll be fine. You'll love having the house to yourself – it'll be so tidy."

As if I ever made a mess. I knew better. I glanced at her hands, knuckles raw from endless cleaning. Her sleeves were still pushed up from the washing and I could see her scars. I looked away quickly and she tugged her blouse down over her wrists. She still hadn't met my eyes.

She cleared her throat. "I was hoping…"

"Hoping what?"

"That you wouldn't get in," she said eventually, lifting her eyes to mine. "Hoping this wouldn't be an issue."

My cheeks went cold. "An issue?"

"You *know* you can't go." Her eyes were defiant. "You'd be too far from your brother. He needs you."

"But … you let him apply early."

"I'm not holding Will back," she snapped. "Not for…"

"Not for me." I swallowed back the threat of tears, bitter and salty. "I'm going to Cardiff."

"I won't pay."

"Dad will."

"Hah. He can't even afford his new family. And he's helping with Will's—"

"I'll get a job, then."

"And manage uni on top of that? Be sensible." Mum leaned forwards and caught my hand. Her fingers were hard. "You know in your heart, Ben,

30

that you can't leave your brother. How would you feel if something happened?" Her eyes narrowed. "You know I'd *die* if something happened." Her eyes flicked, just for a moment, to the drawer that held the packets of pills: pain relief, sleeping tablets, antidepressants. "I love you, Ben, but we have to look out for your little brother. He's your responsibility as much as mine."

"*You* could move to Oxford." I looked up but I already knew…

She gasped. "Move?"

Mum barely left the house these days: her clean bubble, where she had total control.

She shook her head. "I'll buy you a car. Think about it. And you can be a mechanic. That's only what you'd end up doing in the end. This way you'll be earning money while you learn."

Feeling a hundred years old, I took the letter out of my pocket, balled it up and added it to the recycling.

Mum smiled. "You're a good boy, Ben. I don't know what I'd do without you. Most boys your age wouldn't be as responsible as you are. I did something right bringing you up. Didn't I?"

I nodded and went to grab my skateboard from its place by the door. "I'll be back for dinner."

"We need you, Ben. Remember that." Her voice rose and I looked back. Her sleeves were pulled up and her wrists turned out. *See, Ben? See what happens when you drop the ball.*

▼

How could I explain things to Lizzie? How could she understand? Eventually she pulled ahead to walk with Carmen, leaving me alone.

My foot came down with a splash. Around us, pools of water had appeared, reflecting the rain-heavy sky.

"Will, is the tide coming in?" I failed to keep the worry from my voice.

"Can't be." Will waved his arm without looking at it. "My alarm hasn't gone off."

"We had … an hour and a … half," Grady panted.

"So how long have we got left?"

Will glanced at his wrist, then frowned. "That can't be right."

I halted. "What can't?"

"It still says quarter past." His eyes widened. "Uh…"

"What's the matter?" Lizzie turned.

"My watch is frozen."

"Will!" Grady's voice was a wail. "Watching the time was your *job*."

"So, what time is it *actually*?" Lizzie snapped.

I pushed up my sleeve. Grandad's watch was ticking reliably. I swallowed. "Will's alarm should have gone off ten minutes ago. We've already had almost an hour and a half."

"Right." Lizzie's expression set into lines of grim determination. "We'll have to pick up the pace."

Even during the short time we'd stopped to talk, the sand on top of the crossing had become wet. When I put my left foot down again, it squelched and water dampened my socks.

Lizzie and Carmen took the lead, marching swiftly. They were lighter and their rucksacks smaller, making it easier for them to walk on the wet sand.

"This is already *not fun*," Carmen called.

A fat raindrop splattered my forehead and I looked up. "Perfect." I turned to check on Grady.

He was staring back at the bank of solid grey that stretched from the island we had left to the horizon. "C'mon, Grady, get a move on."

He took a faltering step, wobbled and fell.

"Grady, are you all right?" Carmen called.

"Grady! You're slowing us down." I grabbed the back of his rucksack and hauled him to his feet, trying not to lose my own balance. "Why'd you have to bring all this extra stuff."

"We might need it."

"Dammit, Grady." The puddles around us had started to run together, like the parts of a movie monster, forming ominously into one. On our right, the crossing was now the same level as the water. "Swap bags with me for a bit."

Grady brightened. "Are you sure, Ben? You don't have to." On his cheek a long smear of wet sand looked like camouflage paint against his black skin.

I was already undoing my chest strap. "Will, give us a hand," I shouted.

Will had kept walking, but when I called he came back and took hold of my rucksack while I helped Grady lift off his. I grunted as I twisted it into place on my shoulders and settled into the soggy straps. I could smell Grady's sweat on the canvas. Instantly I was heavier, my feet crunching into the road.

"Thanks, Ben. That's better."

"We're changing back as soon as we're on dry land. You brought it, you carry it." I rolled my shoulders, trying to get comfortable. "What've you *got* in here?"

"It'll be a bit lighter on the way back," Grady said brightly.

"You brought extra *food*?"

"I can't function without sugar," Grady said as he marched past.

"But did you have to bring a whole sweet shop?"

"Come on, Ben," Lizzie shouted and I followed the line of her pointing arm. Ahead of us puddles were turning into pools.

"How much longer till we reach the shore?" I muttered to Will.

Will frowned. "We've come three-quarters of the way and it's taken us seventy-eight minutes."

"So how long?"

Will barely paused. "At this pace – twenty-six minutes."

"But the tide will be in … in twelve?"

Will nodded. "The crossing will be completely underwater."

I looked at our route towards the island; there was a shorter way on our left, and it was drier – the crossing was holding back some of the tide. I stared at the water forming between us and the beach. The other path would put us a little bit further round the coast, but at least we wouldn't have to finish our walk underwater.

"What if we go that way?"

Chapter Two

"Not far now," Lizzie called. "Think about how great it's going to be when we get to the island."

The route back to Fetlar was completely cut off. To our right, buoys had started to bob; the crossing was covered now. Ahead, the sea level continued to rise. As I watched, the last of the dry patches on our new route, the one that had led us away from the crossing, was submerged.

I groaned as my shoulders screamed under the weight of Grady's rucksack.

Jellyfish had been drying all over the boggy sand to either side of me – fat, slimy, transparent. Now they bobbed in the water, trailing stinging tendrils around my trouser legs.

I kept my eyes on Aikenhead as I pushed myself to move faster. Our new route was taking us towards an enclosed inlet surrounded by seaweed-covered rocks. The plan was to climb the cliff and walk from the top to the official starting point.

A faint beeping caught my ear.

Carmen shoved her hand in her pocket. "I set an alarm, too," she whispered.

It was officially no longer safe to be out on the sand. We were out of time.

"Guys, we're going to have to run," Lizzie called.

Carmen nodded and splashed ahead of me. I tried to keep up, but with Grady's rucksack I could barely lift my feet out of the water, let alone run.

Because the rucksack was set up for Grady, the straps were biting into my armpits and I could feel blisters. If I carried on and they burst, I could end up with an infection and that could cause real problems for the team. The water was up to my knees now, but I had no choice; the others had reached the rocks but I had to stop and adjust the pack.

I unclipped the chest and hip straps, and shifted so that the pack slipped down to my elbows. I groaned with relief.

"What are you doing, Ben? You can't carry the bag like that! We have to get off these rocks before they get cut off too." Lizzie was balanced on a boulder studded with barnacles. The rain lashed her shoulders and painted her hair to her head.

She was right. I loosened the straps and resettled the pack on my shoulders. But when I tried to take a step, I couldn't move.

"What the…?" I tugged at my left foot. It was cemented in place. The water splashed up to my thighs.

"Ben?" Lizzie's voice shifted up a register.

"I can't move."

"Are you serious?" Carmen stepped gingerly from one rock to another, coming closer to the sea. "What's the problem? *¡Vamos!* Let's go!"

Will's expression was calculating. "The old man said it wasn't safe to leave the crossing," he said and tilted his head. "Ben must have stopped in quicksand."

Carmen's hands flew to her mouth. "*¡Dios mío!*"

"He's right, I'm sinking." I could feel the sand clutching at my calves. "I'm going to have to take off your rucksack. Come and get it, Grady."

"All right." Grady removed my pack and handed it to Will. Then he climbed back into the water. He gasped and shivered, then stopped a few steps out, his arms around his chest. "Wait – if I come to you, won't I end up in the quicksand, too?"

"You're right." I was sinking fast but I didn't dare struggle. Everyone knows struggling in quicksand makes it worse.

"Don't struggle," Lizzie called.

I rolled my eyes. So did Will.

Carmen looked at Lizzie. "What should we do?"

Something brushed past me under the water and the current pulled me sideways. I fought to stay upright as the sea crept past my stomach. Fear chilled me. I'd heard about tides rising faster than a man could run. I hadn't believed it though.

Lizzie didn't answer and I could see Will thinking furiously, assessing options and dismissing them, his eyes flickering like a computer.

My heart raced. Surely Gold wouldn't risk one of us drowning here? There would be someone watching, someone coming to help. Then I remembered all the disclaimer forms we'd had to sign.

"I'm coming, Ben!" Lizzie propped her rucksack high on a rock and rain hammered on the canvas. She stuffed her glasses into a side pocket, then jumped into the water. She hissed as the cold slammed into her but waded forwards. She passed Grady without looking at him.

"What are you going to do?" Grady called.

When she was about a body length from me, Lizzie stopped. She held her arm up to protect her face from the lashing rain. "This is where the sand softens."

"Move back." Carmen wrung her hands.

"How'd the rest of us miss this?" Lizzie shook her head. "Dumb luck, I guess. Can you push Grady's rucksack over to me?"

"It'll be caught by the current," I said. "Go that way." Lizzie sidestepped and I shoved the rucksack towards her. Instantly its weight took it underwater and the current pulled it sideways. Lizzie reached for it and tried to pull it out of the water but staggered with the weight.

"Take it, Grady!" she yelled. Grady splashed to her side and she shoved the bag at him.

"My electronics!" He looked stricken.

Lizzie pushed him back towards the rocks. "We'll dry out what we can when the rain stops. Go."

Freed from the weight of Grady's bag, I remained stuck just past my knees. Water lapped my chin.

Lizzie was fighting the current, moving her arms

frantically in the water to remain in place.

Suddenly Will pulled his foam bedroll from the top of his pack, then waded into the sea. When he drew level with Lizzie, he stretched it out to me.

I managed to snag the end. Immediately I saw what Will intended. "OK, let go." I wrapped my arms around the buoyant foam and the sand loosened its grip a little. It wasn't enough to free me, but at least I wasn't sinking any more.

"Now what?" Lizzie's face was pale. "We're running out of time." She grabbed at Will as her legs were swept out from under her.

"Carmen," Will shouted as he yanked a spluttering Lizzie back to her feet. "My folding shovel is in the front pocket of my bag, with my tent pegs and axe."

Carmen crouched by Will's pack. After a minute, she pushed sodden hair out of her eyes and held up the shovel.

"Pass it to Grady."

The world seemed to shake as a growl of thunder reverberated across the sky.

"This is the worst August *ever.*" Grady pushed his soggy rucksack on to the rocks and took the shovel. "Where's the *sun*?" He suddenly frowned. "You know the US military defence programme HAARP has a project that controls the weather. I bet Gold has something similar – this could be—"

"Not now, Grady," Lizzie yelled.

Rain battered harder and I blinked water from my eyes.

Will grabbed the shovel from Grady and opened it out. "I'm going to dig you out. Don't struggle."

Before I could say anything, my brother took a deep breath and bent. He grabbed my thigh to hold himself in place and I felt the sharp edge of the tool against my knee as he started digging.

I counted thirty seconds, forty. The water around me darkened with the sand Will was disturbing. Lizzie was holding her breath, her eyes on mine. My leg started to feel looser and I tensed to hold it steady. Then Will came up for air.

The buoyancy of the bedroll may have stopped me sinking but the water was still rising.

"This is going to take too long." My lips were numb as I formed the words, my teeth chattering.

"Who else has a shovel?" Will asked.

"We only agreed to bring one," Lizzie said. "But we can use other stuff – bowls, pans…" She started to wade back to shore. "Carmen, have you got your mess tin?"

Another roll of thunder clattered across the sky and gulls took off from the cliff edge with eerie cries.

Carmen pulled out a bowl and tossed it to Lizzie, then she secured her pack and climbed into the water with her mess tin in one hand.

They waded out towards me, holding on to one another as the current yanked at them. Carmen's long hair pulled out to one side, an oil spill in the water, pink ends like the tendrils of an exotic jellyfish.

When they reached the edge of the quicksand, they both took deep breaths and went underwater. They wrapped their arms around my thighs as they worked. I felt like a drowning sailor with sirens below.

Grady was searching in his backpack. "I knew we'd need an extra spade," he yelled. "It's here somewhere."

I choked as water splashed into my nose. My left leg was almost free but that meant it was even harder to resist the current pulling at me.

"Got it." Grady started to swim.

"Grady, no!" I shouted. Too late, Grady was dragged into the rocks by the force of the current. "You have to wade…"

Grady came up spluttering, gripping the spade with one hand and his elbow with the other.

Lizzie and Carmen appeared and gasped for air, cold hands clutching my chest and shoulders. Then they went under again and Will followed.

There was frantic activity beneath me but all I could do was float and spit seawater.

Slowly my right leg began to lift and then, abruptly, I was free.

I had a single second of sheer relief before I realized that I had been anchoring all of us against the current.

I tried to shove Lizzie back towards the rocks, but the current fought me. I still had Will's bedroll in one hand and I managed to catch Carmen as she was pulled past. I pushed the bedroll into her hands and held on to the string so that she bobbed with me like a kite.

Will was swimming hard, his jaw clenched, going nowhere.

"*Grady!*" I cried.

Grady clambered back on to the rocks, turned and fumbled to undo his belt. He tugged it from around his waist but it wasn't until he whipped out his penknife and cut the ends that I realized what he was doing. Parachute cord spooled out as fast as he could pull it.

"Nice one!" I choked on a surge of surf.

Grady threw the line towards Will, who swam frantically, made it a little way against the current, and managed to catch the floating end. He gripped Lizzie with one hand and I snagged his right foot. Will wrapped the line around his elbow and we hung on while Grady pulled us back in.

Lizzie, Carmen and I kicked, trying to help. The water rose higher, waking crabs in the rock pools and Grady pulled. The cord cut through Will's shirt and into his skin, his blood muddying the water.

My leg slammed into a hidden rock and I cried out, but released Will and scrambled for a handhold. Will's fingers found a fissure and we floated for a moment, free of the current. Carmen scrambled over me, into a rock pool, then reached down to help Lizzie.

"Are you OK?" Grady called.

I nodded, then looked up. "Our rucksacks!" The rocks beneath them were submerged, water lapping at the packs. We hauled ourselves up and staggered to our kits.

I grabbed my bag and hauled it further up, out of the water's reach, then collapsed against the cliff wall. I looked at Will, who was slinging his backpack over his shoulder. "Quicksand!"

Will nodded.

Lizzie crumpled next to me. She pushed her glasses on to her nose.

"We could've *died*!" Carmen grabbed Grady and placed a huge wet kiss on his cheek. "You saved us, Grady." Then she wrapped her arm around Will. "And you, Will."

"This wasn't a good start," Grady said seriously.

I snorted a laugh and suddenly we were all giggling.

We stopped when we realized that the tide was still rising – and fast.

"I'm not walking across those rocks," Carmen said. "They are like teeth."

"There's a way up the cliff." Lizzie pointed. "If you're up to it, Ben?"

I nodded. "It'll save us some time once we're at the top."

Before we set off, I looked back. Through the wind and rain, I could just about make out the smudge of the phone box on the other side of the crossing and, making patterns in the surf, Grady's paracord belt, tangled in the rocks. With numb fingers I set an alarm on Grandad's watch. The second time it went off, the crossing would be safe again for our journey home.

Chapter Three

No one argued about the climb but Grady held his injured elbow close to his chest. The rain hammered on his lowered hood.

"Best to go now, Grady, before your arm stiffens up any more," Carmen said sympathetically.

"I know." He swallowed. "We can't wait anyway, the tide…" He glanced at Will and then at me.

"Don't blame Will," Carmen warned.

"He should've noticed his watch wasn't working." Grady didn't meet her eyes. "And Ben was the one who suggested the 'shortcut'."

"I'm sorry, guys." I clipped the straps of my rucksack closed over my chest, relieved that my blisters weren't rubbing underneath.

"Ben carried your rucksack for you, Grady," Lizzie reminded him in a quiet voice. "If he hadn't, you might still be back there." She pointed and we all stared. It seemed that the waves had always been behind us – impossible that we had walked here. Grady clamped his lips together.

I looked towards the top of the cliff. "Are we free climbing?"

Lizzie nodded. "It's only four metres or so and it looks like there are plenty of handholds." She was already pulling on light gloves. "Remember not to grip too hard – it'll wear out your forearms.

I raised my eyebrows. "What else?"

"Keep your body close to the cliff and your knees pointing away from it." She rubbed her eyes and replaced her glasses. "Move your arms or legs and *then* shift your body weight. Don't do both at the same time. Follow me up, try to use the same hand-and footholds." She glanced up, assessing the route. "If you *do* fall…" She tailed off.

"If we fall?" I prompted her.

"Push away from the wall as hard as you can. That way you might not crash into the person below you and there's a chance you'll hit water, not rock. Try to keep your feet pointed downwards."

"That's it?" Grady cried. "Try to keep your feet down?"

"You don't want to break your back, do you?"

Lizzie was already seeking the first handhold. I tucked my own hands under my armpits to warm them up a bit. Will was flexing his, getting the joints moving. The left arm of his shirt was bloodstained.

"Will you be OK, Will?" The question was automatic.

Will raised his eyebrows. "The tendons aren't torn. I can use the arm." And for him that was that.

Lizzie hoisted herself on to the rock.

"I'll go last," I said. "I really hurt my leg on a rock. I'm not sure how much of my weight it'll take."

Lizzie looked down, worried.

"Either I make the climb or I stay here." I said, spreading my hands. Eventually Lizzie pulled herself upwards.

Grady was ahead of me, then Will. Carmen was right behind Lizzie, imitating every move she made. Will was watching her closely. Looking at him now, I could almost forget what he'd been like when he was little. Almost.

I would have been four the first time I noticed something wasn't right. I don't remember why I had the day off school, but for some reason I was with Mum and Will at a Mum's and Tots group. I was playing alone in a corner, pushing a truck up and down, when I realized that the background chatter had quietened. Tension filled the air – I could feel it right up my neck. Suddenly my T-shirt wasn't warm enough. Mum's voice, as she talked about the new slide in the park, had turned brittle.

Curious, I turned. The parents were all watching Will, their conversations fading.

He was peering intently at another little boy, who had a blue lorry clutched to his chest. Will liked the colour blue. I jumped to my feet. "Give the lorry to Will!" I yelled. So, yeah, I guess I *had* known before then.

The boy shook his head and Will clenched his fists. His face grew redder and redder, then he started to shake. Instantly the mothers were on their feet, grabbing their children and lifting them on to their knees. They knew.

The mum of the boy with the blue lorry was slow to react.

"Kate!" someone called, but she only made it halfway to her son before Will erupted. I watched, frozen, as my brother punched, bit and kicked until he was dragged away, screaming.

Later, when it had all calmed down and Mum had a cup of tea in her hand, Will walked up to the other little boy. He offered the blue lorry back to him. The other boy shook his head. Will insisted. Finally, when the boy reached for the toy, Will looked around, made sure Mum had her eyes on the biscuit plate, then stamped on his foot.

▼

My boots were wrong for rock climbing. They were army boots from the surplus store, with huge steel toe caps. I could walk in them for days, and you could drop a tank on my foot, but I couldn't feel with my toes and all the grip was underneath. I should've changed into my trainers.

Four metres hadn't seemed that far, but, balancing halfway up in the rain, the water seemed very far below me. I stopped, rested my weight on my right leg and pressed my forehead on to the rock face.

"Ben?" Lizzie shouted. "You OK? I'm at the top."

"Just taking a breather." I tried to relax my forearms; I was gripping too tight, my muscles threatening to spasm. I tilted my head back, careful not to lean too far. Lizzie had one arm over the edge of the cliff, holding out a hand for Carmen. Will and Grady weren't far behind them. Breathing deeply, I pulled myself up to the next hold.

The moment Will tugged me on to flat ground, I flopped on my back like a turtle on its shell, my rucksack beneath me. The rain was finally lightening and the cloud was breaking up.

With a groan, I sat up and looked at Aikenhead.

Shafts of sunlight-bruised moorland stretched out for ever; wet heather and coarse grasses in a patchwork of purple, green and brown. To our right, trees crowded together, deformed by the wind. Crumbling drystone walls drew lines that meant nothing to wandering sheep.

Birds screamed and I looked up in time to see a great skua chasing a gull, scolding it until it dropped whatever it had been carrying in its mouth. The skua landed, cried at us, then snatched up the food and launched again, the white dashes on its wings flashing.

Lizzie laughed. "Bully!"

"Can you guys walk?" Carmen asked. "I hate to

rush you, *chico*, but if we miss the introduction, we'll have lost before we've even started."

"Carmen's right." Lizzie climbed to her feet. "We have to catch up."

I pulled my medical kit and water bottle from my rucksack. "Just let me take some paracetamol and I'll be OK." I offered the pills to Will and Grady.

Will took two, but Grady shook his head and reached for his rucksack. "I've got my own."

Grady's medical kit was three times the size of mine. Lizzie stared. "What have you got in there? Are you planning on opening a chemist?"

I stared at painkillers, anti-inflammatories, plasters, bandages, different kinds of antiseptic, arnica, butterfly stitches, sting relief, sterilising tablets, even allergy tablets organized in colour-coded pockets.

Will pointed. "Those are antibiotics."

Grady nodded. "Dad prescribed them on a 'just in case' basis. Did you know that there's a cure for cancer, but big pharma has it locked down so they can make more money?" He said it almost absently, a reflex of speech as he selected a packet of high-strength painkillers and took some. He winced as he flexed his elbow, then folded the kit back up and stuffed it inside his pack, but instead of closing up his bag, he dug around some more. His face fell.

"Everything's wet." He pulled out an iPad.

Lizzie raised her eyebrows. "An iPad?"

"Will it turn on?" Carmen touched his shoulder.

Grady sighed. "Of course not."

Lizzie frowned. "Has *anyone* got a working phone?"

Carmen shook her head sadly.

"I hadn't even thought about that!" I said. Mine had been in my pocket the whole time. I pulled it out and tried the power button, even though I knew it would be useless. "Will, what if the Gold Foundation call Mum when they realize we didn't arrive on the crossing? She'll be worried *sick*." I shoved it back in my pocket.

"You think they would?" He frowned, then turned to Grady. "Weren't you bringing a satphone?"

Grady unclipped a side pocket and pulled it out. "The Iridium Extreme." He held it up. "Shockproof, dustproof and ... waterproof!" He turned it on with a flourish.

"Call your dad," I said. "Tell him we're OK."

Grady was frowning at the phone. "This can't be right." He shook it, then switched it off and on again. "This thing's meant to work at the North Pole."

"What's the matter?" Carmen asked.

"It's got one hundred per cent *global coverage*!" Grady was yelling at the phone now. "It's impossible. Iridium satellites are *low-earth orbit*. There's literally no way I could have no reception."

"No GPS?" Lizzie asked.

Grady growled. "Nothing, I've got nothing. There's something weird going on here."

Carmen's face fell. "We can't let anyone know we're OK?"

Lizzie shook her head and strode towards the cliff path. "We'd better find the starting point, before they start making calls."

No one bothered unfolding a map; we knew the crossing should have taken us straight to the gridpoint. We just had to head round the cliff and we'd find our way.

▼

"Hey, you guys, is that another team?" Carmen

57

pointed at five big lads, all dressed in camo gear, heading in our direction. One of them, marching at the head of the group, stood out – his hair redder than mine. We'd pass above them. Carmen shouted and waved. They looked up, then put their heads down and started to jog.

"Well, same to you!" Carmen yelled.

"It's a competition, Car." Will grinned. "I guess they don't want to cosy up to the enemy."

"Waving is not cosying up, it's being polite." She grimaced. "I hope they fall off the cliff."

"Where d'you think they were going?" Lizzie frowned. "Do you reckon that's the way to the first checkpoint?"

"Should we follow them?" Grady turned to look at their vanishing backs. "They look like they know what they're doing."

"No," Lizzie said after a second. "There might be something we need at the official starting point. We can catch up later."

"Yeah, they looked slow," Grady grumbled sarcastically.

I fell into step with Lizzie, Carmen dropped back to walk with Will, and Grady thudded along in the middle, grunting with the weight of his rucksack.

Lizzie looked up at me. "Is this going to be more dangerous than we realized? I mean, no one came to help us back there. You could have *died*."

Will turned. "For five million pounds, it isn't going to be an easy ride," he said.

"I know, but ... I expected *some* supervision."

"We don't need supervision, *chica*." Carmen grinned. "Adults would just cramp our style."

"We haven't got to the official starting point yet," I reminded her. "They're probably waiting for us there."

Above us, the sun burned the last of the clouds away, allowing some August warmth to reach us. A smile played on my lips – maybe our clothes would dry out after all.

"Look!" Grady cried. In the distance a whale blew a fountain of foam. Carmen squealed. Even Will stopped to look as the whale's calf carved an arc from the water and landed with a crash of surf. Carmen fumbled for her digital camera. She aimed it at the glinting sea, then stopped and looked at it miserably. "This got wet too. I should have put it in a plastic bag."

"Look, puffins!" Lizzie cried.

"They're so *cute!*" Carmen was already smiling again. "OK, *compañeros.*" Carmen clapped her hands. "We got off to a bad start, but it's fun all the way from now on and a million pounds for each of us!"

"Do you think we can still win?" Grady raised his eyebrows. "None of the other teams managed to get stuck in the sand."

"Of course we can!" Lizzie said firmly. "That was our one mistake. We got it out of the way. From now on, we'll be a well-oiled machine."

"OK then. I can't wait for the first puzzle." Grady pulled a packet of strawberry laces from a pocket and offered it around.

"I was looking forward to climbing, but we already did that." Lizzie laughed as she chewed.

"Will, what are you looking forward to?" Carmen nudged him.

Will shrugged. "The challenge of beating the other teams?" He looked at me.

"Yeah, the whole game." I faked a heel-flip, as if I had my skateboard with me. "This is going to be the best three days of our lives."

Chapter Four

We kept walking. Will put his shades on and Lizzie rammed a baseball cap over her hair. I knew it was because she hated her freckles. I thought they were cute, even though I'd never tell her so.

I bent down and picked a pale yellow flower. Without thinking, I tucked it behind the arm of Lizzie's glasses.

"You aren't supposed to pick wildflowers, you know," Grady commented.

"We're on holiday, Grady! Relax." Carmen rolled her shoulders.

"I can see other islands." Lizzie shaded her eyes.

"That's Unst," Will said.

I stared. "Too far to swim."

Will nodded. "If it wasn't for Grady, those currents would've taken us out to sea."

I shuddered. "Right."

We rounded the headland and Carmen gave a

whoop. Beneath us six seals basked, undisturbed by her joyful cries. "I wish my camera hadn't got wet. Do you think they would let us swim with them?" Her eyes were round.

"I wouldn't get in the water at all," Grady reminded her.

Carmen sighed wistfully. "I've just never seen a seal in real life. I've never been on a plane before today either. Even if we don't win the money, it will have been worth the trip for me."

"I've never been on a plane before." Carmen craned to see out of the window.

"You never went to visit your family in Spain?" Lizzie asked.

"They come to us. We were going to do a cheap flight at Christmas, but it didn't work out with Papi's shifts—" She gasped as the small plane banked sideways and then giggled at her own fear. "Is it always this rough when you fly?" Carmen caught her camera as it slid off her lap, then posed for a selfie with Lizzie.

I shook my head as they laughed into the flash.

"No, this is a small private plane. A big one wouldn't be nearly so ba—" I choked on my own words as turbulence bumped us in our seats and Carmen laughed again.

I focused on the back of the empty seat in front of me. A Gold Foundation logo was embroidered on the headrest.

We were the only ones on the plane. As she had settled us in, the flight attendant had explained that teams were flying in from six airports across the country. We were the only ones from the southwest and so wouldn't see them until we reached the island.

The plane jumped again and I looked across the aisle at Will.

"This is better than a rollercoaster." He stretched out his long legs.

The attendant had reminded us that we would land on one of the bigger islands and then hike over the estuary.

"I don't know why we can't land directly on Aikenhead," Carmen said.

"It's not big enough or flat enough." Will pushed his map over to her. "See."

"*Great*." Carmen rolled her eyes. "I won't need to use the cross trainer again for weeks."

I leaned over Lizzie to look. "Are those caves?" I pointed.

Will nodded. "The island's riddled with them."

"We might not need to use our bivvies at all." Grady grinned. "So, what do we do when we get to the island?"

"Get to the starting point as fast as possible, get the coordinates and head to the first checkpoint." Lizzie looked at him. "I want to complete at least one before we camp."

I nodded. "At *least* one."

"We'll head out as early as we can tomorrow. If we keep to under six hours' sleep a night, it should give us an edge against the other teams."

"You don't think they'll be doing the same thing?" I asked.

"Maybe." Lizzie shrugged. "You think we should go for even less?"

"*Dios*, no." Carmen shook her head.

"It's only three days, Car." Lizzie laughed. "You can handle a bit of tiredness for a million pounds, can't you?"

"Well, when you put it that way." Carmen nodded.

"Should we be teaming up, you think?" Grady asked.

"What?" I looked at him.

"I mean with another team. Should we find another group to work with?"

"Why would we need to?" Will tilted his head. "We've got all the skills we need. And this is a competition. You want an awkward scene at the end?" Will put his head back. "Get a nap in," he said. "Sounds like we'll need it."

We drew level with the seal colony, which shifted warily and slid one by one under the water. Carmen watched them go with sadness in her eyes.

Next to the rocks a drunkenly tilted sign showed us where we *should* have arrived if we'd made it to the end of the crossing. It indicated a small jetty and a wooden building down the hill.

Lizzie frowned as our eyes followed the arrow. "Where are the Gold Foundation people? I know they said we'd have to cross the estuary alone, but surely someone would be here to greet us."

"Maybe they're inside." I shrugged.

"Let's find out." Lizzie took the lead and strode down the slope. The rest of us followed.

The gradient made my strides longer and I had to stop myself from tumbling into a run. I gripped the straps of my rucksack.

"What do you think the other teams will be like?" Carmen combed her fingers through her hair and slipped into step with me, Lizzie on my other side.

"Like us, I suppose." Lizzie smiled. "I doubt there'll be many younger than Will."

"What are you talking about?" Grady shifted into a jog to join us, his rucksack clanking, face shining with sweat.

"The other teams." I lifted my own rucksack higher. "Just wondering what they're like."

"They're our competition," Will called. "It's not as if we're going to sing campfire songs with them. What do you care?"

The end of the marked path across the estuary was right in front of us now, the weathered sign sticking out from between two rocks, a lonely marker. The door was on the other side of the wooden building, but I could see through the windows. There were no signs of movement.

"*¡Hola!*" Carmen called. "Is there anybody there?"

Silence.

"Where are you, handsome boys?"

Lizzie glared at her.

"I'm just having *fun!*" Carmen laughed. "Of course we have the most handsome boys right here."

"There really *doesn't* seem to be anyone here." I stepped on to the shingle with a crunch of gravel.

"Have we missed everyone? I mean, we saw that team going the other way," Grady said.

"I hope not." Lizzie seemed alarmed.

"There should be someone waiting for us, right?" I peered around. "We haven't got the next coordinates yet." I rubbed my arms, chilled. "Maybe we're in the wrong place. What does the sign say?"

Lizzie squinted at the splintered wooden board. "It doesn't say *anything*." She spread her hands. "It's an arrow and it points to the building." She touched the sign and it moved on its axis, easily spinning a full 180 degrees. "Or back the way we came." She sighed. "One of the other teams might have turned

67

it to confuse us."

"Cheats!" Grady snapped. "That must be why we saw them going so quickly the other way."

"We should at least check inside before we go after them." I started walking round, heading for the door just as the sun returned and lit the decking.

"It could be pointing to something behind the building," Carmen suggested.

"Hey." I reached the door. "There's a notice."

Beside the door, a poster was fixed behind a perspex frame, protected against the weather.

IRON TEEN

Welcome to Aikenhead

Well done, Iron Teens, for reaching the first of seven checkpoints. The game began the minute you left the airstrip and you are expected to reach the end of the course without help.

Teams will set off from this checkpoint one by one. Your progress will be timed from this point. In order to ensure appropriate staggering, each team will be provided with the coordinates of the second checkpoint in a time-locked box. Your own time will begin the moment your box opens. The boxes will remain open for only two minutes. Boxes will open at the following times:

Team	Time
Team 1 Prisha Sadana	1220
Team 2 Hugo Lancett	1240
Team 3 Wang An	1300
Team 4 Curtis Wellington	1320
Team 5 Frances McCarthy	1340
Team 6 Theodore Chase	1400
Team 7 Liam Jones	1420
Team 8 Reece Armstrong	1440
Team 9 Elizabeth Bellamy	1500
Team 10 Otto Warner	DISQUALIFIED

"I wonder what happened to Otto Warner?" Carmen touched his name.

"What's the time?" Lizzie gasped. "Quick, Ben."

I looked at my watch. My eyes widened. "One minute to three."

"We've only got a minute to find that box!"

Lizzie, Carmen and I ran into the building. Will and Grady started to follow, but Lizzie held up a hand. "Search the area, you guys. We don't need all of us to look inside."

"It's not in here!" Carmen cried.

"It *has* to be." I scanned the room. Shafts of sunlit dust slanted from cracked windows. The peeling walls were bare and the floor was empty.

"Will, any luck out there?" Lizzie yelled.

"Nothing," he shouted back.

"Everyone out." Lizzie pushed Carmen towards the door. "Quick!"

"Wait." I tilted my head, but the girls had already gone. Still, there seemed to be something…

I held my breath, looked at my watch and heard a very quiet *click*. It was three o'clock: somewhere in this room, the box had opened and would stay open for only two minutes.

70

"It's here!" I ran into the centre of the room, scanning frantically. I could feel the seconds ticking by on Grandad's watch, vibrating on my wrist. Where was it? Then I saw it: a knothole in the floorboards and an odd pattern in the wood. I crouched, stuck my fingers in the hole and pulled. A whole section of the floor began to lift. I yelled as my shoulders took the strain, it was moving so slowly. Finally, I managed to get my back under it and shoved the trapdoor open. It slammed into the wooden floor. I held the edge and leaped inside the hold, which barely came up to my knees.

Inside there was a row of nine boxes. The last in the line stood open, but there was no time to look in. I tipped the contents on to the floor. Seconds after I dropped the box, the lid snapped shut.

Had any of the other teams been fooled by the trapdoor and missed their turn? If so, where were they? If it had been me, I'd have simply followed the next group out. Was a team watching right now, waiting for us to leave?

I looked up. Will and Lizzie dropped to their knees behind me. Carmen and Grady clattered into the room as well.

"Did you find it in time?" Grady called.

I held up two folded pieces of paper.

Carmen clapped. "That was close!"

"Let's go outside," I said. "The light's better and we've still got some drying-off to do."

We made for the door.

"Hey, you know what this means?" Carmen called, almost skipping as she burst into the fresh air. "The times were staggered. We aren't behind!"

"We missed our chance to size up the other teams," Grady muttered.

"We already know the most important thing about the other teams," Carmen winked at him. "They are not as good as us."

I put my hand on Will's arm. "Here you go. You have the info."

We sat in a circle on the decking outside the wooden hut. A light breeze cooled my face and I stretched out my bruised leg. The sun warmed my damp clothes and birds cried overhead. A small boat with a white sail tacked across the horizon. Lizzie allowed her hand to fall next to mine and I smiled.

"This is so exciting," Lizzie whispered.

"So far so good." I grinned as Will opened one of the papers.

IRON TEEN

Checkpoint 1

1500

Team leader: Elizabeth Bellamy

Congratulations on reaching the first checkpoint.

From now on the boxes you find will not open automatically – you will need to solve a riddle to open them.

On top of each box you will find an android monitor. Only Elizabeth Bellamy's thumbscan will activate the monitor. A keyboard will appear on screen. Type in the answer to the riddle. A game will then be activated. Solve the game and the box will automatically open.

Inside each box you will find a geocache box and either the coordinates of, or a clue to, the next checkpoint. You must complete the geocaching task – remove the contents of each box and replace it with something of equal or greater value.

After you have done this, close the box and scan Elizabeth Bellamy's thumb to relock the checkpoint box.

Each team that finishes the course must provide evidence that they have done so by supplying their full collection of geocache contents.

The winning team is the one that completes the course in the shortest time and with all the contents.

Good luck!

Marcus Gold

"Riddles!" Carmen rubbed her hands. "Excellent. We have Will with his head full of brains!"

"And no game has defeated me yet!" Grady cracked his knuckles delightedly.

Will's lip quirked upwards and he opened the second paper.

IRON TEEN

Checkpoint 2

43.26: -65.10

What can be felt, but not seen?

And destroy, but cannot be destroyed?

"The coordinates and the riddle," Will said. "The answer should activate the game on the next box. Let's think about it as we walk."

He stared at the map of Aikenhead. His hair flopped into his eyes and he pushed it back impatiently. "The coordinates don't make sense. They put us in the sea."

"Let me see." Lizzie held out her hand and took the map.

"He's right," Lizzie said eventually. "We walked over the spot they're taking us to — there wasn't anything there."

"Quicksand," I reminded her.

"But no box. This can't be right."

"So … we have the wrong coordinates?" Grady got to his knees, as if he wanted to find someone to complain to.

"We must be missing something. Some other instructions, or a clue." I looked around, as though I expected the correct figures to fall from the sky.

"Was there anything written in the box itself?" Will asked.

I groaned. "I didn't have time to check. If there was, there's no getting it now."

Lizzie stood. "I'll have another look at the box. Maybe there's something under it, or on top of it."

Will pulled a pencil from his rucksack and started to scribble furiously. Carmen took off her jacket and lay on her back.

"It could be a code of some kind. Why not try some variations?" Grady leaned towards Will, who glared at him.

"What do you think I'm doing?"

"I'm going to look at the room." I stood, leaving my rucksack on the deck. "There could be a clue on the wall or floor."

"But it was empty." Carmen lifted her head.

I spread my hands. "We weren't looking for *clues*. Don't worry, this is just the start of the game. There'll be something, somewhere to tell us what to do."

Lizzie stood behind the trapdoor, holding the box up to a shaft of light, turning it over and over. She hummed low in her throat. An Ella Fitzgerald song.

"Nothing?"

"Not a thing." She put it back down. "This can't be *that* hard. The other teams have already worked out the problem and gone."

"At least one team headed in the direction of the sea though." I tilted my head towards the sound of waves. "We saw them." I started to walk around the walls.

"What are you doing?"

"Looking for patterns, a message – something like that."

"OK." Lizzie sped to the other side of the room and started running her hands over the peeling walls. "Time's slipping away." She pulled off her cap and tugged at her short hair.

"You don't know how long it took the others," I reminded her. "We probably just missed the last group." I touched her hand. "Some of them likely raced off without checking the coordinates first. Better to get it right now than go speeding off in the wrong direction."

"I know." Lizzie groaned. "It's just there's *nothing here.*"

I scanned the walls, floor to ceiling. Tried counting boards, but nothing seemed to form a pattern, let alone a clue. Of course, this was Will's area. If there was something here, he'd be the one to spot it, not me.

We heard a sharp burst of Carmen's laughter from outside.

"Glad *she's* having fun." Lizzie's shoulders slumped.

"You're not having fun?" I put shock into my voice. "I mean, we almost drowned, we climbed up a cliff, we're soggy, all our electronics are ruined, we seem to have fallen off the earth to a place even the satellites don't recognize, we can't leave until the crossing is raised again and we have no idea where we're going. Other than that, what's *not* fun?"

Then Carmen from outside again: "Come on out, you guys. *I've* worked it out."

Lizzie's eyes met mine. "*Carmen* worked it out?"

I shrugged.

Carmen was standing by the old sign, spinning it first one way and then the other. She smirked like a cat. "Have you got it yet?"

I frowned. "No."

She looked at Will. "Have you?"

Will glowered at her. "Just *tell us*."

Carmen clapped her hands. "First, say I'm the cleverest."

"We don't have time for this." Grady folded his arms.

Lizzie grinned and jammed her cap back on her head. "Just say it, guys."

Carmen pirouetted as we chorused the words. Her hair flew around her, lifted by the strengthening wind, pink tips like a swarm of butterflies.

"I am, aren't I?!"

"Carmen, we need to get moving," Lizzie

reminded her.

She pouted. "Fine." She spun the sign again. "We didn't need this arrow to tell us where the notice was." Carmen looked at us expectantly.

"So, it's pointing at something else," Grady said.

Lizzie's eyes widened. "It doesn't point to anything – it spins."

"Uh-huh," Carmen said. "But not all the way."

"One hundred and eighty degrees." I hit my own forehead.

Will was already scribbling on the paper, holding it close to stop the cold Atlantic wind from stealing it. He held it up for me to see: -01.56:62.34

"You flipped it."

He nodded.

"And does it make sense?"

He put a finger in the middle of the map. "If we're right, there's the second checkpoint."

"Brilliant!" Lizzie threw her arms around Carmen and gave her a squeeze. "Can we get there before dark?"

"No problem." Will put the map in his pocket. "Let's go."

Chapter Five

"Earthquake!" Carmen shouted.

Grady looked at his feet.

"She's talking about the *riddle*, Grady." Lizzie stifled a laugh as she hopped over a boulder that was half-blocking the path.

"It can be felt, but not seen. It destroys, but you can't destroy it." Carmen nodded smugly. "I am on a *roll*."

Will hummed. "Not a bad suggestion, but we should keep thinking." He paused and looked at the map. "We leave the coastal path here – we have to go this way." He pointed towards the moorland.

"At least it should get us out of this wind." Lizzie shivered. "It's freezing."

"The sun's warm." Grady turned his face to the sky. "We just need to get off the clifftop."

I pulled out my binoculars, wiped the wet lenses, and held them to my eyes. When I had adjusted the focus, an expanse of moorland came closer. A lake glimmered ahead. We would be walking alongside it in less than an hour. "I see another team." I pointed at a cluster of trees.

"Proves we're going the right way." Carmen grinned.

"If that's team eight, they're more than twenty minutes ahead of us," Grady said as he handed a bag of pear drops around. "We're losing time *already*."

"*If* it's team eight." I put a sweet in my mouth. "For all we know, that's team one and we're catching up."

Lizzie nodded. "We just have to keep going – no second-guessing ourselves."

"For five million pounds, we could pick up the pace," Carmen suggested.

"OK." Lizzie tightened her rucksack. "Who's up for a run?"

Grady put his sweets away and we sped over the moor, feet pounding on the grass, kicking up clumps of mud and grunting with the weight of our equipment.

The ground passed in a blur under my feet; I trampled flowers, thistles and oatmeal-coloured grass. Soon we were jogging beside a rushing stream and I couldn't resist. I paused, kneeled and splashed water on my face, cooling off.

Lizzie saw me and held up her hand. "Quick break, guys?"

Carmen flopped down beside me and drank from her bottle. She allowed her head to tip back when she was done, her pale throat open to the sky. Lizzie filled her own bottle from the stream and added a water purification tablet.

"You don't think this water's pure enough already?" I raised my eyebrows. The stream was as clear as a screen.

Lizzie snorted. "Even with my glasses I can't see bacteria, can you?"

"Guess not." I smiled as she put the bottle back in her rucksack and copied me, splashing her face and hands. Droplets clung to her wrists, which seemed fragile and delicate, like the bare veins of an autumn leaf.

An otter was a dark flash and gone, winding sinuously between the rocks and speeding away from us upstream.

"You know … they fill the water at home … with

special chemicals to feminize men?" Grady gasped as he took a drink. "That's why there're hardly any protests against the government these days – not enough … testosterone in the population."

Lizzie shook her head with a smile. "How're you getting on with that rucksack, Grady?" she asked. "Is this pace all right for you?"

"I'll manage." He put his hands on his knees.

"We're making good time." She checked her watch. "It's not sunset for a while yet. We might even get to the *third* checkpoint today – what do you think?"

Will stood a little apart, waiting for us to get running again. He tapped his useless watch. "Five million pounds?" he said.

Lizzie leaped up. "Show me where we're heading."

Will pointed to the map, then off into the distance. "See that lake?" Maybe three-quarters of a mile away the lake shimmered. "That's where we're going."

By the time Will was four, Mum didn't have many friends left – only a couple of diehards from when she had me: Auntie Ros and Auntie Anne.

I remember the last play date I had with my best friend, Matthew. Auntie Anne was pregnant with Matthew's little sister. Will walked up to her, cocked his head to one side and asked, "Is there a baby inside your tummy?"

Auntie Anne nodded. "Yes, there is, Will. You were inside your mummy's tummy once too."

Will looked at her for a long time. Then he walked away without saying anything. Auntie Anne smiled at Mum, and Matthew and I carried on playing with my trains.

The next thing I knew, Auntie Anne was screaming. Will had wandered back up to her holding a thick hardback book and hit her across the stomach as hard as he could.

The whole time, the thoughtful expression never left his face.

"I can't do this any more, Carrie." Auntie Anne hustled Matthew away, sobbing and clutching her belly. "He's out of control. You've created a monster – you never tell him off, never punish him. If you let this carry on, what's he going to be like when he gets to school?"

The last thing she said as she propelled a shocked

Matthew out of the door was that he wasn't going to be able to see me again.

Mum cuddled Will for an hour after that. No one seemed to care that my best friend was gone.

▼

By the time we were nearing the lake, we had all slowed to a jog.

"I need to get fitter," Carmen gasped as she staggered to a halt.

"We'll walk for a while." Lizzie wiped her steamed glasses on her sleeve. "But we should keep up a good pace, at least until we reach the trees." She kept her feet moving, jogging on the spot.

Grady was barely able to speak. He put his hands on his knees and wobbled.

"*Dios*, Grady, are you having a heart attack?" Carmen stared.

Grady held up a hand. "I'm … all right."

"Five million pounds is all very well –" I patted Grady on the shoulder – "but we don't want to kill Grady."

"Wait a minute!" Carmen rushed to a patch of grass sheltered by a leaning rock. Mushrooms clustered beneath the overhang. "Check these out."

"Don't pick wild mushrooms, Car." I rolled my shoulders. "Could be poisonous."

"These aren't poisonous, *chico*." Carmen bent and picked three. "Don't you recognize them?"

Will leaned close to her hand. "Psilocybin mushrooms."

"That's right – magic mushrooms. A little for each of us."

"Are you kidding?" But Lizzie's eyes had brightened with humour. "We have to stay focused."

"Just a tiny bit, *chica*, enough so all this running becomes fun. You *promised* me fun." Carmen was already lifting the shiny brown top to her lips.

"I don't think you should, Car." I frowned. "If that *is* poisonous—"

"It isn't." Will's eyes were on Carmen's mouth now.

"But what if it *is*?" I insisted. "We have no way to call for help. Some mushrooms are *lethal*."

"Let me see." Grady had got his breath back and he pulled Carmen's hand closer to him and squinted. "It does look like the pictures Dad made me memorize. And I do have this." He patted the pocket of his rucksack that contained his medical kit. "I can at least induce vomiting."

"If she poisons herself, she'll already *be* vomiting." I glared.

"I'm taking it." Carmen bit the mushroom. "If I'm still OK in five minutes, you can take some too."

"*Carmen!*" Lizzie cried. But she swallowed and there was nothing any of us could do.

We stared at her in horrified fascination. Nothing happened. Nothing continued to happen.

"See, I'm fine." Carmen laughed. "Give me half an hour and the fun should kick in. Then I can run again."

"Or you'll be falling over a lot," I muttered.

Carmen wrapped her mushrooms and put them in her jacket pocket, then we all started to hike around the lake towards the trees.

"It's really beautiful here, isn't it?" Lizzie murmured as she strode beside me. Her nose piercing sparkled in the same light that caught the lake, and her hair stood up in wild, wind-blown spikes.

I nodded. "In a desolate way."

The lake lapped the shore beside us. I allowed my hand to brush against hers and she leaned slightly towards me. At least, I thought she did. Internally I was at war – sometimes I wondered if I should push things between us before she went to university and someone else got there first. Most times I knew I'd be ruining everything if I did. She was my best friend.

She tensed up in the way that told me she had something to say.

I sighed. "Spit it out."

"You're *really* going to give up your future to keep an eye on Will?"

I opened my mouth, but she kept going.

"At least tell me that once Will graduates, you'll try again with civil engineering? If we win, you could use your money to pay your tuition fees – you wouldn't have to rely on your mum."

I closed my eyes briefly. "I don't know, Lizzie. I don't want to be three or four years older than everyone else on the course and … what if Will decides to do a PhD or something?"

"Haven't you heard of mature students?" Lizzie hit me with her cap. "This has been your dream for *three years*, Ben. And it's important. You could be doing some real good in the world. Can't you plan a cut-off point? Like, when Will is eighteen you've done your time."

"It's not *prison*, Liz. I—"

Grady gave a shout. "There's another team!"

They were approaching the trees from a different direction around the coast and it looked like they would reach cover before us.

"Hey, Will, d'you think they went to the wrong coordinates?" I called.

Will gave his lopsided smirk. "Looks like it."

A girl walked in front with a very long black ponytail. Her skin was brown and she was slim and long-legged. Her rucksack was bright purple. There was a smaller girl on her team and a boy who looked like her twin – or brother, at least. Two larger guys marched alongside the younger girl like personal bodyguards, one dark-skinned, one light.

"Could be team one," I said. "Prisha something, wasn't it?"

"And they're not much ahead of us." Lizzie grinned. "That's excellent."

She called over to Carmen. "How are you feeling?"

Carmen was staring at the water, her head on one

side, mouth slightly open.

"Car?"

"It's so pretty. You guys need to try this. Look at the sparkles."

I laughed.

Lizzie took Carmen's arm. "C'mon, babe – we're walking."

Carmen giggled. "Your voice sounds like bells."

Lizzie laughed. "Can you run?"

Carmen shambled happily into a jog. Lizzie guided her towards Will.

"*You* keep an eye on her."

Will lifted his head from the map. "Dreamer-says-what?"

"*You* said she could take the mushrooms," Lizzie snapped. "So you're in charge."

"I'm reading the map."

"We can all read a map," I said. "Give it to Grady."

Carmen started to sing as she ran. "Grady, Grady, give me your answer do..." Then she forgot the rest of the song and switched to a Spanish lullaby. "*Din dan, din don dan, campanitas sonarán...*"

When she finished her song, she quietly translated the final verse. "*Close your eyes and go to sleep, because the night is coming soon.*" She paused. "*Din, don, dan.*"

Will sped up to catch her.

"I'm tempted," Lizzie whispered. "She's definitely having the most fun."

I looked at Will and grinned. He was already frustrated with preventing her from wandering off.

I watched for a moment as Will slid his arm around Carmen's waist, under her rucksack. He looked back at me and our eyes met. Then he smiled and turned his attention back to guiding Carmen. He was fine.

I squeezed Lizzie's shoulder. "I do want that million pounds. You're right, I can do the course later and what's left could be seed money for important projects, once I've got some experience under my belt."

She smiled at me. "I'm so pleased, Ben. I'm not sure you'd be *you* if you weren't planning to save at least a *bit* of the world."

"We're going to have to leave the lake and head for the trees," Grady said, flapping the map importantly. "There's quite a dip ahead; I think we should go around."

"Will?" I couldn't help checking.

Will looked up from Carmen and nodded. "That was my plan."

"See." Grady sniffed.

"OK, sorry."

We stepped out in the direction Grady pointed and Carmen started to sing again. An old song and a favourite of Lizzie's. Lizzie joined in, her voice higher than Carmen's. Grady hesitated and then he too started to sing. Will met my eye.

I grinned. *"Run to the rock, rock won't you hide me…"*

We were all singing loudly as we jogged across the moor towards the first leaning copse of rowan, long-trunked and red-berried. Birches clustered behind them, silver-grey. The ground underfoot became boggier, making it more difficult to maintain the pace, but Carmen's singing kept going.

"Did you know," Grady's voice raised above the singing, "Paul McCartney has been dead for years? He was replaced by a lookalike in 1966."

Chapter Six

By the time we got to the trees, the sun had slipped behind the hill. As the sun dropped, so did the temperature, and the wind found us again. Shivering, I ducked gratefully under the shelter of the canopy. As the day turned to twilight, the first moths fluttered around us. Carmen squeaked as a bat flew low between the branches.

I swung my bag from my shoulders and found a jumper.

"It's going to get properly dark in an hour or so," I commented as I pulled it over my head. Colours were already bleeding from my vision, leaving only muted greens and reds among shades of grey.

"We could set up camp here." Grady shifted his rucksack. "It's sheltered, at least."

I returned my pack to my shoulders, as Lizzie shook her head. "I want to reach the second checkpoint. We've still got light – we should keep going."

"Lizzie's right," Will said. "The other teams won't

be stopping yet."

"I'm tired," Grady groaned.

I patted his shoulder. "We all are, but we agreed to push ourselves."

"The trees are breathing." Carmen was leaning close to a birch, her arms wrapped around the trunk.

"Think of the money, Grady," Lizzie said as she found her torch. "You can rest at the checkpoint."

"I think I'd almost *pay* a million pounds for a rest," Grady muttered, but he set off, still clanking.

Lizzie slapped her face and arms as she strode. "I hate midges!"

They clouded around us with tiny bites, getting in my eyes and up my nose.

"This is disgusting," Will muttered as he wrapped a travel towel around his neck and over his mouth.

"I'm going to be itching like the devil in the morning," Lizzie groaned, slapping her neck. Already I could see marks on her pale skin where she had been bitten.

Only Carmen didn't seem bothered by the midges; she was skipping ahead, occasionally wafting her hand in front of her face to clear them away.

"Grady, you OK?" I looked back. He winced

as he re-shouldered his rucksack, then he sprayed himself with insect repellant. "Can I have some of that?"

Grady held out the bottle. "Sure. This is the good stuff."

"Thanks." I did my own face and neck, then Lizzie's, Will's and a squirming Carmen's.

Lizzie gasped with relief. "Thanks, Grady!" She swung a stick she had picked up. "We ought to think about eating. We haven't had anything except sweets since lunch on the plane."

"You want to break for tea?" I looked up through the trees – I could see the moon, but it wasn't yet night.

Lizzie shook her head. "Not just yet. We can't be far from the check—" She cried out and grabbed my arm as her leg buckled beneath her. Her eyes were wide with alarm and sharp pain lined her face. Carefully I lowered her to the ground and she bit her lip as she touched her right ankle.

Lizzie's walking boots weren't as strong as my army boots. A dark hollow showed me what had happened: she had stepped over a tree root and into a rabbit hole.

"I think I twisted it!"

Immediately Grady was on his knees beside her, pulling out his medical kit. "It's not sprained?"

"I hope not." Her voice was as pale as her face and her hand was shaking where she touched the swelling.

Grady frowned. "I *said* we should stop. Should I undo your laces?"

"No." I closed my hand around Lizzie's ankle. It felt hot even through her boot, and I could feel the swelling pressing against the leather. "Her boot is keeping some of the swelling down."

Grady handed me an instant cold pack. I squeezed to break the water pouch inside and shook it. Quickly it became ice cold. I pressed it against Lizzie's ankle and she groaned.

Grady passed her some paracetamol and ibuprofen. "Alternate these, every two hours."

Lizzie nodded. "You should be a pharmacist, Grady."

He snorted.

Will tapped me on the shoulder and I looked up. He was holding a long birch branch with a perfect Y-shape at one end.

"You found me a crutch!" Lizzie exclaimed.

"You don't have to use it tonight." I frowned. "We can stop now and keep going in the morning."

"We need to keep moving." Lizzie held up her hand and, reluctantly, I pulled her to her feet.

Grady sighed. "We *need* to stop injuring ourselves. Even *my* medical kit isn't bottomless."

Grady put his supplies away and found himself a cereal bar. I put one arm around Lizzie's waist. "Let's find this checkpoint then."

We were almost out of the trees and the full moon had risen higher, casting shadows of its own. Twigs cracked underfoot and I noticed that the scents of the island had changed – become colder and fresher. The sounds around us had changed too. The gulls had gone, but now I could hear the buzz of bats' wings and the distant hooting of owls.

We moved more slowly as Lizzie carefully tested each step with her stick.

"Are you sure you want to keep walking?" I asked again as I helped her over a rotting trunk.

"I'm sure." Lizzie forced a smile. "I'm excited to

get to the second checkpoint, aren't you?"

"Absolutely. It's just that I know how much you're hurting – remember last year?"

I'd wiped out doing a fifty-fifty grind on my skateboard and landed hard, with my wrist twisted under me.

"Lucky you didn't break your arm that time." Lizzie grinned, then flinched and paled again as she put too much weight on her ankle.

Finally, we stepped into the open. The wind ruffled my hair again, but gently now, as though it too was considering turning in for the night.

"Can you see any other teams?" Lizzie whispered as if leaving the trees meant we had to drop our voices.

Reluctantly I released her and put the binoculars to my eyes. "I can't see anyone."

The river was directly ahead, too long to walk around. "We're going to have to ford that, aren't we?" Lizzie sighed.

Will nodded.

We made our way to the river, no longer trying to push the pace. When we got to the bank, I touched Will's shoulder. "You want to test the depth?"

He tilted his head. "You'll have to watch Carmen. Give me your crutch, Lizzie."

I balanced Lizzie as she handed the stick over.

Will waded into the river and used the stick to measure the depth. When he came out, he was shivering.

"How deep is it?" Grady called.

Will held up the wet crutch, to show the hip-high waterline, then he handed it back to Lizzie. "It's deep, cold and fast-moving." He sniffed.

"We've forded rivers before," Lizzie said. "In DofE last year."

"But we don't want to get everything soaked again." I plucked at my trousers. "We won't dry off at night."

"So, we take off our clothes," Lizzie said simply.

I started to ask if she was sure, but Will was already taking off his rucksack and kneeling to unlace his boots.

"Keep your boots on," I said quickly. "You'll need the traction and there might be sharp stones."

"I'm removing my socks and insoles." He pulled one out to demonstrate. "To keep them dry."

"Oh, right."

"What about Lizzie's boot?" Grady asked. "She can't take it off."

"The cold water should keep the swelling down enough so we can get it back on again," I said.

"One of us could piggy-ba—"

"No." Lizzie shook her head. "That's too dangerous. I can walk in the middle of the group." She unhooked her rope from the side of her bag. "We'll go in a line and hold on to this."

I nodded.

"Ben should go in front with the stick," Grady said.

"What about my knee?" I pulled down my trousers to reveal the bruising. The pattern of purple, red and blue circled the knee and decorated my leg to the shin.

Grady caught his breath. "Remind me to give you some arnica when we set up camp." He looked at me for a long moment. "Even with that knee, you're strongest."

"All right then." I took off my jumper and shirt and folded everything in a precise pile. Will had done the same. Habits learned at home. I sometimes wondered if we'd ever be able to be messy.

"Carmen and I are keeping our vests on," Lizzie called.

Will packed his clothes neatly into his rucksack. "So long as you have something dry to put on when we're across."

"F-fine." Lizzie's teeth were already chattering.

"Are you ready yet?" Grady clutched the straps of his rucksack and edged self-consciously into the deepest shadows.

I repacked my own rucksack and settled the straps back over my shoulders.

"Nasty blisters," Will commented, looking at my chest and armpits.

I nodded as I took Lizzie's crutch and turned so that he could tie the rope to the straps of my bag. Then he linked up Grady's pack, Lizzie's, Carmen's, and finished by attaching his own.

"We're just like paper dolls," Carmen whispered.

"You back with us?" I asked.

"Pretty much," she replied, looking at the river.

"Let's get this over with." I faced upstream and strode into the river, using the stick to check my footing. Within three steps the icy water was up to my thighs.

The rope on my back gave a tug and then loosened as the others trailed after me. Grady held up his torch so that I could see ahead.

I moved at a slight angle downstream, but faced upstream. Leaning into the current, I shuffle-stepped sideways, keeping my feet in contact with the riverbed.

I didn't dare look back; the gentle pressure on the rope told me that the others were still there, still on their feet. I focused instead on our first destination, the sandbank in the middle of the river.

The water rose until it was hip-deep, and my rucksack was getting wet again. I was glad I had my dry clothes in the top. Plants brushed against my legs, drawn past me by the current. They felt like wet fingers. I shuddered.

"This is an adventure!" Carmen shouted. "Cheer up."

I shook my head, but had to smile. Carmen was right. This was what I had wanted: an exciting challenge. Three days playing a life-size game with no Mum to nag at me, Will acting like a human being and Lizzie by my side 24/7.

Suddenly there was a cry behind me – one of us

had fallen. I dropped to one knee and gripped the stick, digging it into the sand.

"Grady, who is it?" I called.

"C-Carmen," Grady stammered. "Will's got her. She's OK."

I felt the rope slacken as Grady moved closer. They were walking again.

Will hadn't been at school very long when Mum was called in to see the head. I would have been around six or seven. With no one willing to babysit and Dad at work, she had to bring us with her. We sat outside the office, kicking the chairs with our heels, trying to listen.

"All little boys lash out," Mum snapped suddenly, loudly. "It's *normal*! It's called *rough-housing*!"

"Well, I hate to compare children, Mrs Harper, but we never had this trouble with Ben." Mr Hutchinson sounded annoyed.

"They're *different*. Will's *very* bright."

I glanced at Will.

"Two of the other boys have been taken to the nurse *this week* alone."

"Well then, you aren't keeping Will occupied, you aren't pushing him. He's says he's bored." Her voice was shrill. "This is *your fault*."

I heard Mr Hutchinson sigh. "We're just asking you to work with the teachers, to support our disciplinary actions with further intervention at home."

"I don't punish my boys." She caught my eye from inside the office.

I patted Will's tense little shoulder and knocked on the office door. "Mr Hutchinson?"

Mr Hutchinson looked surprised. "Hi, Ben. We'll just be another few minutes. Why don't you take Will and go and look at the fish in the tank?"

"I thought…" I swallowed. "Maybe I could take my work to Will's classroom for a bit. He's usually calmer when I'm around."

Mum's face lit up.

Mr Hutchinson leaned back in his chair. "I'm sorry, Ben, it's a really kind offer, but that's not how it works in school."

"You could talk to his teacher," Mum said. "She can make sure Ben has work to do."

Mr Hutchinson looked shocked. "Mrs Harper."

He frowned. "Ben's education will suffer if he misses his own class time. The focus in reception is on socialization and learning through play."

"There you go." Mum sat back with an expression of triumph. "That's why my Will is bored."

Mr Hutchinson looked hard at his paperwork. "Will *is* one of the older reception children. Miss Scott tells me that he is reading at the level of a seven- or eight-year-old and is already doing column addition."

"And long division," Mum said smugly.

"But it's not just about maths and literacy, Mrs Harper." Mr Hutchinson twitched as if he wanted to destroy the paper in front of him. "His social skills are terrible." He rubbed his eyes. "All right. For two weeks, we will allow Will to go up to Ben's class for literacy and maths *only*. For the rest of the day, he will be with children in his own year group. We'll meet again in a fortnight, unless there is cause to meet sooner."

"There won't be," Mum said confidently.

"If there is an improvement in his behaviour, we'll talk about next steps."

"You mean moving him up permanently?" Mum

leaned forwards.

"We'll see." Mr Hutchinson folded his hands. "Ben, how do you feel about having Will join you in your class for literacy and maths?"

I felt Mum's eyes on me, but I didn't look at her. If I said it was fine, I'd be a joke: the boy whose little brother was better than him at school. But then I thought of the other kids in my class. Will was even cleverer than Abigail Chaney, who knew all her times tables quick as a click. They'd soon stop laughing.

"It's OK, he can sit by me," I said.

On the other side of the bank, I dumped the water out of my boots, put the insoles back in and got dressed, using my shirt as a makeshift towel. I was shivering uncontrollably.

I heard Lizzie's teeth chattering and when I turned round, she was still struggling to get her trousers on. "Need a hand?"

Wordlessly she handed me her clothes. She hadn't bothered trying to dry herself, so I opened out her checked shirt and began to rub her arms. Her body was rigid with cold. Finally, she began to breathe more easily. She turned her back, pulled off her wet vest and put on the shirt. Then she stood up on one foot. I dried her legs and carefully pulled her trousers up.

She fastened them with trembling hands, then sat back down to put on her boots. She ground her teeth as she pulled her right boot over her ankle. I held my breath, but the boot went on. She tied the laces loosely.

As soon as everyone was ready, Will pointed up the hillside. "That's the way to the checkpoint."

"Are you sure?" Grady frowned at him. "You don't think we should look at the map again?"

Will turned, his face expressionless. "The moon is full. That means it's 180 degrees away from the sun, and twelve hours behind it. The moon rose over there an hour ago, so that's east." He gestured. "According to the map, it's a straight line across the river and up the hill to the coordinates."

"There's a shape up there." Carmen squinted towards the top of the hill.

I looked through my binoculars. "It's a cairn or something, halfway up."

"That'll be it." Lizzie smiled tiredly. "You can't see any other teams?"

I shook my head. "Looks like we've got a clear run."

Grady opened the map, then closed it again. His stomach rumbled. "Then let's get up there so we can eat!" He started to walk, his torch throwing a jerky light across the ground.

I took Lizzie's elbow and she smiled gratefully as she lurched forwards, using the crutch to bear her weight once more. "I'm slowing everyone down," she grumbled.

"Nah." I squeezed her arm. "If it weren't for you, we'd have let Grady set up camp an hour ago."

"I'm not sure I can climb this hill." She raised her torch and sent a beam of light racing over the rocky slope. The gradient was steeper than it had first seemed.

Will, Carmen and Grady had forged ahead and were already quite a long way above us. My bruised knee throbbed.

"One step at a time," I said.

Our breath came faster and harder as we climbed, and Lizzie's crutch thudded with every other step.

"Are you still looking forward to next year?" I asked. "Making new friends and that?"

Lizzie kept her head down. "It's weird. Knowing you were going to be going through the same thing made me less worried. Now..."

"You're more nervous about going to Swansea because I'm not going to Cardiff?"

"It's stupid."

"I'll come and see you every weekend if you like."

"But..."

"What?" I frowned.

"We won't be doing the same stuff... What if we—"

"'What if we what?" I said hoarsely.

"What if we don't have anything to talk about any more?" she said in one long breath. "You'll be working, I'll be studying." She looked at me. "Told you it was stupid."

I swallowed. "I'm not worried about that. Worst case, you can talk for both of us, like usual."

"Hey." She glared.

I cleared my throat. "What I'm scared of is ... what if your new friends think I'm a loser for working in a garage?"

Her eyes narrowed. "I wouldn't be friends with anyone who thought that. Anyway, what if they do? You think that would change what I think of you? You think I look down on Car because she works in Cutz?" She pulled her arm from mine and wobbled. "I'd never!"

I caught her before she fell. "I'm sorry, Lizzie. I know you're not like that. I just meant – I'm worried, too." I shuffled forwards. "We have to make sure we don't drift apart. I'll be there for you as long as you want me to be."

"Ben, that's—"

There was a whoop from above us. Carmen and Will had reached the cairn.

Lizzie nodded at me. "To be continued." She looked up. "Is the box there?"

"Yes," Carmen shouted. "But we can't open it without you – we need your thumb."

"Don't rush," I warned her as she tried to pick up the pace.

I could hear Grady ahead of us, panting with the effort of the climb.

"You all right, Grady?" I asked as we drew level.

"Yeah, I'm … fine."

"Nearly there," Lizzie said cheerfully. "Then you can take that bag off and eat something while we work on the box."

Grady brightened and nodded.

Will and Carmen were sharing a huge bag of mixed nuts when we reached the checkpoint. Grady unclipped his rucksack and lay panting as Carmen offered the packet round.

"Mmm, protein." I took a handful of nuts and tossed them back while I used my binoculars to look for other teams. I couldn't see any movement, but to our right I spotted the glow of a campfire. So at least one of the teams had stopped on the moor and others were likely camped on the other side of the hill, out of the wind. Were we the only ones still going?

Lizzie touched my shoulder. "You can see the sea from up here."

I adjusted my gaze. In the distance, the lights of a cargo ship floated above the black water and the town on the bigger island lightened the sky. Behind us the hill sloped back towards the estuary. I dropped the glasses and returned my gaze to the pile of stones that formed the cairn. My torch lit up a chain linked to a metal box about the size of a lunchbox, with a small black screen on the top.

Carmen clapped her hands. "Let's open this thing."

I helped Lizzie to take off her rucksack and sit by the box. She pressed her thumb on the top to activate the monitor and immediately a screen lit up with the words WELCOME, ELIZABETH BELLAMY.

"It worked." She breathed a sigh of relief.

Then a keyboard appeared on screen.

"Loving the tech!" Grady grinned. "Gold must have had the boxes designed especially." He leaned closer. "Type in *earthquake*."

Carefully Lizzie typed in each letter. When she had finished, she pressed the return key and waited.

Chapter Seven

"Shouldn't something be happening?" Carmen leaned over Lizzie's shoulder.

I groaned. "It must be the wrong answer."

Carmen frowned. "It *has* to be earthquake. It fits."

"Well, it's not." Will pulled the paper out of his pocket and unfolded it. "*What can be felt, but not seen. And destroy, but cannot be destroyed?*"

"*Earthquake* – see?" Carmen sniffed.

"Other things fit, too." Will pushed his fringe out of his eyes.

"Like what?"

"Time!" Lizzie cried. "We can feel the passing of time, right? But not see it. And ultimately it destroys everything."

"Or something like a virus or a germ," Grady offered. "You can feel its effects, but not see it."

I shivered again and ducked into the shelter of the cairn as a gust of wind whipped past.

"*Time*'s good," Will said. "Try that."

Lizzie typed in the four letters. There was a slight whir from the screen and then it lit up with just two words: *Strike two*.

"That's bad." I sat back on my heels. "Three strikes and we're out?"

"Only one more guess, then." Lizzie took off her glasses and rubbed them on her shirt. "I've got nothing."

"Hey! It could be *nothing*." I looked at Will. "Or nothingness?"

Will shook his head, frowning. "Can you *feel* nothingness?"

I folded my arms.

"So … *germ*, then?" Grady reached for the box, but Lizzie's hand snapped out and caught his wrist.

"That doesn't feel right."

"It's all we've got, *chica*," Carmen pointed out.

"If it's wrong, we're out of the game. We have to be absolutely sure," Lizzie said.

"Vote?" Grady turned to Will.

Will shook his head. "Keep thinking. See if we can come up with something better."

"At least we've got these rocks to keep us out of

the wind." Carmen pressed closer to me, rubbing her arms.

Will and I looked at each other. I began to laugh.

"Wha—" Lizzie started to ask. "Oh, right."

She reached for the keypad and started to type. W-I-N-D.

I held my breath. There was a long moment when nothing happened. And then the screen cleared and an image of a door appeared.

"I know this game!" Grady leaned forwards again. "You've got to solve the puzzle to open the door." He gently nudged Lizzie out of the way. "Let the master work."

▼

After ten minutes, Grady threw the box down and stamped towards us.

"No luck, Grady?" Carmen was leaning against her rucksack, eating a sandwich.

"It's ridiculous," Grady hissed. "I'm brilliant at these – all you have to do is swipe things around in the right order and find the key."

"Maybe it's because you're hungry," I said. "Eat something while you think."

"And in the meantime, Will can have a turn," Lizzie added.

Jerky with frustration, Grady opened his rucksack and pulled out a gas stove and his mess tin. He opened a tin of stew and began to heat it up. Lizzie got out a mini stove of her own and boiled water for tea. The bluish light looked cool but warmed the side of my face.

I had planned to do all my cooking on a campfire, so I was making do with a cold, half-crushed Cornish pasty. I looked at Grady enviously as the scent of beef filled the air.

"You want me to cook another tin?" Grady asked.

"Thanks, but that wouldn't be fair – it's yours." I bit into my pasty again.

Will and I were lucky Mum had seen sense and let us bring the pasties. I'd also talked her into couscous and instant noodles for the other two days, insisting that on a hike, the Atkins diet was not going to be our friend.

She had still made me pack a big hunk of cheese wrapped in plastic and more beef jerky than we'd ever be able to eat.

"Here, Ben." Lizzie pressed a cup of tea into my

hand. The first sip burned my tongue, but heat wound down my throat and settled in my belly like a hot-water bottle.

"Any luck, Will?" Lizzie handed him a cup of his own.

Will shook his head. "Grady's right. I've tried everything."

Carmen tucked her sandwich wrapper back into her rucksack. "Let me try."

"Whatever." Will backed off ungraciously.

Carmen twisted her hair in one finger and leaned close to the box. She touched the screen experimentally.

"*¡Hola!*, little box," she breathed.

Then she tilted her head and sat up with the box held in both hands.

"*¡Hola!*" she said again breathily, a question in her voice.

Then she smiled and blew hard on the screen. There was a click and the box opened.

Will stared. "How did you do that?"

"I'm not stupid, you know!" Carmen tossed her head. "The answer was *wind*, wasn't it?"

"But that was just to activate the game." Grady

looked up from his dinner. " Not to solve it."

"It was *both*." I cupped my hands around my mug. "Well done, Carmen!"

"The image moved a little when I breathed on it," she admitted.

"What's inside, Car?" Lizzie asked.

"More coordinates and another riddle, etched into the lid. There's a coin glued to the inside and … another box." Carefully Carmen tipped the smaller box on to the ground. I held my torch close to the open lid and stared at the information written on it.

IRON TEEN

Checkpoint 3

78.20: 52.05

FYALWURTOILOECSLTCKE

I held it up for everyone to see. "That's not even English!"

"Well, at least the coordinates don't *seem* to need messing with this time," Will muttered as he and Grady shone a torch on the map. He pointed. "There. Right on the coast."

"What about the riddle?" Grady stared at the letters.

"Not now." Lizzie carefully copied it into a notebook, took a pencil rubbing of the coin and tucked the book back in her rucksack. "Let's get *this* box finished with, then find somewhere to camp for the night. I don't think we should go for the next checkpoint till the morning – does everyone agree?"

"Definitely." Grady nodded.

"But I still think we aim for no more than six hours' sleep and set off early."

"Works for me." I was relieved I'd wrapped my sleeping bag in a plastic bin bag – at least it would be dry.

Carmen was holding the smaller box. "This is so exciting." She stroked it with a finger. "I wonder what's inside?"

"Our first geocache." Grady rubbed his hands

together. "Five more and we've won the game."

Lizzie grinned. "All we've got to do is replace what's in there with something of equal or greater value. What do you think it is?"

"If they're clever," Will said, "it'll be a compass or torch."

"It's too small to be a torch." Carmen turned the box over in her hands. "And it's really light." She held it to her ear and gave it a shake. It rattled.

"Just open it!" Will was impatient.

An owl shrieked in the woods below us. Carmen jumped and clutched the box to her chest as the wind dropped to almost nothing. Holding her breath, she unlatched the box. Almost reverently, she opened it.

Her hair fell in dark curtains around her face as she peered down and her hands started to tremble. Then she snapped the box shut and shoved it at Will.

"W-Will?" Lizzie's voice quivered. "What's in the box?"

Will opened the lid, then he looked at me. His eyebrows rose, ever so slightly. I'd never seen Will disturbed before.

"What is it, Will?" I tried to remain calm, but my mind was racing.

"What's in the box?" Grady yelled.

Wordlessly, Will held up the small metal container for us all to see.

Inside, still bloody, with pieces of gum hanging off it and a corroded silver filling glinting in the torchlight, was a tooth.

Chapter Eight

"That's a *human* tooth," Grady said weakly. "It's got a filling."

"Well … it's not a compass." Will cocked his head to one side, then looked around. "Is someone pranking us?"

"It's a *tooth*, Will. This isn't a prank." I wrapped my arms around my chest.

"It's one of the other teams. They're trying to make us give up," Lizzie breathed.

"Dirty tricks!" Grady's eyes flashed.

Carmen was shaking and mumbling "*¡Dios mío!*" under her breath.

"Someone's taken out the original item and replaced it with something we'll never be able to match." Lizzie shut her eyes. "It's the only explanation."

"But *who*?" I felt numb. "Who'd pull out their own *tooth* to sabotage another team?"

"Someone we don't want to run into." Carmen rubbed her elbows as if she was cold.

"A team who *really* want to win," Grady added.

"We really want to win, but we wouldn't do this. It's … cheating." I clenched my fists impotently.

"Actually, it's a pretty good plan," Will said thoughtfully. "I mean, what do *we* do now? Either we have to do the same or give up. We've no idea what was in that box before they got to it, so we can't put in something of equal value to the original item."

"Can we guess what it was?" Lizzie pulled off her cap and started tugging at her hair. "I mean, it's a small box – it *might* have been a compass."

Grady rubbed his temples. "It could have been almost anything – a watch, food, jewellery, the map, an iPod, money, insect repellent … *anything*."

Carmen sat down. "This was meant to be *fun*!"

"It still can be." Lizzie crumpled her cap in one hand. "We just have to work this out – like another puzzle. Then we show we won't be put off and move on to the next checkpoint – there are five more to go after this one."

"This could even work in our favour," Grady added. "Thin out the crowd a bit."

I shook my head. "I don't know, Lizzie, this has kind of ruined the game for me."

"You want to give up?" Lizzie stared.

There was silence, broken only by the buzzing of the midges and the distant shush of the sea.

"If we're not, then we have to follow the rules," Will said eventually. "Replace the tooth with something of equal value."

"But ... what's of equal value to a *tooth*?" Lizzie looked at him.

"Someone's boots?" Grady suggested.

Lizzie rubbed her eyes. "What if the judges don't agree – we could lose the money."

"And how are you going to get *boots* in that box?" Will sneered.

"Money, then," Carmen said.

"But how much?" Will tilted his head. "How many pounds for one tooth?"

"Fifty?" Grady offered.

"Did you bring fifty quid with you, Grady?" I asked. "I mean, the shopping opportunities here aren't great."

He glared. "I bet we all brought money for the airport. We should have enough between us."

"I've got about a tenner." Lizzie scratched her head. "But is fifty pounds going to do? Is that what they want?"

"I hate to say this, but it feels like money is an easy way out," I mused. "It doesn't have the feel of *sacrifice* that I think they'd be looking for."

"You want sacrifice, *chico*?" Carmen stared. "You think Lizzie or I should have packed a white dress?"

"Funny." I shook my head. "You know what I mean. Whatever *was* in that geocache, the Gold Foundation weren't looking for *money* to replace it. This game doesn't feel like the kind of set-up rich kids could just pay their way through."

"So, we go home?" Carmen asked shakily.

"No!" Grady snapped. "We keep thinking."

"There's really only one thing we *can* leave in the box." Will rubbed his chin again. "A tooth."

Carmen surged to her feet. "That's *loco*."

"If we leave something else," Will said, "we run the risk of getting it wrong and being disqualified at the end of the course. If we leave a tooth, we're following the rules. We can argue that we left something of equal value to *what we found*. They can't take us out of the running for that."

"Then what if we say we *found* a compass or an earring?" Carmen said.

"Don't you think they're monitoring us?" Will asked. "They must know what's in the box now."

"I don't care," Carmen snapped. "They can't expect us to—"

"Maybe we should vote on it," I heard myself say. "Our choices are to give up and go home or leave a tooth ... right?"

Carmen looked defiant. "I don't like this."

"How badly do you want to be a vet?" Lizzie asked her, and her shoulders sagged.

"How do we vote?" Grady asked.

I picked up some smaller stones from around the cairn and handed them out. Then I lifted the checkpoint box, empty of everything except its glued-in coin. "We all turn our backs and I'll pass the box around. If you think we should leave a tooth, put your stone in the box. We'll count the votes when the box gets back to me."

I stared from the box to the stone in my hand. Give up, or go on? We were stuck on the island until the estuary cleared safely – another two days. But we could set up camp near the deck on the beach, chill out and then walk back the way we'd come. Not what we'd planned, but at least we'd have had a holiday.

▼

"*How* many T-shirts?" I stared at Lizzie's bed, where she was laying out her things ready to be packed.

"It's August. It'll probably be hot and we *will* need changes of clothes this time." Lizzie raised her eyebrows, a reminder of the first time we went camping, when Will and I had brought only one shirt and one change of pants each. My argument that turning my boxers inside out was the same as putting clean ones on hadn't gone down well.

"What else are you bringing?" I had the master list with me. It had taken almost a whole day to put together – all the things we thought we might need for the trip. So long as the whole list was ticked off, between us we'd have everything.

"Climbing gear, obviously." Lizzie pointed to the pile. "We'll each need the basics, but I'll take my full kit: the carabiners, hexes and the rest." She grabbed a stove and tucked it into her rucksack.

"You're taking a stove?" I sat on the floor.

"We might not have time to make a campfire at every stop. Right, medical kit, spare socks, food, energy drink, mess tin, spork, cup, teabags, milk powder, phone, notebook and pencil, pack of cards." She scanned the bed. "What am I missing?"

"Compass, torch, bedroll."

"Under the bed from last time." She pulled them out and added them to the pile. "What else?"

"Towel?" I asked.

"And toothbrush." She made a note on a piece of paper. "I'll add it to the medical kit once I've used it in the morning." She bounced over to her dresser. "Deodorant, moisturiser."

"Seriously?"

"It's important." She opened a drawer. "Swimsuit."

"You think we'll need one?"

"Maybe. One of the checkpoint boxes could be underwater."

There was a crash as her door swung open. Carmen stood in the doorway, one hand on her hip.

"Your mami sent me up. You're not done yet? *I* am all packed and I finished my last shift. Now we just need to win and I won't need my terrible job back!" She raised her phone and made me take a selfie with her. I grimaced into the lens.

"Mrs Arnett let me dye her hair," she said as she put a filter on the photo, then held it up to show me. "It came out very purple. She complained, but Rosa had warned her I was only learning. She was so ungrateful. I would have been happy with purple hair." She smiled widely. "I will much prefer working with animals, who don't complain."

Lizzie laughed. "Did you pack a swimsuit, Car?"

Carmen shrugged. "No. If I need to swim, I have my underwear."

Lizzie tucked her swimsuit into her rucksack firmly.

"I did pack vodka." Carmen nudged me.

I rubbed my hands. "Cards, vodka, music on our phones... Plenty to keep us occupied around the campfire then. I can't think of a better trip."

Carmen looked around. "Where's Will?"

"With Mum. She's acting like she's never going to see him again."

"Seriously though." Carmen leaned forwards. "This is going to be fun, right?"

"The best." I looked at Lizzie.

"We could even get together with some of the

other teams in the evenings," Lizzie suggested. "Make a *real* party of it."

"It's a *competition*," I reminded her.

"Yeah, but I'm sure they'll all be good guys." She finished rolling up her bivvy and attached it to the top of her rucksack. "There, something to sleep in, that's everything."

I ticked her items off on the master list. "Is there anything else you think we should take to help us with the riddles?"

"We've got our phones," Carmen pointed out. "Wikipedia is our friend."

Lizzie frowned. "You reckon we'll have reception?"

"We could pack a dictionary and a calculator," I suggested. "Just in case."

"Good idea." Lizzie found a little pocket dictionary in one of her desk drawers.

"Why do you have *that*?" Carmen stared.

"Won it in a school competition," said Lizzie as she added her calculator. "Anything else?"

"Um … tools?" I said thoughtfully.

"Why would we need *tools*?" Carmen said. "You're just adding weight for poor Lizzie, *chico*. You have your Swiss army knife, don't you?"

"Yes. But we might have to build a raft or—"

Carmen snatched the list from me. "Look, Grady has a pick and pliers, Will has a shovel and axe, we've got rope that we can use for tying logs together. I have my own Swiss army knife. What else would we need? Stop worrying!" She returned the list. "We've thought of everything. We have our strategy – to keep moving and do as many checkpoints as possible each day. We know what to do. We can win this."

"It feels a bit too much like we're winging it." I glanced at Lizzie.

"We can't make much more of a plan." She shrugged. "We don't know what the checkpoints will be like or where they are. Our priority is getting to the last of those seven coordinates as fast as we can."

"And winning five million pounds," Carmen said.

"Three days to set us up for the rest of our lives." I held out a fist, beaming, and Carmen knocked it with hers.

▼

Now, if we went on, someone would have to lose a tooth.

When Will was seven, he developed an abscess. The dentist said he needed the tooth out and Mum insisted we both had to be in the room with him to make sure he wasn't frightened.

The dentist told Will that the numbing injection would hurt more than the extraction itself and that even then he'd only feel a little prick. The dentist's smile was very wide and blindingly white, and his hair was rigidly slicked back. Will cried out when the needle went into his gum. After the dentist removed the syringe, he poked Will with his gloved finger to make sure that the area was numb. Will bit him as hard as he could.

When the dentist's partner came in to complete the operation, I sat on the chair at the back of the room and watched Mum hold his hand as Will shuddered and shook and finally screamed – a high-pitched note that shivered through my whole body.

"It isn't hurting him," the new dentist insisted. "It just feels weird. A lot of kids don't like the sensation." She gave a twist and a yank and held Will's tooth up for him to see before turning to put it in an envelope so he could take it home.

The look Will gave her...

▼

I'd never forgotten that look. Having that tooth out had hurt Will. If we decided to keep going, someone would have to go through the same experience with no anaesthetic. Maybe it would even be me.

Did I need the money that badly?

Or rather, did I want to fix cars my whole life?

If we kept going and *won*, I could study civil engineering, Carmen could go to vet school, Lizzie could pay off her parents' mortgage and her own uni fees, Will could start his working life without debt and Grady ... well, he could entertain the trolls by exposing the world's conspiracies.

OK, I didn't much care about Grady's ambition, but everyone else's felt important.

Part of me wanted to keep going just to show the team that left the tooth that we wouldn't give up so easily. I thought about the other teams. How many of them would go back when they saw a tooth in the box?

Right now, our chances of winning were one in

nine. If some of the other groups dropped out and we kept going, then our odds would go up.

Quietly I put my stone in the box and passed it to the next person.

How would everyone else vote?

I tried to listen for stones going in. The box was rattling as it went around the circle. At least one other person must have voted to keep going. What would *Will* do?

Finally, Carmen put the box back in my hands. I swallowed.

"Everyone turn back round." I shook the box. There was more than one stone inside. If there were only two, we were giving up.

I opened the lid so we could all see at once.

Three stones. I gasped in a mix of relief and fear. Keep going.

I tipped the box so that the stones fell on the floor. "OK, then." I rubbed my face. "We've got another decision to make."

Eventually Grady spoke. "We could draw straws."

Lizzie straightened. "I'm the team leader. It should be me."

"No," I insisted. "*Not* you. You *are* our team

leader, so we need you to be at the top of your game and you've already hurt your ankle."

"Carmen's going to have to pull the tooth," Will said. "She's our medic. You can do it, can't you, Car?"

Carmen paled. "*Si* ... probably."

"OK." Grady wrapped his arms around his chest. "Me, you or Will, then? Straws?"

I shook my head. "If Will comes back missing a tooth, Mum will lose it big time."

Lizzie looked up sharply. "Ben, that's—"

"Perfectly true," Will said mildly.

I looked at Grady. "So, it's you ... or me."

His eyes were frozen on mine. Then I picked up a stone, showed him and turned my back. I tucked the stone into one fist. "Choose a hand." I turned back round. "Whoever ends up with the stone loses a tooth."

Grady reached out a finger and held it over first one fist, then the other. I could feel the stone digging into my palm. His hand was trembling.

"Get on with it." Will sounded bored.

Grady smacked my right fist.

My heart thudded. I slowly opened my left hand

135

and tipped the stone from my palm.

Grady whooped, Lizzie shushed him.

"Are you all right, Ben?"

"Sure. It's only fair." I forced a smile. "I did vote to keep going."

Carmen let out a tiny moan. "I don't feel good about this, *chico*."

"Would it make everyone feel better if Ben had a financial incentive?" Will cocked his head. "How about if he does this, Ben gets a percentage of everyone's winnings? Say, two and a half."

Grady frowned. "That's twenty-five grand each."

"Ben gets another £100,000 and we all get £975,000."

Carmen's lips curled upwards. "That does seem fair."

Lizzie nodded.

Matthew was laughing at me. "Ben's got to copy his answers off his *little brother*." He was waving his arms around. *"Ben's a dumbo!"*

The oldest girl in our class marched across the playground. Her hair was long and she wore it in a dark plait that never stayed neat. Stray strands flew mesmerizingly around her face. Her glasses had blue *Star Wars* frames; she had campaigned for months to get the Disney ones replaced.

She put her hands on her hips. "Matthew Harris, you are a complete idiot," she said and then she kicked him as hard as she could in the shin.

Lizzie stood beside me as Carmen held Grady's pliers in a tin of boiling water.

"We shouldn't even be considering this," Lizzie said again miserably. "What kind of people are we?"

"It's OK, Lizzie. How bad can it be?" I raised my torch to search for Will, hoping he'd tell me his own experience hadn't been as terrible as I remembered.

Will shrugged. "It'll be bad, but it'll be over fairly quickly. And there are things we can do to make it hurt less."

"Like what?" Lizzie demanded.

"We've got painkillers – he can take some now."

Grady opened his medical kit. "Hold the torch here, Will. How about some Tramadol?"

Lizzie stared. "That's what Nan was taking after her operation. How do you have that?"

"Dad." Grady slid the packet out. "He filled the prescription – just in case."

"There you go, Ben," Will said. "You'll hardly feel a thing."

"What else?" Lizzie said.

Will's mouth twisted into his little smile. "The brain produces its own painkillers, but for that, Ben needs to be relaxed."

"The Tramadol should help with that too," Grady said and I looked at the two pills I'd cracked into my palm.

"I've got something else to relax him!" Carmen laid the pliers in a clean mess tin and pulled the magic mushrooms out of her jacket. "Here!"

"I'm not sure about that." I frowned.

"You saw me take them. They're fine." She broke one in half. "Here, that should be plenty."

Lizzie put her arm around me and I leaned closer to her. "Take it, Ben," she insisted.

I took the mushroom with my other hand and examined it.

"It'll take a little while to kick in," Carmen said.

"Eat it now."

I ate the mushroom. It was the most disgusting thing I'd ever tasted. Carmen clapped her palm over my mouth. "Don't spit it out."

"Yuck." I retched and pulled away from her.

"Quick, drink something." Lizzie looked around for a water bottle, but Carmen had already produced her bottle of vodka. The label gleamed gold in the torchlight.

"Have some of this."

"He's going to be tripping his nuts off," Will remarked.

I tipped the Tramadol on to my tongue, let the capsules sit for a second, then upended the cheap vodka.

Lizzie looked at Will. "What else can we do?"

"Distraction," he said.

"We can hold his hands," Lizzie said and Carmen laughed.

"Is that the best you can think of to distract a boy?" She began to pull her top and vest over her head. Her voice was muffled by her T-shirt. Will and Grady stared at the lacy bra that was revealed little by little. The torch, quickly aimed by Grady, showed that the bra was bright red. I couldn't take my eyes off it. The colour glowed against her olive skin. Were the mushrooms starting to kick in?

I stared between the bottle of vodka and the red lace. I started to feel light-headed and the world began to slide sideways.

Carmen swallowed. "You're sure you want me to do this? Wouldn't you prefer it to be Will?"

"You do it." I found a wide, flat rock to sit on and thumped down.

Carmen touched the pliers. "Which tooth, Ben?"

"Not one of the front ones," Lizzie said.

"The ones at the very back will be hardest to get." Grady frowned, shining the torch at me.

"How about the third molar in?" Will pointed to his own mouth. "That one."

I took a deep breath, which made my head spin, and nodded. I handed the vodka to Grady, who took a long drink of his own. "See you on the other side."

Lizzie's fingers were twisting like snakes. "I don't like this."

I tried not to notice that Carmen's hands were trembling as she picked up the pliers. "Will, you'll have to hold his head still."

Will nodded and walked behind me. I gave an involuntary shudder as I felt Will's hand on my shoulder. Not comforting me; pinning me down, preventing me from running.

An insect, long and scuttling, raced across my hand, from one nook in the rock to another. I pulled my hand up and blinked at my fingers.

Grady put my hand around the vodka bottle and guided it to my lips. "Drink up."

My head thumped like a drum as I suckled the bottle. The front of my shirt grew wet. I was spilling more from my numb lips than I was swallowing. I fixed my eyes on Carmen. Her black hair slid forwards to tickle my cheek, the pink tips grey in the darkness.

I looked for Lizzie. She was shifting from foot to foot behind Carmen. I raised an arm towards her. "Hold my hand?" My words sounded odd to my ears, far away and blunt.

Lizzie dropped to her knees on the damp grass and caught my fingers in hers.

Finally, Carmen pulled the bottle from me. "How do you feel, *chico*?"

"Pretty great." My gaze shifted from Carmen's bra to Lizzie's blue eyes.

"Sing to me?" I mumbled. Something I never would normally ask her. I had to be careful, my tongue was loosening. What if I said something even more stupid? Like *I've always loved you, Lizzie.* That'd be just brilliant. Quickly I opened my mouth and pointed with my free hand. Do it.

Immediately Will's hands caught my temples like a vice. I could no longer see Lizzie, but she began to sing, her low voice twining into my ears. An old song, one that she often sang along to in the car. We both knew all the words.

Then Carmen inserted one hand to hold my mouth open and put the pliers in with the other.

Bats whizzed past, swift blurs against the sky. My stomach lurched and I began to feel sick. I tried to wrench my head around, but Will held me still. Vomit swelled in my oesophagus. Lizzie's fingers in mine. I thought frantically. Carmen's bra. The moon. The … *pain!*

The pliers were clamped around my molar and Carmen was pulling. At first I'd felt nothing, as if she was tugging at a lump of food in there, then the nerve endings came alive and shrieked.

I bucked like a bull and gagged on a scream.

"Quick, Car!" Lizzie cried.

Will pulled me back hard and I felt his knee on my chest, the rock against my back. I started to tremble, my heels drummed on the ground.

"Hurry," Lizzie cried again.

I focused on Carmen's face. She was sweating, wrinkles between her eyebrows, her eyes narrowed.

"I ... can't," she ground out. "It's not ... coming. Grady, I need you."

Grady moved into place and Carmen wrapped his fingers around the pliers. "Pull."

He braced himself on the rock and leaned back. I howled between his fingers. Thrashed.

"Not good, not good," Lizzie was repeating like a mantra. Her hand was crushing mine.

My eyes bulged and Grady yanked again, rotated this time. I felt something come loose and blood filled my throat, coppery and thick. I choked.

"Almost there." Grady twisted once more and I wailed.

Grady grew horns. His skin turned crimson and his teeth elongated. Blood filled his eyes, black veins traced his forehead.

Midges crawled over Carmen's naked chest and blood began to run down her throat from a thousand bites. I tried to turn my head. Only my eyes went to Lizzie.

Her blue eyes had gone white all over, the glaze of death. Water ran down her face; tears that turned into an ocean. Her clothes soaked, everything wet. Ice-cold water running from her hand to mine. I shrieked and Will's face appeared above mine. Impassive. Normal Will, his eyes cold and dark, his mouth warped into that small smile that didn't know what to make of itself.

"I think he's hallucinating," Carmen cried.

Will's eyes bored into mine. "Not surprising with everything he's taken."

Grady gave a final yell of effort and my tooth tore from my mouth by its roots. He fell backwards, still gripping the pliers and blood flew in an arc, spattering Lizzie's shocked face and Carmen's chest.

Will released me and I rolled on to my side, thudding from the rock to the ground, spitting blood into the mud and vomiting on to the grass. My gut uncoiled and I vaguely felt Lizzie's hands on my back, stroking me. Vodka, blood and shreds of mushroom spilled around my knees, hot and acidic.

"It's all over, Ben." Lizzie's words were soothing.

I tried to stand up, but my limbs weren't my own. I fell back, my mouth filling with the taste of blood and an aching void where my molar had been. I spat again.

"Here." Carmen's T-shirt, still warm from her skin, wadded up, shoved into my mouth.

"Hey, look at that." Grady staggered to his feet, holding up my tooth. The roots were long, like legs, and blood and gristle clung to the branches. "I did it."

"Well done, Grady," Lizzie said without looking at him. "Put Ben's tooth in the box and take out the other one. Wrap it in my glasses cloth – it's in the case in one of the side pockets of my bag – and leave it there for safekeeping."

"Will." Carmen's voice was worried, and her hands, which had been holding her T-shirt in my mouth, looked as if they had been dipped in ink. "Why is Ben still bleeding?"

Will narrowed his eyes. "Uh-oh."

"What?" Lizzie snapped, turning on him.

"How much vodka did he have?"

Carmen held up the bottle. "About a third."

"It's a blood thinner," Will said. "I should have thought of it before."

Lizzie looked at Carmen's blood-soaked T-shirt, then at Grady's medical kit. "Haven't you got anything in there to stop the bleeding?"

Grady shook his head.

Chapter Nine

"Ben needs to eat, drink and rest." Lizzie took control. "We can't set up camp right here – other teams could be arriving any time. Will, Grady, can you guys go to the bottom of the hill and pitch somewhere on the east slope? Light a fire and get some food started. Carmen and I will bring Ben."

Will and Grady shouldered their packs, then hung mine and Lizzie's on their fronts, sandwiching themselves in equipment.

"We can't take Carmen's," Will warned as Grady grunted and bent his knees.

Carmen put her own rucksack on. "That's fine, *querido amigo*, I am not walking wounded. I'll set up my own bivvy when we get down."

Will nodded and turned away. "Don't forget to relock the box," he called as they started downhill.

I watched through foggy eyes as Lizzie picked up the small box that now contained my tooth. She dropped it back inside the checkpoint box and closed the lid. Then she pressed her thumb down on the screen. The lock clicked.

"I feel bad," she said after a moment. "We're leaving the next group with the same problem."

"What do you think they'll do?" Carmen asked. She was wearing a green jumper. When had she dressed?

"Hopefully they'll give up."

I pictured other people pulling out their teeth because of one stupid dirty trick. I swallowed and the taste of more blood made me retch.

"Poor baby." Lizzie stroked my forehead and I leaned towards her.

"Can't rest here, *chico*." Carmen pulled me on to my feet. I staggered and Lizzie steadied me. She had her crutch under her arm. "We just need to walk downhill," she murmured encouragingly. "One step at a time."

The ground beneath me appeared spongy and I staggered and sat down hard, almost pulling Lizzie off her feet.

"We're going to have to leave it a little while," I heard Lizzie say. "He's off his face and losing blood.

148

We'll be lucky to get him moving in a straight line."

"He threw up most of what he took," Carmen replied seriously.

"But how much got into his bloodstream before that?"

Lizzie sat next to me and put her arm around my shoulders. "I think the bleeding's slowing," she said. "Come on, Ben."

"Water," I whispered hoarsely. I wanted my mouth cleaned out.

"Not yet." Carmen squeezed my hand. "Your gum has to clot first."

Lizzie and Carmen hauled me back to my feet. I swayed. Little lights burst all around me and I held my hand in front of my face; it left a trail of lights like fibre optics.

Carmen sighed and put her shoulder underneath mine. "I know you did this partly for me, *chico*." Her voice was low. "I'm going to make sure we win this."

"He did it for me, too," Lizzie said. "He knows I want to pay off our mortgage."

Carmen stared at Lizzie over my head. "Why do you want to do that? Your parents aren't short on money, are they?"

Lizzie looked at me and then at Carmen. "Don't tell the others, but Dad's not well. It's his prostate." She swallowed. "He needs to give up work, but he won't until the mortgage is paid off."

"*Chica!* I didn't know. Your poor papi."

"It's OK." Lizzie shrugged. "Mum's looking for a full-time job, but at her age… All the interviews she's got have been for low-paid positions."

"And you haven't even told Ben?"

Lizzie shook her head. "I didn't want him to worry … and…"

I tried to lift my hand to comfort her, but my arm felt like spaghetti and there were moths flying around our torches. They looked like fluff, leaving puffs of dust in the air. When I looked back at Lizzie, she was talking again. What had I missed?

"…our relationship isn't like that. I mean, he's my best friend. Apart from you, of course. But we don't talk about family stuff. He's had *something* going on at home since before his dad left, but he's never talked to me about it – he shuts me out every time I try to mention it."

"So you don't talk to him?"

"Not about Dad's illness, no."

"Well, he knows now."

Lizzie laughed. "I don't think he'll remember much about this at all." She caught my hand. "Come on, Ben. We'll try to get a bit further this time."

At first each step seemed like a huge effort, the three of us half-walking, half-reeling through the darkness. Carmen held the torch so that we could see the ground, Lizzie tested the footing with her crutch.

Her dad was sick and she hadn't told me. She felt like I didn't confide in her, so she didn't confide in me. I hadn't known that by holding back my own problems, it would hurt us. But it had.

After a while my movements started to blur, as if the ground were flying under me. Then the slope evened out and it was as though all the stones wanted to trap my feet.

Carmen and Lizzie were panting; Carmen lurched under my weight, but I couldn't move without her guidance. "Sorry," I said. "Sorry, sorry, s—"

"It's not your fault, *chico*." Carmen grunted as my foot caught on another rock. "You'll feel better in the morning."

A fire glowed in front of us.

"Will?" Lizzie called. "Come and help."

▼

Mum was shrieking. "Have you seen this?"

I looked up from my spellings. She was holding Will's bag in one hand and a letter in the other.

"Dean, have you *seen this*?" Mum was still yelling.

There was a thumping upstairs as Dad left his study. He glanced at me as he came into the kitchen, then at Will, who was standing in a corner by the door.

"What's up?"

"*What's up? What's up?*" Mum mocked. "That interfering cow at the school." She shook the paper. "She made Will see —" her voice lowered — "a *counsellor.*" Like it was a dirty word.

"Without our permission?" Dad frowned.

"It's a school thing," I said cautiously. "Miss Clark comes in every Wednesday and does Nurture Group with some of the..." I trailed off.

"Yes?" Mum said dangerously.

"Some of the kids who..." I tailed off again. "Kids like Norah," I said.

Norah wore bottle-thick glasses and threw screaming tantrums five times a day.

"The more challenging kids?" Dad asked.

I nodded.

"And now they want *us* to have an appointment with her." Mum crumpled the letter in her fist. "How *dare* they!"

Dad started forwards. "Can I see?"

Mum snatched the letter back. "Why?"

"I want to see what it says."

"It doesn't matter what it says. That Clark woman thinks there's something wrong with my boy. I'll *sue*."

Will's eyes flickered to me.

"Well," Dad said slowly, dragging his fingers through his flop of bright red hair, "she is a professional... Maybe we should—"

"Are you *insane*?" Mum shoved the letter into the kitchen bin, pulled out the bin bag, tied it tightly and marched out of the back door. We all watched as she slammed the bag into the wheelie bin then strode back in. "There, gone."

"But the issue hasn't gone," Dad said softly, looking at Will.

Mum trembled. "You're calling my boy an *issue*?"

"Something must have happened to trigger this."

He looked at me. "Ben, did something happen at school this week?"

I tried not to look at Mum, who was tapping one foot and glaring at me.

"Ben?" Dad took my chin. "Tell me."

I spoke in a whisper, not meeting his eyes. "He cut Anna's ponytail off."

"He what?" Dad stared.

"Anna wouldn't give him her crisps."

I was going to get in so much trouble. Mum's eyes were boring into me and Will had his arms folded, expressionless.

"Did you know about this, Carrie?"

Mum sniffed. "I went into the school. It was all sorted out."

"Why wasn't I told?"

"It was sorted out." Mum's own face had lost all expression. She looked exactly like Will.

"What happened, *exactly*?" Dad asked me. He wouldn't let me look at Mum.

"She should have given them to him," I muttered. "He asked nicely."

"But it was Anna's lunch," Dad said gently. "She didn't have to give it up if she didn't want to."

"But she should have," I shouted. "Everyone knows—" I clamped my lips together.

"Everyone knows *what*?" Dad pressed.

"I want to go to my room," I begged. My feet jittered against the chair legs.

"Leave your son alone," Mum snapped. "Let him finish his homework."

"What does everyone know?" Dad asked again.

I swallowed.

Dad stood up. "It's OK, Ben." He looked at Mum, then at Will. "What does everyone know?"

It was Will who answered. "They know they should do what *I* want."

"… or else," I whispered.

"We can deal with this at home," Mum said. "He doesn't need a counsellor. He needs his family. I'm calling the school. If that woman comes near Will again, I'll ruin her!"

I opened my eyes. My gum throbbed like it had a spike in it. I touched the hollow with my tongue and tried an experimental swallow. I no longer tasted blood. That was good. I rolled over with a groan.

My head was *killing* me and for some reason I felt sad. But why? I searched my memory. It was full of holes.

I was tired, but I wasn't getting back to sleep without a painkiller. I reached for my torch and my hand knocked over a water bottle. It reminded me of the last thing Lizzie said to me before I passed out. "I'm leaving some drugs right here. Take them if you need them."

Blindly I felt around until I found the little packet. Without switching on the torch, I popped two pills out of the foil, opened the bottle of water and took them gratefully. I was glad I hadn't needed the torch – my eyes ached. Every muscle was sore and I was hungry, but I could feel sleep pulling me back under. My body wanted to heal.

Before dreams took me, I sensed movement and fought my eyes back open. In the darkness, a figure was moving, rustling among the backpacks. Who else was awake?

"Grady?" I whispered.

Then I fell asleep.

▼

Towards the end of March, Will officially joined me in Year Two and he asked to bring home the class pet: a bright orange guinea pig called Chewbacca. He played the baby card first, appealing to the teacher with wide grey eyes and a wobbling lip.

"It's Matthew's turn," Mrs Heap said. "You and Ben aren't on the list for this term."

And never would be. Mum hated pets and I was sure she'd asked to be excluded from the timetable.

Will retreated, tears unshed. Then he spent the whole day on a charm offensive. Matthew was offered the chocolate bar from his lunchbox, Mrs Heap was given a handmade card that he'd constructed during his lunch hour. It had a picture of flowers on it, and a glued-on heart with the words *I luff you Misuss Heep*. He could spell perfectly well.

Will put up his hand for every question. At tidy-up time he won a sticker and during PE he took the blame when Matthew's ball went over the fence.

At the end of the day, Matthew went to Mrs Heap and told her that he didn't want to take Chewbacca any more.

On the way home, Chewbacca bit Will's finger when he poked him through the cage.

▼

As I slept I dreamed of dead guinea pigs with hair the same colour as mine, and blood. Lots of blood.

▼

I woke to the smell of bacon, coffee and woodsmoke. It was barely light. When I rolled over I saw Grady and Carmen by a smouldering fire. Carmen was slicing open bread rolls with the blade of her Swiss army knife; Grady was poking a pan with a long fork. I was dragged into full alertness by my nose: bacon sandwiches!

Experimentally I lifted my head. It no longer ached. I felt nauseous, though, and my gut clenched like a fist. I wriggled out of my bivvy into the pre-dawn chill and crawled to the fire.

"Ben!" Carmen looked up. "We let you sleep for as long as we could. How are you feeling?"

"OK," I croaked. "Hungry."

"Here." Carmen snagged some bacon from the pile on the plate beside her and slapped it on an open roll. "Eat."

Grady handed me his coffee. "I'll make another."

"Thanks." I took the sandwich from Carmen and as I took my first bite, I automatically looked for Will.

"It's his turn for a wash in the river." Carmen answered my unspoken question. I froze, the sandwich sticking to the roof of my mouth. It was my blood that they needed to rinse away. For the first time, I looked at my own hands. Dried brown flakes followed the lines on my palms.

Quickly Grady handed me a pan of water. "Use this. We can refill it."

"Thanks." I put down the sandwich, dunked my hands and watched the water muddy. Then a sound from Lizzie, half a sob, caught my attention. I paused, my hands dripping. There was something about Lizzie, something I needed to remember. I looked around.

She was kneeling by the pile of rucksacks, still in the grey tracksuit she wore to sleep in. Her pixie hair was half-glued to her head.

"I *told you* mine was at the bottom," she cried. "I *said* they'd been moved."

"Who would move the rucksacks?" Carmen raised an eyebrow.

I frowned as a memory surfaced. "Didn't Grady get something in the night?" The vision was hazy, part-dream, but I was sure I'd seen him. Hadn't I?

"Nope. I passed out like a rock. Didn't move till dawn." Grady forked more bacon on to the plate. "What's the problem with the rucksacks, anyway?"

Lizzie turned, her face stricken. "The tooth – it's missing."

"It can't be." I frowned. "Maybe you moved it…"

Both Carmen and Grady were staring at Lizzie in horror.

Lizzie shuffled back. Her rucksack had been emptied, the contents were strewn around her knees. "It's not here." Her voice was dull.

I lurched to my feet. "It has to be!"

"Grady, are you sure you put it in Lizzie's rucksack?" Carmen looked at him. "Maybe you put it in your pocket by mistake?"

Grady shook his head, but he stood up and started to go through his clothes. "It's not here. I put it where Lizzie told me – I remember doing it."

"Check again." I swallowed. "Check everywhere."

"You saw someone last night, didn't you, Ben?" Grady's eyes narrowed as he turned out his shirt pocket. "You thought it was me, but it wasn't."

"I thought I did – but…"

"He was off his head, Grady," Carmen said gently. "He could have been dreaming … or hallucinating." She stood and walked over to Lizzie. "Will carried your rucksack for you, *chica* – it might have fallen out." She snapped her knife closed and put it in her pocket. "I'll go back up the hill and see if I can find it." She stood and ran off.

"The bags have been moved," Lizzie insisted. "My side pockets have been opened. We've been robbed!"

"No." I clenched my fists. "Carmen will find it."

"What if she doesn't?" Grady murmured. "What if you really did see someone?"

"How could they have known where the tooth was?" Lizzie was crying.

Grady swore. "They must have been watching us."

"From where?" I spun abruptly, scanning the rocks.

"It was dark." Lizzie rubbed her face.

"In the trees, maybe," Grady said. "If they had night-vision binoculars, we'd have been clear as day." He swore again.

161

"But *why* would anyone be watching us?" I shivered.

Will strode back to our camp, rubbing his hair with a towel. He heard my question and his eyes flicked over us, drawing conclusions. "They couldn't get in the box," he said finally and tossed his towel down on top of his rucksack. "So they waited to see how the next team did it." He made himself a bacon sandwich and began to eat.

Lizzie put her head in her hands. "They watched Carmen blow on the box, then saw us pulling Ben's tooth and where I put it. They decided to take ours so their team didn't have to do the same."

"It makes sense." Grady dropped his shirt on the floor. "They'll be long gone by now, with the coordinates of the third checkpoint and *our* geocache tooth."

I sat on a rock. "What do we do?"

We looked at one another. Then Grady groaned. "The way I see it, we have four choices."

Will nodded. "Someone gives up another tooth."

"No!" My hands flew to my mouth. "Think of something else."

"OK." Grady held up his right hand. "Three

162

options then." He extended a finger. "One, we give up and go back to the beach."

Lizzie pressed her lips together. "Or?"

"Two, we keep going, tell the invigilators at the end that one of the other teams stole our first geocache and hope they let us off."

"We haven't any proof," Will pointed out.

"Except Ben's missing tooth," Lizzie said.

"All *that* shows is that Ben's had a tooth out. It could have happened before we left." Grady shook his head. "It won't be enough."

"Then what's option three?" Lizzie scrutinized Grady.

"Find those bastards and make them give us the tooth back."

There was a long silence. I stared at my uneaten sandwich. I couldn't bring myself to pick it back up.

"Grady," Lizzie said quietly. "Let's get real. Between my ankle, Ben's knee, Will's arm and your elbow, we're not going to scare anyone into giving us anything, especially if they're bigger than we are."

"And there are eight other teams out there." I rubbed my eyes. "How do we know which of them did it? We catch up with someone, they deny having the tooth and … then what?"

"It was that team we saw ahead of us – the one with the girl leading them," Grady growled.

"Probably." Will crossed his ankles. "But we have no way to be sure."

"There *is* another option." I leaned on my knees. "We carry on as normal, complete the other checkpoints, then, if we get a chance to search someone else's stash, we get a tooth that way."

Lizzie rubbed her hair into even spines. "Steal someone else's, you mean."

"It's not ideal," I admitted.

She sighed. "It makes us no better than the thieves who took from us."

"It's our best choice," Grady said.

"We just need to be on the lookout for opportunities." Will took another sandwich. "If we find other teams, we can wait for them to leave their bags unguarded."

"And if we don't *get* opportunities?" Grady asked.

"*Then* we decide – give up another tooth or tell the invigilators about the theft," Will replied.

"OK." I stood. "Last night was awful, but we found the second checkpoint and I don't reckon every team did. I'm feeling a lot better this morning. Lizzie, how's your ankle?"

"Stiff and sore, but I can manage with my crutch."

"Great! Then let's get our heads back in the game. What's the plan for today?"

"Break camp and go." Lizzie started re-stuffing her rucksack. "We've got two more days and five more checkpoints. We should be able to get to three today. One by mid-morning, one after lunch and one this evening. Then six hours' sleep and the final two tomorrow."

"With any luck, we'll overtake the team playing dirty this morning," Grady said as he collected our rubbish.

"You're sure you're up for a hard hike?" I stepped towards Lizzie.

She nodded and grinned suddenly. "The sun's coming up, it should be a nice day. Let's make it a good one."

I laughed as I started to roll my sleeping bag. "You're right. Let's have a great day."

After a few minutes Lizzie looked up. "Hey, guys … shouldn't Carmen have been back by now?"

Chapter Ten

"Carmen!" My knee was less swollen than it had been. I ignored the remaining discomfort as I forced myself to jog up the hill. Will was ahead of me, Grady behind.

Lizzie had stayed in the campsite to pack our gear and wait in case Carmen returned. She hadn't been too happy about it, but Grady had suggested she take the opportunity to properly bind her ankle so she could move more easily.

"Carmen!"

We should have been able to see her by now. The trees and river were behind us, the cairn ahead; if Carmen was still out searching for the tooth, she'd have been right here.

I pulled to a stop and Grady puffed up next to me. "Where is she?"

"If you were Carmen and you were searching for the tooth, where would you go?"

"It was wrapped up in the glasses cloth. Maybe she thought the wind blew it." Grady looked around with a frown.

"So, we split up." I pointed. "You go east around the hill, I'll go west."

Grady nodded.

The hill looked even starker than it had the night before, when it had been lit only by the moon and our torches. The sloping ground was spotted with tufts of stubby beige grass. Thistles provided the only colour, and the eastern side was mainly gravel and scree with some larger protruding rocks.

"What if she fell? She could be unconscious anywhere." Grady wrung his hands.

"I'll come to help you look when I've checked my side."

Will was still powering upwards, already passing the cairn with barely a glance.

"Will, can you see anything?"

He turned. "Let me get to the top – I'll have a better view."

"Other teams are going to be coming." Grady looked around worriedly. "I don't want to meet anyone else right now. What if they make us tell them how to get in the box?"

I gave him a small push towards the rocks. "Go and look for Carmen. We can think about other teams once we've found her."

On my side of the hill, the view was of the sea, dull and black. The sky above was early-morning white, the world on its way from black and white to colour. Mist clung to the grass and pale cobwebs stuck to my boots. It was still early, but we should have been well on our way to the next checkpoint. We were losing time.

"Carmen!" I called again, then stood still and strained my ears, listening for a response. Nothing. If Carmen *was* in earshot, then she had to be, as Grady had suggested, unconscious. "Car, can you hear me?"

Something tickled my memory, something about last night. Carmen and Lizzie had been talking over my head. Carmen was worried about Lizzie. No, not Lizzie, Lizzie's dad. He was sick.

Lizzie hadn't told me. I'd thought she told me everything, but there were things about her I didn't know. And it was my fault for keeping things back.

▼

Dad inhaled sharply. "You said Will was fine at school." His hands shook. "You said he was only acting up at home. That he just had a problem with *me*, that we *clashed*. You showed me that article – *Good in School, Bad at Home*. I have it on my computer."

Mum looked at me and Will. "Go to your rooms."

I leaped to my feet and bolted. Will followed more slowly.

At the top of the stairs I stopped. Will came to stand next to me and we stared down at the closed kitchen door.

"If *I'm* not the only one he's hurting—" Dad's voice was raised.

"You should have had more to do with school if it bothers you!" Mum yelled.

"You never *let* me." We heard Dad thump the table. "You said school business was *your* business. You even booked parents' evening appointments when you knew I was working."

I couldn't hear Mum's reply.

"I mean it, Carrie. I don't see why it would traumatize him. We can speak to someone together."

Mum's voice, rising and falling, but the shape of the words escaped me. I could feel Will's eyes on me, looking for clues. I flinched as his hand appeared on my leg. His sharp little nails started to dig into my thigh.

Mum's voice carried this time. "Trust me, Will's fine. He's normal. He acts up a bit, but he'll settle down."

▼

The side of the hill was steep. I had to hold on to the bank with one hand as I picked my way around. Rabbit holes pitted the scrub. I could imagine the wrapped tooth being blown and snared in one of them. If the tooth *had* fallen from the rucksack and tumbled into the wind, it could be here.

But there was nothing. I looked up again. "What can you see, Will?"

"Three other teams are on the move." He pointed at the treeline behind us and then off towards the third checkpoint.

"What about Carmen?"

He put his binoculars to his eyes and searched downwards, around the hillside, then further out. "I can't see her," he said at last.

A horrible scream trembled through the air. My head whipped up, trying to trace it. Automatically, I looked for a seabird, assuming I had heard a new call, but something inside me knew better.

I started back around the hillside, heading as fast as I could towards Grady. He was scrabbling and tripping his way through the rocks to meet me. "Was that you?" he shouted.

I shook my head. "Will?" I bellowed.

Will was half-running, half-slipping down the hill towards us. "There are plenty of other people on this island. Any one of them—"

"Any one of them isn't missing!" My eyes stung. "Where *is* she?"

Abruptly Will stopped behind the cairn and bent over. When he rose back to his full height, he was holding something in one hand. It was Carmen's Swiss army knife, open – the blade bloody.

"We have to find her," Grady wailed.

"I know." I said as Will shoved Carmen's knife into his pocket. "She can't be far. Will couldn't see her from the top of the hill, so she has to be beneath a ledge or something."

We searched, looking at any spot that might be able to hide a person. I checked Grandad's watch: over an hour had passed.

"Lizzie's going to be wondering where we are," I said.

"Keep looking," Will said evenly. "Lizzie's fine. Carmen needs our help."

"It might not have been Carmen who screamed." Grady wiped his shining forehead with the back of his wrist. "It could've been anything ... a bird ... or a seal..."

"Yeah." I ducked under another ledge, hoping. It was empty except for a broken bird's nest; twigs and smashed eggs. "Where *is* she?"

"We aren't all the way around yet." Will was more methodical than we were, zigzagging as he walked.

"There's another team." Grady pointed. All big lads, they were crossing the river and heading away from us. "How did we miss them?"

"They must have come around the other side of the hill." I stood. "Maybe they've seen Carmen. Should we go after them?"

Will thought. "She's not with them. If they're good

172

guys and they found her hurt, they'd have taken her with them."

"And if they're *not* good guys?" Grady cleared his throat.

"Then either they found her and left her or…"

"Or one of them has a cut from Carmen's knife," I muttered darkly.

As we searched on, the incline steepened until I realized that we weren't so much circling a hill as the first of a series of plateaus. To the west the land sloped towards jagged cliffs and now I could see two higher peaks ahead of us, one to the north-west and the other almost directly north.

I slumped on to a rock. "She isn't here."

"Where is she, then?" Will demanded.

"Those lads didn't have her, but another team might have taken her with them," Grady said, his face brightening. "If we head to the third checkpoint, we might catch up with her."

"And they got by without us seeing them?" I shook my head.

"You're assuming it was Carmen we heard before." Grady clenched his fists. "It *could* have been a bird. Carmen might have been taken by another team ages ago."

Will said nothing, only patted the pocket where he had stashed the knife.

"She fought," I murmured. "Why would she need to do that?"

Abruptly a great skua shrieked shrilly, flew towards us, then tilted and vanished below our feet, only to reappear moments later, cawing furiously. It took off again with an angry cry.

"We're sitting on top of a ledge." Grady leaped to his feet. "We'd better take a look beneath us."

Grady saw it first, a black mark in the rock that turned out to be a shadow. "There's a cave!"

We started to run. Will pulled his torch out of his trouser pocket and switched it on. "There's room to go inside." He stepped out of view.

"Is she there?" Grady tried to see around me. "Can you see her?"

"Yeah." Will's voice was oddly subdued. "She's here."

The entrance to the cave was narrow, and sharp juts of stone tore my shirt. Inside, Carmen was curled up, her back to us. Will was kneeling next to her.

Grady nudged me and I stepped sideways to let him in.

The light of Will's torch showed that Carmen was lying in a puddle. It shone crimson when the beam caught it.

"I-is she alive?" Grady whispered. He clutched my arm, fingers digging into my skin.

"She's alive, but she's not conscious." Will touched her face. "Carmen?"

Grady kneeled beside Will. "What happened?"

I held my hands to my chest. "Why would anyone hurt Carmen?" I mumbled.

With his eyes on mine, Will lifted Carmen's right wrist.

Her arm ended in a stump. Even her kestrel tattoo was missing.

My hand over my mouth, I reeled backwards until I hit the rough wall. I made desperate *huh* noises – half-sob, half-heave – trying to clear the lump from my throat. "W-what do we do?"

With shaking hands, Grady took Carmen's wrist from Will. "I-it's been cauterized. Burned. See?"

Now that he said it, the smell that had been filling

my nose made sense. Burned wood, meat, copper. I retched again.

"It's not bleeding any more?" Will leaned in for a closer look.

"No, but she needs properly cleaning and bandaging and..." Grady pointed to the cave floor. "She's lost a lot of blood."

Will nodded. "They didn't mean to kill her. Maybe they burned her arm quickly enough. She needs rest and, I guess, lots of water and iron."

"So ... steak and green vegetables?" Grady said.

"Yeah, we've loads of that," I snapped.

"I'm doing my best," Grady cried. Then he raised his head. "Wait. I've got iron tablets in my kit."

"OK ... good." I looked at Carmen's face. She was still passed out, a frown crease between her eyes. "She's going to be in terrible pain. She needs something to help with that. We've got to get your bag, Grady." My eyes widened. "Lizzie's on her own out there!"

"We can't leave Carmen," Grady said. "And we can't move her. No way!"

"*You* stay with Carmen; Will and I are going back for Lizzie and the bags." I was already out of the cave and moving.

"But what if they *come back*?" Grady's howl followed us along the path and out on to the hillside. This time I put my head down and sprinted without even thinking about my knee. *Please, God, let Lizzie be all right.*

▼

Lizzie raised her head as I staggered into our camp, Will on my heels.

"Did you find her?" Her worried cry greeted me as I rushed forwards and swept her into a hug.

Will was already shouldering his rucksack. He slung Carmen's over his front. "Lizzie's fine, Ben. Let's go." He started back, kicking dry earth over the fire as he passed.

Lizzie shoved me away from her. "What's going on? Where's Carmen? The next checkpoint is *that* way." She pointed.

"We're not going to the next checkpoint." I picked up my pack and grunted with the weight as I lifted Grady's into my arms as well. "Get your things. We need to get out of here." We were right out in the open.

Lizzie started to shake. "Tell me where Carmen is."

"She's on the other side of the hill." I handed Lizzie the long stick she was using as a crutch. "*We're going to her.*"

"Is she all right?" Lizzie's eyes were wide.

I shook my head. "No, she's not."

Chapter Eleven

The cave was crammed with all of us inside. Will and I had made a barrier across the entrance with our bags and we had every torch on, chasing the shadows into corners.

Lizzie was pacing, swear words tumbling from her lips. "Who did this?" she pleaded. "Why?"

"What do you think, Will?" My voice trembled.

"Well..." he said. "*I'm* wondering what's in the second geocache box."

Lizzie stopped and took off her glasses. "What do you mean?"

Will leaned back. "We figured the geocache boxes would contain normal stuff, even after the tooth. But what if we were wrong? What if the next box contains something like a tooth but ... bigger?"

"You mean ... a hand?" Lizzie replied faintly.

"Something like that."

"You honestly think someone cut off Carmen's

hand to put in a geocache box?" I stared.

Will looked at me curiously. "You don't?" He shrugged. "Either someone decided to raise the stakes of the first geocache box ... or all the boxes are going to keep on containing things like this, because they're meant to."

"What do you mean 'they're meant to'?" Lizzie slid her glasses back on with shaking hands.

"The boxes could all contain body parts," Will said.

Lizzie sat down beside me with a thump. "But the Gold Foundation organized this – there's no way." She shook her head.

But Grady groaned. "I should've known. A big corporation like that."

"That doesn't make any *sense*, Grady." Lizzie glared at him. "What reason could they possibly have?"

Even Grady had no answer.

"Lizzie's right, Will, that doesn't make sense. Maybe there was another reason." I took Lizzie's hand. "What if someone *had* to do that to Carmen ... and left her here to keep her safe."

"Why would anyone need to cut off—"

"I don't know, OK, Grady? Maybe she had a … a snake bite, or it was being crushed under a rock and she couldn't escape. We won't *know* until she wakes up."

Grady hung his head.

"If it *is* the boxes," Will said eventually, "you realize they left her here for safekeeping? When they know what they need next, they'll be back."

Lizzie bolted upright. "We need weapons."

"We *need* to get out of here!" Grady rasped. "But … we can't." He looked at Carmen, then at Lizzie. "Can we?"

She glared at him. "No. We can't."

"I'm getting Will's axe." I crawled to his pack.

"I've got my stick." Lizzie huddled it against her.

"Here." Will pulled string from his jacket pocket and tossed her his penknife. "Attach that to the end. Make a spear or whatever."

"I–I've got a pick. For rock climbing," Grady mumbled.

"Perfect." I rolled his bag towards him. "What about you, Lizzie, where's your climbing stuff?"

"My pick's in the bottom, on top of the rope and crampons," she said.

"Give that to Will." I clutched the axe to my chest. It wasn't big, but the blade would cut through wood. If I swung it hard, it would do someone a real injury. Could I do that?

"How could anyone hurt Carmen?" Lizzie whispered as she wrapped string around the knife. "She's a good person. She's going to be a vet."

I caught my breath. "Can she do that now?" I asked.

Will shook his head. "I don't think she can."

In Year Four, we went on our first residential trip. Two nights at Oxley Farm Outdoor Centre. Mum had panicked about letting Will out of her sight, but he'd learned how to charm by then, so he went with the rest of us.

On the first day, we were introduced to a climbing wall. Lizzie was delighted, as was our friend Tommy.

"I'm going to beat you up there," Tommy called to me.

I laughed. Will didn't.

When we got to the wall, Will insisted on going first. Tommy went after him. I followed, then Lizzie.

I had just started to enjoy the climb, looking down to see how far below me my other mates were and waving at them, when I looked up and saw Tommy overtake Will.

I put on a burst of speed, trying to catch up, but I'd been messing around and was too far behind. Tommy reached the top first.

My brother looked at me, his face flushed. I climbed like the devil was after me, but I was too late. I didn't see what happened exactly, but somehow Tommy's rig got unhooked.

He screamed as he tumbled past me. One of his feet hit Lizzie in the back and she spun out, caught by her rope. When Tommy hit the ground, we all heard the crack as his wrist snapped.

I slid backwards, to put Will between myself and the entrance to the cave.

Once we were armed, we kept our ears tuned to the outside, but the day wore on, Carmen didn't wake and all we heard were the cries of gulls.

"Do you think it's lunchtime yet?" Grady asked.

"Why? Are you hungry?" Lizzie frowned.

"No…" There was still the faint smell of cooked flesh in the cave. "Just thinking that we should be on our way to the third checkpoint by now."

I looked at Grandad's watch. "It's half eleven." My shoulders sagged. We'd lost any advantage gained by completing the second checkpoint and waking early. I pictured all the teams passing us and probed the throbbing gap in my teeth with my tongue. What a waste.

My gut felt empty and not because I was hungry. I could feel my future slipping away.

Then I looked at Carmen and jerked. I shouldn't even have been thinking about the competition right now.

"We should go home," I said.

Will frowned at me.

"We're already half a day behind. We aren't going to win and … would you really want to?" I pointed at Carmen. "What if you're right and the other geocaches are worse? What then – would *you* start giving up body parts?"

Will shook his head. "No, but—"

"But *nothing*," I snapped. "What did you think would happen if we carried on?"

Grady swallowed. "We could—"

"What? Do what this team did?"

"No! Steal from another team's stash."

I paused.

"Wasn't that what we were planning to do anyway?" Grady frowned.

"That was before this." I indicated Carmen, who was groaning in her sleep.

"You're forgetting something, Ben." Lizzie squeezed my hand. "We *can't* go home. Not yet. The crossing is raised every three days. If we try and get to Fetlar without it, there's quicksand and who knows what else. We can't call anyone to come and get us. Whatever we decide about the competition, we're stuck on this island for now."

"We've got flares," I said stubbornly.

"Right." Grady looked at the bags. "But…"

"But what?"

"But if we set off flares, the other teams will know where we are. They'll know we're weak."

"One team already knows where we are – or at least where they left Carmen." I bit my nail.

"One team," Grady said. "That leaves another eight. Who knows how many of them are out there

185

looking for 'body banks' too."

"Do you really think they are?"

"I don't." Lizzie took off her glasses again and rubbed her bloodshot eyes. "I'm sure Will's wrong – the other checkpoints won't be like the last one. We won't know what really happened to Car until she wakes up, but I don't believe someone amputated her hand for a geocache. That's just *sick*."

"Then what do you want to do?" I looked at them.

"There's only one thing *to* do," Lizzie said. "We've got to reach the last checkpoint. I know we have to do the course alone, but there's bound to be someone at the end, waiting for the winners – if we find them, we can get help."

She put one hand on Carmen's hip and leaned on my shoulder.

Grady lowered his voice and spoke to Will. I couldn't make out his words, but Will nodded.

I opened my mouth to ask, but a distant scream silenced me. I clutched my axe tighter and put an arm around Lizzie.

"How's Carmen doing?" I whispered to Will.

He looked over at her. "She's crying in her sleep."

186

▼

We ate a subdued lunch: cold beans, packets of trail mix, corned beef, sweets.

"Did you know," Grady said quietly as he unwrapped a chocolate bar, "a lot of leading scientists think reality is a huge computer game?"

"I read that." Lizzie snorted.

"It would be nice to think so right now, wouldn't it?" I put a tin of beans to one side. "We could do with a reset."

Will looked towards the cave entrance. "I wonder how many lives we get?"

I was silent.

"Give us another one, Grady." Will laid the pick on his knee and put his hands behind his head. "One we haven't heard before." He stretched his legs. "Go on."

Grady checked Carmen's temperature, then leaned back. "There're some who reckon dinosaurs never existed."

"Seriously?" Lizzie lifted her head from my shoulder.

Grady cracked a slight smile. "They were made

187

up by the CIA to discourage time travel."

Lizzie shook her head. "That one's more insane than usual. How would the bones have been planted *inside* cliffs?"

"Anyway," I added, "the first dinosaur bones weren't found in America."

"That's what we're *told*." Grady folded his arms. "Remember, you can't believe anything you don't see for yourself. You should question all the time."

"But you believe these nutters on the Internet," I said. "Why don't you question *them*?"

"If I *could* time-travel," Will said, "I'd quite like to go back and see the dinosaurs. I mean, I'd take some really big guns with me…"

Suddenly my watch started a shrill beeping. Quickly I switched it off.

"What's that?" Lizzie tilted her head.

"My alarm. The tide's going out. Exactly two days till we can use the crossing."

Lizzie wrapped our rubbish and put it in her rucksack. "What have we got that Carmen can eat when she wakes up?" She tugged out her washbag. "I've got my daily multi-vitamins – can she have a few of those?"

"Can you overdose on vitamins?" I looked at Grady, who shrugged.

"Ben and I have jerky," Will said. "What else?"

"There's Peperami, too." I nodded at Will, who pulled out our cook pack and handed it over.

"And we've still got bacon from earlier." Lizzie bit her lip. "But she can't eat it raw and we can't cook it in here. What did *you* bring, Grady?"

We looked at his huge rucksack.

"Have you got any beef stew left?" I asked. "That'd be good."

Grady wiped his hand over his forehead. "I've got another couple of tins. Some ravioli, cocktail sausages. The rest is … well, mainly sweets," he admitted. "You know what I'm like. I've got lots of gummy bears…" He tailed off.

Lizzie put her finger to her lips, and her eyes widened. "Listen!"

I gripped my axe. Voices drifted faintly from the other side of the hill.

"They're trying to get into the checkpoint box," she whispered.

"You mean there are still teams behind us?" Grady lifted his head.

I frowned at him and gestured at him to keep quiet.

"They're *fighting.*" Lizzie clutched her stick.

"Did they get into the box?" Will slid towards the barrier of bags, listening.

The yelling was louder now. A higher male voice was screaming at other, deeper, voices.

"They want his tooth." Will picked up his weapon, but moved no nearer to the daylight.

I put my hand to my face; my gum still ached.

The yelling intensified. We could hear grunts, calls of encouragement, shouts and cries. Lizzie shivered.

Suddenly, from behind us, a scream ripped through the cave. Carmen had woken up.

Grady scrambled to cover her mouth, but she writhed, arched her back and struggled to escape Grady's grasp. With her one hand, she clutched at her bloody wrist. Tears dampened her cheeks and she made terrible sounds: half-scream, half-sob.

"Carmen, it's us," Lizzie whispered.

I joined my voice to Lizzie's. "Car, whoever they were, they've gone. It's Ben."

Carmen calmed slightly, but still writhed and

sobbed under Grady's hand.

"Tell her to be *quiet*," Will snapped. He remained by the entrance. "If they hear us…"

"Carmen, I know it hurts, but you've got to hush." Lizzie was crying too now. "There's another team on the hill – we don't know what *they'll* do if they find us."

Carmen's brown eyes met Lizzie's blue ones. Her chest rose and fell in pain, panic and her efforts to be silent.

"Painkillers, Grady." I grabbed a water bottle and Grady pushed the medical kit towards me with his free hand.

I fumbled the Tramadol out of the packet. "Take these, Car."

Grady took his hand from her mouth as she twisted towards me, her teeth gritted. I pushed the pills past her lips and forced her mouth open. She gagged and I poured water into the corner of her mouth. "Swallow them, please."

She gulped awkwardly and then gripped Lizzie's collar with stiff fingers. "They thought … I was … you!"

"Say that again." Will turned to stare at her.

"They wanted … to stop us … from…"

"Opening any more boxes," Will finished with a nod. "Without Lizzie's thumbprint we'd be screwed. Clever!"

"And … they wanted … my fingers … for geocaches."

Then Carmen's eyes rolled back in her head and she passed out again.

Chapter Twelve

Carmen was sitting up in Lizzie's arms, shuddering violently. Lizzie stroked her head with one hand and steadied an open tin of stew with the other.

Grady held the spoon. "You have to eat," he cajoled.

"I'll be sick." Carmen looked away from the food.

"What do you remember, Car?" Will leaned closer.

She trembled harder. "They called him Reece."

"Reece Armstrong," Will said. "Team eight."

"He was big. He kept calling me ... Elizabeth. I said I wasn't, but he didn't listen."

"You don't have to tell us if you're not ready," Lizzie whispered.

Carmen shook her head. "They said they'd seen another team with a girl ... on a rope ... a-a lead. Reece called her Spare Parts. He said they weren't dumb enough to use someone from their own team like that. I-I'm *his* Spare Parts." She choked into silence.

"Two teams ahead of us, then," Grady said.

I glared at him.

Lizzie started to brush Carmen's hair with her fingers, trying to untangle the bloody knots. "I don't understand," she said. "What do these idiots think is going to happen when we all get home? As if no one is going to speak to the police!"

Will raised his eyebrows.

"OK, Will, I get it," Lizzie snapped. "You think 'Spare Parts' and others like her won't get home to tell the tale."

Will leaned on his knees. "Not necessarily – some of the teams might not be thinking further than the win. Maybe they're even planning to buy their victim's silence. But Reece is being clever. If you're going to use someone like this, it's best to use a stranger. That way, in a week's time you have a traumatized victim who doesn't actually know you – who could be confused about exactly who they saw while they were being attacked."

Grady nodded. "You can argue you're one of dozens of blokes on the island wearing camo gear, and you have your whole team to back you up."

Will cocked his head. "Worst case, each team member can blame the other one."

"Something like that was in the news recently," I said. "Three suspects. They all blamed each other. There was no way to know who was the murderer so they all got off."

Carmen gripped my hand. "It's afternoon, right?"

I nodded.

"They've had hours to find the next checkpoint." She looked at Lizzie and then at me. "He'll be back soon. If Will's right, then you guys are witnesses he can't afford."

Her hand shook and I pressed it between mine. "Do you think you can walk?"

"Of course not!" Lizzie glowered, but Carmen's eyes hardened. Grim determination dried her tears.

"If I have to," she said.

Reluctantly, Lizzie helped me get Carmen to her feet. She sagged between us.

"Let's at least decide where we're going before we head out." I looked at Will.

He opened the map. "We've a number of choices."

"What are they?" Grady leaned over his shoulder.

"West – we can head towards the cliffs to look for another cave."

"Not a bad idea," Lizzie said. "Weren't there meant to be loads of them? And we'd be hard to find."

"But it could take ages to find one big enough and we'll be out in the open the whole time we're looking for who knows how long," Will finished.

"Oh!" Lizzie dragged her fingers through her hair and Carmen shuddered.

"What's our alternative?" I gripped my axe.

"Walking back to the jetty." Will put his finger on the map. "If we hide out in that building where we found the first box, we should be all right. Other teams are likely to be going forwards, not back. If we bump into anyone, it'll be a team doing the same as us – giving up and hiding. Or one that hasn't yet found that first checkpoint."

"And they wouldn't be a danger to us." Lizzie brightened.

"Good thinking." I bent to pick up my pack. "Let's go."

Will didn't move.

"What's the 'but'?" Lizzie sighed.

Will shrugged. "It's a long walk for Carmen." He looked at Lizzie. "And we know there's no medical help there. If there *is* help at the final checkpoint, this would take us further from it."

I narrowed my eyes. "You still think we should go for the money, don't you?" I said.

Grady flushed. "What if he does?" He pointed at Carmen. "She's going to need the prize even more after this."

Will held up the map. "There's another option: just under halfway between here and the next checkpoint, there's probably a cottage or barn."

I shook my head. "What if Reece and his team are heading back from the next checkpoint now? We could walk into them."

Will handed me the map. "We can avoid them. If you were going from here to the next checkpoint, which route would you take?"

I frowned. "Depends – do I want the quickest way or the easiest?"

"*We* were going to go around the river, past the small loch and across the fields," Grady pointed out.

"So, if we go across the river and directly to the cottage, we should miss them – and it's almost all downhill," Will said.

"It's a huge risk," I said as I handed back the map.

Lizzie nodded. "Ben's right, there are *eight* other teams – we could run into any of them. I vote we go back to the jetty."

"This isn't a vote." Carmen spoke up, her voice low and rasping. "You think we should hide until the competition is over while they get a million pounds *each* for doing this to me?" Her voice rose.

Grady looked anxiously at the cave entrance. "Quiet!"

"No!" Carmen's eyes chilled me. She roughly shoved blood-matted hair from her cheek. "We're going to that building. We'll rest until I have enough strength. Then we run the course, ignore the geocaches, and beat everyone to the last checkpoint. We won't win the prize, but if we can find a way to hide the last box … or destroy it, then no one else will either."

There was a long silence.

"You know," Grady said thoughtfully, "if *no one* completes the geocache challenge, they might just give the money to the people who get to the end in the fastest time."

"And it'll get us to help quickly. Let me see the map." Lizzie bowed her head over the paper. "If you're sure about this, Carmen, we'll go north-east first. It'll mean we have a little more walking to do, but we're less likely to run into anyone else." She folded the map and handed it back to Will.

Carmen watched in silence as I clipped my rucksack over my chest, then I picked hers up and weighed it in my hands. "Is there anything you want from in here? Your vodka?" I touched her pocket where she still had her mushrooms stashed. "You could have a mushroom?"

Carmen looked sick; she shook her head.

I swung her rucksack on to my front and found my balance, then tested my knee.

"Will could take it," Lizzie murmured. She was leaning on her stick. Or, with Will's knife strung on to the end, should I have called it a spear?

I shook my head. "Not a chance. If we meet Reece, Will's arms need to be free."

Lizzie pushed her glasses up her nose. "You're bigger than he is."

"But I'm hurt." I said nothing more.

It was my ninth birthday. My stegosaurus cake was in crumbly green pieces on the kitchen floor and Dad was sitting at the table, blood running from a cut above his eyebrow. Mum was disarming Will. He had the cake knife.

I tried to dab at Dad's face with a tea towel, but he pushed me away. I could feel his anger.

"He went for Ben," Dad said in a whispery voice. "I only just got in the way in time."

"He *didn't*," Mum insisted, one arm around a red-faced Will. "He was only threatening. If you hadn't got between them…" She tossed the knife into the sink.

I looked at Dad. "It's my fault. Sorry."

Dad stared at me, his face white. "Your fault, Ben?" He stood up. "It's your birthday. You should be able to blow out your own candles."

I tried not to look at the floor. Dabs of blue wax were sticking to the lino. There was a Will-sized footprint in the middle of the cake.

"This isn't fair on Ben," Dad said.

"I understand Will," Mum said. "You know I do. *I* can deal with this. He's been so much better."

"Has he?" Dad looked at me.

"I guess." I nodded. Will hadn't hurt anyone in weeks. He was learning.

"I don't know how much longer I can..." Dad tailed off.

▼

There was a reason I never fought with my brother.

I bit my lip – *was* I making the right decision in taking Carmen's bag? What if something happened to Will?

But we needed weapons and that's what Will was.

"Everybody ready?" Lizzie looked around.

Grady stood by the entrance, shoulders hunched under his pack and misery on his face. "I don't want to go out there," he muttered. He clutched his pick to his chest.

"We can't stay." Will offered him a rare half-smile, his eyes glittering. "Look at it this way – we *know* they're coming back here."

Grady nodded.

"Carmen?" I glanced at her.

"I'm ready." She faced the entrance.

Lizzie caught her shoulder. "One minute. Let's

listen first," she whispered.

We stood silently. The air stirred, luring us outside. Birds sobbed hauntingly and I heard the distant bleating of sheep. The hill itself was quiet.

"Let's go," Lizzie said.

It was still bright, and we squinted as we emerged from the dark of the cave. Will and Grady led, with Lizzie and Carmen in the middle. Moving slowly, I brought up the rear.

We went without speaking, awkward steps broken only by occasional grunts and groans, and the clatter of Grady's clanging rucksack.

"This isn't going to work." Lizzie leaned on her spear with a groan. "Grady's too loud."

We were still on the plateau. A ribbon of water glimmered below and to the right. To the left, another rise in the land, another peak, more cliffs.

We stopped, and Will started to unhook pans, a dangling coffee-maker, a camp stove and carabiners from Grady's bag. "We're leaving these."

Grady nodded. "You're right."

He stood still while Will dumped his equipment beside the footpath.

"Can we hide it?" Lizzie's knuckles whitened on

her spear. "We don't want anyone to know which way we went."

"Hide it where?" Will tilted his head.

I tottered down the side of the rise to where a ditch was filled with stagnant water. "Here."

Grady winced as Will pitched his equipment into the water.

"Have we gone far enough north-east?" I asked Will.

He looked at the map and nodded. "Probably."

"So, we can start going down?" The incline was pitted with rocks, clumps of heather and thistle, rabbit holes and scree. There was no path, so our route wouldn't be obvious to anyone looking for us.

In silence, Carmen stepped on to the slope and began to stumble downhill with her mutilated arm tucked under the other. Her tangled hair whipped in the cold wind. It was black and red now; the pink dye had vanished under blood and dirt.

As I half-walked, half-stumbled down the rise, I had to fight to keep from tilting into a jog. With Carmen's huge rucksack hanging from my chest, it was almost impossible to look for safe footing, so I followed Will as best I could.

My shoulders ached and my neck itched. We were too exposed – there was nothing but the vast sky above, the sweeping hillside and the moorland below. If someone came, we had nowhere to hide.

Somewhere out here, there were eight other teams. One had stolen our tooth from Lizzie's bag. Another had… I looked at Carmen. Those two teams, at least, were ahead of us. We had been overtaken by one more group, maybe more, while we were in the cave. That left five. I reckoned everyone had found the second checkpoint by now.

"I wonder how many gave up?" I murmured.

"What?" Lizzie turned.

"How many teams do you think gave up, you know – when they found the tooth?"

"I don't know." Lizzie shifted her glasses out of the way and rubbed her eyes. "I mean, *we* kept going."

"But I figure some would have stopped right there," I said. "Wouldn't they?"

Lizzie shrugged.

I halted. "Hey!"

"What?" Will turned.

"The teams who gave up – they'd go back to the jetty to wait, wouldn't they?"

"Probably." Will nodded.

"So, once Carmen has a rest, if we go that way, we'll find allies – teams with no interest in hurting us and every reason to want to increase the size of their own group."

Will and Grady stopped walking.

I pressed on. "That second checkpoint wasn't simple. We had to work out the correct coordinates, the riddle, the locked-door game – then there was the tooth. There had to have been dropouts."

"Ben's right," Lizzie said. "If we go to the jetty, we can join forces with another team."

Carmen kept walking.

"You hear that, Car?"

"We're not … stopping." She didn't lift her eyes from the hill. "I'm *not* letting Reece's team … win."

"Car," I pleaded. "You aren't thinking—"

She whirled on me, eyes blazing. "We. Aren't. Going. To. Give. Up."

"I know how you feel, but—"

"Really? Because you lost … a *tooth*, Ben*?*" She raised her arm. "What kind of life am I facing without my hand? Tell me!"

Shame riddled me.

"You can't fight for me," she hissed, "but you *can* run to the last checkpoint and keep Reece from … getting that money." She lurched on down the hillside.

"If they can't get into the next box, they'll still be at the checkpoint," Lizzie shouted. "They'll be waiting for someone who *can*."

Carmen turned round one more time, her eyes narrowed. "I'm not giving up."

I moved to stand beside Will and lowered my voice. "Lizzie's right. If we go to the next checkpoint, we're offering ourselves to whatever team is waiting. It could be Reece, it could be the cheats who took my tooth. It could be someone we haven't met yet."

Will gestured helplessly towards Carmen. "We'll just have to be careful."

Chapter Thirteen

The ground was flat and, from our vantage point between a rock and a cluster of prickly bushes, we could see the cottage tucked inside the bend on the river. It was a stone hut, thick-walled with two storeys. Half the roof had caved in. There had once been a small garden; a riot of wild flowers grew among the broken tiles.

We were lying next to one another. Carmen was exhausted – her head lay on Will's arm and her arm was tucked inside her jacket.

I panned my binoculars around. To the south I could see the lake we'd passed on our way to the second checkpoint.

"Have they gone?" Grady whispered.

I nodded.

Another team had appeared from around the back of the cottage, forcing us to drop to the ground. They had hiked northwards without seeing us. My heart was still pounding.

"Who were they, do you think?" Grady pressed.

"No way to know." I focused the lenses. "It wasn't Prisha's team, and it wasn't Reece's."

The biggest of them, a tough-looking girl with a buzz cut, had worn a machete on her belt.

"Can you see anyone else?" Will asked. He was leaning on his elbows, scanning the river ahead.

"Not yet." I turned my eyes towards the trees that had sheltered us the day before. "I think there's movement over there."

"How long do we have to wait?" Lizzie groaned. "Carmen's freezing."

"We've got to cross the river to get to the house," Grady said. "We're going to have to carry her."

I trained my lenses on the water. "I think there are rocks over there where it forks – stepping stones. It could be a proper crossing."

"You guys go over with the bags." Lizzie gave Carmen's shoulder a squeeze. "I'll stay here with Car – you can come back for us."

"I don't like leaving you alone." I frowned.

"You can't carry your bag, Carmen's bag *and* Carmen. And I'm going to need help crossing, too."

I took one last look around. "All right. Give Grady your bag, Lizzie." I moved up to a crouch and settled Carmen's bag back over my arms.

Lizzie unhooked the rope that had been dangling from my rucksack and threaded it through my belt. I offered one end to Will and the other to Grady.

Grady moaned as he took the weight of Lizzie's pack, but he held on to the rope.

"There's a sandbank on the other side of the river. We'll leave the bags there." I swallowed. "See you in a bit."

"Give me the glasses." Lizzie held out her hands.

I nodded and handed her the binoculars.

"Be safe." She planted a quick kiss on my jaw, then looked away before I could meet her eyes.

We scuttled along the edge of the river, but with every step away from Lizzie and Carmen, I panicked more. What if another team found them?

"Hurry, hurry," I muttered and shifted into a faster jog, forcing Grady to match me, or be dragged behind.

We stopped at the water's edge. To our left the

river forked. A weir foamed a little further along the right tributary. Here, just before the junction, the banks were further apart, the water was shallower and studded with slippery rocks green with algae.

Will stepped out to the first one. It was barely bigger than his foot, and he quickly leaped to the second – wider, but more slick. He waved his arms for a moment, then stabilized.

I looked at Grady, swallowed and leaped out. My balance was good – I was a skateboarder, after all – but I was wearing two heavy bags. I landed on my good leg and left my weak one sticking out into mid-air. I thrust my arms out to either side and fixed my eyes on a curl of fossilized shell in the side of Will's stone.

"OK, Will," I called. The water's rushing filled my ears and the wind seemed to become stronger. Splashes wet my shins.

Will leaped to the next rock; I followed him to the wider, flatter stone and felt the rope behind me tighten and then relax as Grady hopped on to the first one.

My foot slid wildly on the next stone, but I caught myself just before I went to my knees, managing not to grab the rope.

"OK?" Grady shouted.

"I'm good," I replied.

Will jumped again. We were halfway across when I heard Lizzie's cry. My throat closed and I turned to see her gesturing desperately towards the trees at the river bend on her side of the river. We were no longer alone.

The newcomers were still a couple of hundred metres away and they froze when they saw us.

I looked frantically between Will and Lizzie. "We have to go back!"

"No!" Will dived forwards, forcing me to follow him. Four more jumps that I barely registered and we were on the other side, Grady staggering into my back. I dropped the two rucksacks on to the thin line of dry sand that bordered the riverbank as fast as I could, and spun back round.

The other team had put on speed.

Will bounded back on to the stepping stones; I was a second behind him. "Stay with the bags, Grady," Will yelled.

Frantically, Grady looked from us to the team that was now coming up fast. He hopped from foot to foot and eventually settled on grabbing his pick and pressing it to his chest.

I pulled my axe out of my belt as I bounded on to the bank, ignoring the last stone completely and landing half in the freezing water. We had to get to Lizzie and Carmen first. I put my head down and sprinted.

Without our bags, we were fast enough. I skidded to a halt between the girls and the oncoming team, raised the axe and yelled.

Will slid into place beside me and lifted his pick.

Carmen was on her knees. Lizzie braced her spear against the ground and aimed the blade forwards. "Stop right there!" she cried.

The other team leader held up his hand and everyone froze. We faced one another and I stared, chest heaving. He looked Chinese, and two of his team-mates – a boy and a girl – were also Asian. Like us, they held weapons – knives, a small axe, climbing spikes. There was also a tall, blonde, athletic-looking girl and a skinny lad with a bushy monobrow who had twisted himself into a karate pose.

"What do you think, Will?" I asked without

breaking eye contact.

"Wang An, perhaps," Will said. He raised his voice. "Is that right?"

The leader dropped his fists slightly. "You can call me An." He leaned slightly to look around us, then sneered. "You use your team member like *this*!" He gestured at Carmen.

Lizzie's eyes widened. "*We* didn't do this!"

An nodded his understanding.

"What about you?" I rasped. "What did you do about the first geocache?"

The tall girl opened her mouth. She pointed to the gap where her right canine had been. After a slight hesitation, I opened my own mouth. My missing molar was more difficult to see, but she got the idea.

"There're teams out there going a different way." I didn't lower my axe.

"I know, we saw. One team reached the checkpoint ahead of us. The smallest guy on their side wasn't given any choice."

"We think there's something even worse at the next checkpoint," I offered. "Carmen's hand, maybe..."

An looked at his team. "We did wonder..."

"But you carried on?" I frowned.

"A million pounds," the tall girl said, as if that explained everything.

"Then you're still in the game." I tightened my grip on my axe.

"So are you," she snarled.

"We're just getting to the end so we can find someone to help Carmen. There has to be someone waiting for the finishers."

An held up a hand and the girl stepped back. "You aren't going for the money?"

"It's not important any more. Carmen is!"

"Hey." Lizzie called. "Maybe they can help." She looked at An. "Our electrics got wet. Have you got a working pho…" She saw the look on his face and tailed off. "You haven't."

An spread his hands. "Nothing's worked since we got here."

"That's strange." Will frowned. "Don't you think so? A tech billionaire should have a phone signal and Wi-Fi on his private island."

An looked at his teammates. "You reckon this whole thing is something to do with the Gold Foundation?"

"No, we don't," Lizzie snapped. "That's stupid. Some idiots in the first team are playing dirty tricks and people are falling for them."

"Dirty tricks," An repeated thoughtfully.

The Asian girl leaned into An and whispered urgently in his ear. I heard the words 'team up' and caught Lizzie's eye.

An shushed her. "They aren't going for the money," he said. "We are." He looked at us. "There has to be a way of getting the prize that doesn't involve..." He pointed at Carmen.

I looked at An. Sweat patches were spreading under the straps of his rucksack.

"Nervous?" I asked.

An licked his lips. "It's hot."

Monobrow cleared his throat. "Where're you headed? Maybe we can walk together for a while. Get one another's backs." He looked at Carmen. "Looks like you could use the help."

Lizzie opened her mouth, but I jumped in first.

"You seem like nice guys." I glanced at Will and sensed him shift his weight. "If you're still going for the money, what are you planning to do about the next geocache?"

215

An's gaze slid from mine, but Monobrow laughed awkwardly. "Can't we deal with that when we get to it?"

"I think we're better on our own, thanks. Like you say, we've got different aims."

Lizzie tilted the knife end of her spear. "I'm just wondering, did you come from back there –" she pointed in the direction of the second checkpoint – "or have you circled round?" She glared. "What's in the next geocache box, An?"

An swallowed.

"You've been to the third checkpoint already, haven't you?" I said.

"I…"

"Don't say anything," Monobrow snapped.

"You have!" Lizzie spat. "You were coming back to find someone … someone like Carmen."

"You've got us wrong," the Asian girl said. "We aren't bad guys."

I lifted my axe. "Then what did you leave in the box?"

"It was just—"

"Shut up, Casey." Monobrow silenced her.

"We can still do it, An," the boy behind him

urged. "Get them."

"So, you thought you could take us by surprise?" I shifted my gaze to Monobrow. "Harder now we're on to you, huh?"

"What's in the next box?" Will leaned closer. "Is it a finger?"

An nodded, white-faced, and I gripped my axe tighter.

"Do you really think you'll win the money with a bag of body parts?" Lizzie cried. "When you get to the end, the Foundation is more likely to call the police than give you the prize."

"We think otherwise." An shuffled closer.

"That's far enough." Lizzie thrust her spear. "There's no need for anyone to get hurt right now. Why don't we just … go our separate ways?"

"Pretend we never saw each other?" An asked.

He looked at Monobrow and there was a long moment of silent communication between them. Eventually Monobrow nodded.

"All right," An said. "We're heading north."

I stepped to one side, symbolically more than anything, but kept my axe raised as An and his team sidled around us.

As they passed, the other Asian boy turned back. "I'm making a spear, Four-eyes," he called. "*Maybe we come back for you.*"

As soon as they were far enough away, I dropped the axe from fingers as limp as noodles and put my head between my knees.

Lizzie rested a hand on my shoulder. "Well done, Ben."

"Carmen needs to get out of this wind," Will said. He pulled Carmen to her feet and put her over his shoulder in a fireman's lift. "Are you coming?"

"Yeah." I picked up my axe, got back to my feet and began to help Lizzie towards the river.

I looked wistfully at the cottage fireplace.

"Wishing we could build a fire?" Lizzie was cuddled up to Carmen beneath two sleeping bags in a corner clear of rubble.

"Talk about signalling our position." I chewed on a piece of chicken from the snack pack Grady had shared with us while trying not to look at the sheep droppings that covered the floor like black marbles. Carmen had the beef jerky.

Will was sitting by a shattered window, staring out with his binoculars. The glass splinters that stubbornly clung to the frame were opaque with dust and sticky with clumping cobwebs and dried flies.

I sat on the other side of the room, guarding the door. The stairs had long ago collapsed – if another team wanted to shelter in the house, we had nowhere to hide.

From where I sat I had a view towards the small loch. Rabbits, scared by our initial approach, were now hopping around the garden and birds had returned to roost in the roof. A butterfly fluttered across a clutch of heather. I wrapped my arms around my chest and shivered.

I strained my ears and caught the distant shush of the sea. The map had shown an inlet in the cliffs not far from the house.

"How long should we wait here?" Grady asked anxiously.

"Until Carmen feels up to moving," Will answered.

Lizzie shook her head. "I don't want us to set off while the sun's up."

"That's a lot of time to sit things out." Grady

sighed. "We were meant to do three checkpoints today. If we leave them till tomorrow, we have to get through all five in one day and I'm not sure we can—"

"I didn't say we should leave them till tomorrow." Lizzie chafed Carmen's shoulders with her hands. "If we wait till it's almost dark, there's less chance of us being seen. It's the best time to travel – poor light for binoculars, but not dark enough for night vision. We'll head out then and see how far we can get."

"So we're going out when the bats do." I looked up. Seabirds circled.

"It gives Carmen plenty of time to rest," Lizzie said. "And it'll be safest for us. Some of the other teams are bound to be camped out."

I nodded. "We aren't that far from the next checkpoint."

"When we get there, I want to be in and out," Lizzie said. "No hanging around, so if you're bored, Grady, work out the clue."

"I'd forgotten about the clue." I took another look out of the door. Was that movement beyond the garden's drystone wall? I froze.

An old ram raised its head, tugged ivy from the

stone and ambled on. My heart started beating again.

"In my rucksack, Grady." Lizzie nudged it with her toe.

Grady dug around until he found her notebook.

"There was a coin, wasn't there?" I remembered Lizzie taking the rubbing.

"And this nonsense word." Grady held up the book and Will turned.

"See if you can crack the code." Lizzie settled back with Carmen, who had closed her eyes.

Grady nodded, took a pencil from his jacket and started to scribble.

▼

Dad was staring at Mum. "I think I'm seeing you clearly for the first time."

"What a strange thing to say."

Mum was doing the washing-up. I was in the porch cleaning mud off the wheels of my new skateboard. Dad hadn't seen me behind the kitchen door.

"What you said on Ben's birthday last week — that you understand Will. It's because you're the same as he is."

"Don't be rid—"

"The more I look at Will, the more I see you." Dad sighed. "I can see him learning. He's turning into a charmer. And you've had me wrapped around your little finger from the start."

I froze, fingers on my wheelbase.

Dad carried on. "I'm beginning to wonder about some things. How everything always ends up your way, no matter what I think. Everything always on *your* terms. Why haven't I seen my brother in ten years?" He cleared his throat. "I've been trying to remember, but all I can think is that you didn't like him."

Dad had a brother? I laid my board and scrubbing brush down on the step.

"There's nothing wrong with Will … or me." There was a splash. "Why do you make things so difficult, Dean? It's like you're always trying to find fault with me." A little sniffle. "I thought you loved me."

Dad moved towards the door. "That won't work on me any more," he said.

After a while, Will lowered his binoculars. "Swap?" he asked.

I nodded and moved to the window, Grady handed Will the notebook and took my place by the door.

Now I could see back towards the river. The hill with the checkpoint cairn loomed in the near distance. I shuddered.

"What've you tried, Grady?" Will turned the notebook upside down and frowned at it.

"Transposing letters, mainly." Grady shrugged his shoulders.

"The coin has to be a clue," I suggested.

"Probably." Will looked at Lizzie's rubbing.

"Is there a date or some writing or something on it?"

"Just the word *Caesar*."

"So it's Roman."

"Duh."

Suddenly Lizzie snorted. A strange, out-of-place sound. "The coin was stuck on to the box – it's a *Caesar Cipher*. We did it in maths a year or so ago – Mr Goode said Caesar was the first person to invent codes."

Will went still for a moment. "I remember." He started to scribble.

"So," Grady asked. "What does it say?"

"Hang on, twenty letters could make up a grid of two by ten or four by five." He smiled. "All right, it's five by four." Will showed us the paper again.

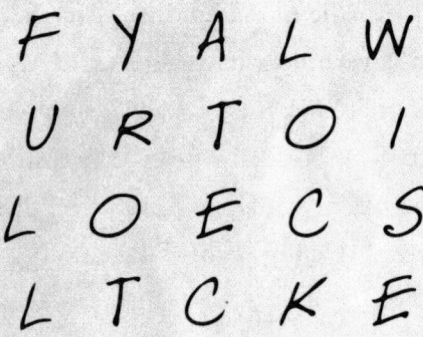

"Fully rotate clockwise!" I laughed. "That wasn't so hard."

"You have to know it's a Caesar Cipher," Grady glared. "It's not *that* easy."

"When we get to the checkpoint, we can quickly grab the next coordinates and go." I nodded. "How's Carmen doing, Lizzie?"

"She's asleep," Lizzie whispered. "We've got another hour or so before it's time to leave. Why don't we try to get some rest, too?"

"You guys should," I said. "Will and I can keep watch."

"Thanks, Ben." Grady lay with his back against the far wall, clutching his pick under his chin. His eyes darted around the room. "You know," he said with a yawn, "the moon landings were faked by the American government because Russia was going to get there first." He closed his eyes.

As Grady's breathing turned into whistling snores, I kept my gaze towards the hill. "I feel like a rabbit in a burrow," I whispered, "waiting to sneak past the foxes."

"I'd be more worried about dogs coming to dig us out," Will said.

"What do you mean?" I kept my voice low.

"An's team – they said they'd be back."

I exhaled shakily. "They'd be here by now if they were coming."

"Maybe," Will said quietly. "Or maybe they're waiting for us to fall asleep."

As the sun sank beneath the hills, the feeling of

being watched grew stronger. "Maybe we shouldn't wake them," I breathed. "I don't think we'll find a more defensible position."

Will shrugged. "We stay here and we'll have to fight eventually – either An comes back or someone else will want the shelter. We go outside and there's a chance we'll sneak past everyone."

"But if we're caught in the open…"

Will spread his hands. "I think we're better off risking the walk."

"You would." I glared at him.

"I won't ask what *that* means," Will said softly.

"He has friends," Mum yelled. "He's *normal*."

"*Ben* has friends." Dad's freckles had vanished in a surge of red. "Will's a hanger-on."

"That's not true." Mum's voice went dangerously quiet. "Will's charming. Everyone likes him."

"Ben said everyone's afraid of him."

"Maybe *Ben's* the hanger-on, have you thought of that? Will's the good-looking one *and* he's intelligent…"

I looked towards the landing at the top of the

stairs. Will was framed in the entrance to his room, scraping the top of a match with his thumbnail. I sat behind the phone table, peering through the gap in the kitchen door. Dad's bags were clumped in the hallway.

"The doctor gave me this printout." Dad tried to hand it to Mum, but she hurled it back at him.

"You went to the doctor without me?" Mum screamed. "You traitor! We don't need this rubbish. *You're* the one causing all the problems. You think you can just *leave* us?"

"I can't stay, not if you won't—"

"You're making me choose between you and *my son*. There isn't even a choice."

"All I'm asking is that you let us get help. Will could have burned the house down last night." Dad's fists clenched.

"I'm not having some *pop psychologist* poking around in my son's head." She spat the words. "Making up lies about him. What if they take him away? I can look after him."

"You have *two* sons, Carrie."

"Torben's fine. He doesn't need me the way Will does." Mum's shoulders formed stubborn lines. She'd

227

made her decision. I looked between Dad and Will. Will's eyes met mine, then he faded back into his room and the door clicked closed.

"Ben should come with me," Dad said. My eyes widened and my heart thudded.

"Are you *mad*?" Mum hissed. I froze. "Will *needs* Ben. If you're going—"

"You admit it, then." Dad sounded triumphant. "You admit that without Ben around, Will's *not* normal."

"He calms him down." Mum folded her arms. "You've wanted to leave for ages, so go. But don't think you're taking Ben with you. *We* need him."

"Yeah?" Dad sighed. "Well, *I* love him."

"Get out!" Mum screamed. "Get out, get out, get—"

Dad strode miserably into the hallway and picked up his bags. He hesitated when he saw me. "I'm sorry you heard all that, Ben."

"Will heard it, too."

"You always think of him first." Dad stood, bags dangling. "You could come with me."

I swallowed. "I want to." My voice was hoarse. "I can't though, can I?"

"You can." Dad kneeled beside me. "This isn't your responsibility."

"No," I said, suddenly angry. "It's yours."

Once Dad had closed the front door, I made my way into the kitchen. The printed paper was crumpled on the floor. A heading was written in sober black: *Your Child's Behaviour: Help and Advice.* I smoothed it out and went to slide it in the 'important-papers' drawer.

"Put that in the bin," Mum snapped.

I didn't take my eyes from the window I was watching. "Will ... you remember when Dad left?"

"Of course." Will's voice was flat.

"You know *why* he left?"

Will looked at me and then peered through his binoculars. "There were a number of factors. It wasn't just one thing." I said nothing. Will put down his glasses. "You think he left because of me." Again, there was no tone.

"That's not what I meant." I rubbed my eyes. "Forget it, I don't know why I brought it up."

"Because you're afraid." Will checked outside,

then turned back to me. "You're worried we might not make it off the island."

"We *are* going to make it off the island."

Will blinked slowly. "I can read you like a book and I know you've had the same thought as me. If the third checkpoint led a team to take Carmen's hand ... what will the last checkpoint involve? Even if the rest of the checkpoints contain normal *stuff* – and I don't think they do – there's a team out there who really don't want us speaking to the police. We'll still be in danger."

"Do *you* think we can make it?" My binoculars dangled from numb fingers.

Will nodded. "No matter what, you'll get us out of here. It's what you do."

"*What I do?*"

"You think I haven't noticed – you've always looked after me. You won't let anything happen."

Perhaps for the first time, I faced the facts head-on. "I have to bring you home. If I don't, Mum will kill herself."

Will snorted.

"*Will!*"

He looked at me strangely. "You really don't see

through her, do you?"

"She tried it before…"

Will tilted his head. "You found her in the bath. She timed it very well."

"She *what*?"

"I think she originally planned to have Dad find her – he was coming to pick us up for the weekend – but then she decided it would hurt him more if it was *you*."

"She wouldn't do that."

Will shrugged. "If you say so."

"Dad's right, there's something wrong in your head."

Will said nothing.

"Doesn't that bother you?"

"Should it?" Will lifted an eyebrow. "I don't think there's anything wrong with me. Maybe when I was little I was more … volatile. But now, I'm in control." He looked out of the doorway again. "Ben, don't worry. It achieves nothing. You're strong and I'm … me. Between us, we'll get everyone home."

Chapter Fourteen

As the bats started to circle the house, Lizzie opened her eyes. "Is it time?" She stretched, then caught her breath as she remembered that Carmen was sleeping against her.

Carmen was jolted awake by Lizzie's movement and her face immediately wrinkled, aged by pain.

"You need Tramadol." Lizzie found the pills in the pocket of Carmen's pack, handed her two and shoved the rest in her khakis.

Before I picked up my binoculars, I kicked Grady's foot. He lurched awake with a cry. "Freemasons!" he squawked. "Illuminati…" He stuck the pick out in front of him and blinked furiously.

"It's OK, Grady. It's time to leave." I stood and dug my fists into the base of my spine. My back cracked. "Are you sure about going for the checkpoints, Carmen?" I held out a hand to help her up. She took it and Lizzie stabilized her as she stood.

"We can always go back to the jetty," Lizzie said gently.

Carmen looked at us through bleary eyes. "No. I want to get to the end. Do you want me to take my own pack?"

I shook my head as Lizzie rolled their sleeping bags away. "I can manage."

Will picked up his rucksack and Lizzie lifted her spear.

"I don't have a weapon," Carmen said suddenly.

"What do you want, Car?" Will asked.

She turned to him. "A blade."

Will nodded. "I've got your knife." He found it in his bag and handed it over.

Carmen closed a shaking hand around the red plastic body. "You … found it?"

"Behind the cairn, on the hill." Will looked into her eyes. "You hurt him with it. Good for you."

Carmen unfolded the blade and held the knife in front of her.

"We'd better go before it gets dark." Will opened the door and I took one more look outside.

"Which way?" Grady asked.

Will pointed. "North-east along the river, until

233

we reach the sea."

Midges formed choking clouds along the garden path. We stepped out into them.

▼

We walked along the river, the banks sloping higher above us with every step.

"I don't like this," I said.

Lizzie raised her eyebrows. "What's the matter? The bank's hiding us."

"Yes," I said, "but I can't see if anyone's approaching from the west."

Lizzie reached out and squeezed my hand, then let it go.

Will had taken the lead once more, Grady was marching at the rear and the girls and I were in the middle – me with two rucksacks and a limp, Lizzie still hobbling and leaning on her spear. Carmen staggered like a zombie, her mutilated arm tucked under her jacket, the other jabbing at invisible enemies.

"Is Carmen OK?" I whispered.

Lizzie shook her head.

I said nothing more as we scuttled along the river. The moon looked like a smudged fingerprint against the sky. Soon it was difficult to see Will out in front.

The longer we hiked, the louder the sea became, until it was no longer a background hush but the boom of surf against rock. Ahead I could just about make out individual seabirds as flashes of white swooping towards the cliffs.

The banks loomed on either side of us until I could hardly breathe with the fear that one of the other teams would drop rocks on us, before leaping down to finish us off.

Then the river opened out to the sea.

I caught my breath as the walls came to an end. Above us natural ramparts were completely covered in roosting birds; white streaks calcified the rock and bush-like nests protruded from every cranny. The noise was incredible: cawing and screeching, crying and jabbering – an unruly audience awaiting a show.

We stood on the scrubby patch of land and stared.

"It's so loud!" Lizzie yelled.

Will was already looking for a way across the tributary. "We need to be on the other side of the river mouth," he shouted.

I couldn't take my eyes from the water. There was

an inky splodge just outside the bay – a tiny island off-shore.

Grady caught my shoulder. "Don't even think about it, Ben. Remember the currents? You'd be dragged out to sea."

I shivered. "Probably not worth the risk."

"Not yet," Will said. "No."

The river mouth was shallow enough to splash across and a quick search revealed a path up the side of the cliff in the direction we needed.

Carmen's breath was coming in harsh rasps now and she was mobile only with Grady's support.

"We could rest here," Grady panted when we reached the clifftop.

Lizzie shook her head. "Not here, we're outlined against the horizon. Let's get to the checkpoint first."

"How much further?" Grady asked.

Will looked at the map. "We're just under halfway."

Grady groaned, Carmen said nothing and we trekked on as the sun began to burn the sea. It wouldn't be long before night-vision glasses would easily pick us up.

Will stopped abruptly at a fork in the path. "I think this is where we head away from the cliff…"

"You're not sure?" I frowned. The two rucksacks I was wearing were compressing my spine; I just wanted to get to the checkpoint.

"Not a hundred per cent – there *could* be another fork further along. This feels a bit premature."

"Then we keep walking." I started forwards.

"If this *is* the fork, we'll have to double back," Grady moaned. He didn't move. "Why aren't you sure? Weren't you reading the map?"

"It's *dark*, Grady," Will snapped.

"Well, why aren't you using your torch?" Grady adjusted Carmen's arm where it lay over his shoulder.

"Because it would signal where we are," I growled.

Lizzie held up her hand. "Maybe we've hiked further than you think, Will? Are there any landmarks that would tell us if this is the way we need to go?"

Will rolled his eyes. "Yes, obviously. If we *are* in the right place, we can mark a direct line east to west, between the second checkpoint, us and the bottom of the holm in the bay." He folded his arms. "Just turn your head to see the holm on one side and the cairn on the other."

I sighed. "You could just *say* it's too dark."

Will gestured with his binoculars. "I can just about make out the shape of the hill."

"Then we can only guess," Lizzie said.

"Let's carry on along the path," I decided. "If we haven't found the checkpoint in the next fifteen minutes, we can come back and look for another fork." I strode off, trusting that the others would follow.

The third checkpoint was a low, wide tree in a weather-beaten copse. The box was chained to the trunk and nestled in the roots.

Grady lowered Carmen to the ground.

"I'm going to keep watch," Will said. He stood a little away from us, looking out at the shadowy moor.

I touched his shoulder. "Can you see anything?"

"No, but they're there."

"How do you—"

"At least one team will be watching the checkpoint. They're going to assume we've got to solve the riddle, open the inner geocache box, freak out, do something about the finger... They're expecting to have plenty of time to sneak up. We should be able to get away before they can reach us."

Lizzie was already kneeling by the box, pressing her thumb on the lid. The screen lit with a pale electronic glow. "What was the answer?" Lizzie poised her fingers over the keyboard.

"Fully rotate clockwise," Grady said, leaning over her shoulder.

Lizzie entered the phrase and immediately the locked-door game appeared.

"If it's like last time and the clue is also the solution to the puzzle," I murmured, "you'll need to turn the box."

We all heard the click as it opened.

The inner box that fell out was bigger than the first one had been: a finger-sized coffin. Lizzie ignored it; instead she flicked on her torch and shone it carefully into the lid.

"Oh no," she whispered.

"What?" It was my turn to lean awkwardly over her shoulder, Carmen's bag jabbing against my thighs. I peered at the riddle.

"Write this down, Grady," Lizzie said.

He grabbed the notebook she tossed at him.

"*My fifth and my third make fourteen. There is one between my fourth and second. My first is one less than twice second, yet my second and third make ten. Altogether I make thirty.*"

"It's all right," I said as Grady scribbled. "This is a maths problem. Will's the maths king."

Will didn't take his eyes off the horizon. "Can we go now?"

Lizzie called out the coordinates engraved in the lid and Grady added them to the notebook, then picked up the geocache box. "Should I open it?"

"We know what's in there." I stepped backwards, picturing the severed finger, tendons tensed so that it curled like a hook. Splinters of bone showing. Blood. A bitten nail.

Carmen smashed it out of his hand. "Put it back," she hissed.

Lizzie shoved her notebook into her jacket, returned the geocache box to the checkpoint box, slammed the lid, pressed her thumb against the screen and leaped to her feet. "Let's go."

As we stood, there was a yell from the moor;

shadowy figures broke from cover and melted out of the darkness to appear on top of a hillock.

"They saw us shut the box," Will called. "They think we have a geocache. They're coming!"

"Run!" Lizzie yelled.

"Which way?" I looked around wildly. We hadn't even identified the next checkpoint.

"That way." Grady picked a direction at random and dashed into the darkness, head down, pack bobbing. I turned to follow, but Lizzie grabbed me.

"You're too slow. You can't run with two rucksacks. Leave one of them." She tugged at Carmen's, but I resisted.

"Carmen's things…"

"*Leave it*, Ben." Carmen's eyes blazed.

I tore the pack off my chest and immediately my shoulders ached less. "Sorry, Car," I said as I dropped it by the checkpoint.

I caught hold of Lizzie's elbow in one hand and clutched my axe in the other. Will slung Carmen's good arm over his shoulder and together we raced after Grady.

"Oi!" The chasing team were shouting after us, as if we'd stop and let them catch up.

"This is … a nightmare," Lizzie gasped. I was half-carrying her. She lifted her spear, trying to stop it from tangling in her ankles.

"Ignore them. They wouldn't be shouting if they could catch us." I propelled her forwards. "We just need somewhere to hide."

Grady was stumbling ahead of us, panting loudly. He was a dark shape, just visible in the grey murk. To our right, Will was hauling Carmen.

"Hey, you!"

Lizzie gave a choking sob and I teetered sideways as her ankle gave way. I yanked her close to my side, put my arm around her waist, and we stumbled on.

The wind died. All I could hear was my own rasping, Lizzie's sobbing pants and the mismatched thud as our feet hit the ground. *Rasp. Pant. Thud.*

My boots crushed moss, tore through grass. I stumbled in a clump of mud.

Lizzie twisted in my arms. "They're … catching up."

"No … they're not." I pulled her harder. Where was Will?

My ears rang, blood pounded. Did I just hear

Grady cry out?

My leading foot came down on air. I couldn't let go of Lizzie. I dragged her with me, hurling the axe sideways to stop us rolling on the blade. We were sliding down a slope. Gravel in my elbows, scraping my face. Lizzie didn't scream, but there was a loud snap as her spear broke.

Finally we stopped and lay tangled together, gasping.

"Ben, is that you?" Grady floundered over.

"It's us," I whispered. Will leaped down the slope after us and Carmen cried out as his landing jolted her arm. I started to stand, but Lizzie grabbed me and pointed.

We had landed in a deep ditch. At one side was a low overhang, crowded with shadow. If we crawled inside, we'd be invisible.

I gave her a thumbs-up and commando-crawled beneath the deep overhang. Lizzie and Grady followed. Will pushed Carmen after us and then rolled inside.

My heart pounded. I pressed my fist into a growing stitch as Lizzie jammed her face against my shoulder.

"Curtis, where are they?"

The voices sounded older – perhaps twenty, the top end of the age limit.

"Split up. Look for them."

Torchlight haloed the sky and then scanned the slope in front of us. My eyes widened as I saw my axe. It lay in the open on the other side of the ditch.

Light gleamed from the iron blade, but there was no outcry. I almost sobbed in relief when the light moved on.

We remained in a silent huddle as time dragged by. Shouts passed us, sometimes far away, sometimes close enough to drive my heart into my throat. I was too afraid to go for my axe.

The gaps between shouts grew longer. "Have they gone?" Lizzie whispered.

"Maybe they're searching the cliffs," Grady whispered.

I checked on Carmen, who had slumped to one side. "Car, are you all right?"

She didn't answer, and I started to crawl towards her. Suddenly I froze.

"Stay right there." The words were almost a hiss.

"I've got a knife."

Behind Carmen, further back beneath the overhang, two figures watched us. We were not alone.

Chapter Fifteen

Very slowly, I retreated.

"Will?" I whispered.

Will switched on the penlight he kept attached to his belt.

"Switch that off!" the voice rapped.

Will directed the light towards the sound and the slender beam picked out two girls huddled together. One was holding a large knife. She kept her other arm around the girl beside her.

"We won't hurt you," Grady said.

"Put down the knife." I held up my hands, trying to look non-threatening. "Are you Prisha? I think we saw your team earlier."

The girl shook her head. "Somia."

"What happened? Where's the rest of your team?"

The knife tip tilted downwards. "Who d'you think we're hiding from?" Somia glared. "Liam and Sanjay wanted to take Pasha's finger. I told them we'd do it in the morning. Then, when they were making camp, we ran." Her eyes went to Carmen, who was sat at the edge of the pool of light, tears welled and the knife swept back up. "You did *that* to *her*?"

"No!" Lizzie crawled to my side. "We're hiding from the people who did … and from the team who were chasing us."

"We're hiding from *everybody*," Grady muttered.

"Well, you can't stay here." Somia gestured. "This is our place. Find somewhere else."

"Why don't you come with us?" Lizzie begged. "You're not safe alone."

"Says you!" Somia glowered. "You can only find this hiding place if you actually climb into the ditch. And if someone *does* try to drag us out, they'll get cut. We're safe enough until the competition's over. One more day. *Then* we'll come out."

"You'd be better off with us. We can protect you." Will flicked his hair and offered her one of his rare smiles.

Somia stared for a second. "Yeah? Like you protected her?" She pointed the knife at Carmen. "And how do I know you don't want some body parts of your own? You're in this too."

Pasha whispered frantically in Somia's ear.

Somia shook her head. "*I* don't trust them." She looked back at us. "They've gone. You can leave." She feinted with the knife and I slid backwards.

"Be reasonable," I begged. "Carmen's out cold."

"Wake her up," Somia snapped.

I started to move forwards.

"Not you!" She held me at bay. "Her." She pointed to Lizzie.

Lizzie started to edge around me, but I touched her shoulder to hold her back.

"It's OK." She slid out from under my arm. When she reached Carmen, she placed her fingers on her pulse, sighed with relief, then shook her. "Carmen?"

Carmen groaned.

Lizzie looked at Grady. "She's burning up!"

"It must be an infection." Almost in tears, Grady pulled his medical kit from his pack. "She should've been taking antibiotics from the start! I didn't think... Can you get her to take these?" He handed two capsules to Lizzie.

Lizzie sat Carmen up and pushed her matted hair out of her face. "Anyone got water?"

I handed her the bottle from the side of my pack. Somia watched, her knife hand unwavering, as Lizzie wetted Carmen's forehead and then poured water into her mouth.

Carmen choked and opened her eyes.

Lizzie tucked the capsules into her mouth and poured water after them. "She's due another painkiller, too," she reminded us.

Grady nodded and Lizzie gave her the paracetamol she had stashed in her trousers.

"Now go!" Somia barked.

"You're really going to make us take her out there?" Grady hunched over his pack, glancing nervously up at the stars.

"You *can't* stay," Somia repeated. "Too many people will draw attention here."

Delirious, Carmen shoved herself away from Lizzie. She crawled out into the open and wobbled to her feet. "*We can't let them win!*" She swayed. "Where's m'knife?"

Lizzie handed it to her.

"I can't believe she's still focused on that." I rubbed my face. "We *can't* go for the next checkpoint. We were lucky to get away this time!"

Carmen started to swear at me in Spanish and Will caught her before her legs folded. "Don't worry," he soothed. "Ben didn't mean it. We are going for the next checkpoint."

"I did mean it!" I snapped. "And no, we're not!"

Carmen swiped at me with her knife, but missed. Lizzie held her arm.

"All right, Car, we'll keep going." Lizzie looked at me. "It won't hurt to at least check it out."

I folded my arms. "We should find a place to hole up. Somia's got the right idea."

"No!" Carmen howled and Grady clapped his hand over her mouth.

"Stop upsetting her, Ben!"

"*You are going to bring people here!*" Somia cried, furious.

Pasha whimpered.

"Fine." I ground my teeth. "Give me the map. I'll show you where the checkpoint is." I checked the numbers, then tapped my finger on the folded paper. "*There.* It's right at the other end of the island near that chapel. We'd have to walk north half the night to get there." I looked at Lizzie. "Do *you* want to carry Carmen?"

"*I* will." Will tightened his arm around Carmen and they both glowered at me.

"I'm not the bad guy here!" I growled.

Lizzie took the map and Will's torch. "We can go through those trees." She pointed. "And look – there's another building *and* the chapel. Loads of places to hide."

"Yeah?" I muttered. "Loads of places *marked on the map*. Places all the other teams will like the look of too. We'll probably walk right into someone else's camp."

"We just have to be careful," Will said.

"The faster we get to the end of the route, the faster we find help." Lizzie took my hand.

"If we get to the last checkpoint in the fastest time we could still win." Grady avoided my eyes as he clipped the straps of his bag over his chest.

"This isn't about winning any more. It's about *surviving*. Haven't you been paying attention?" I dragged my hand through my hair and reached to pick up my axe.

"We're *not* letting *them* win," Carmen grunted.

"Yeah, but, Car, what are you willing to risk to stop them?" I exhaled, trying to regain control.

Lizzie held my gaze. "We're going to take it slowly and be careful. We'll go from one hiding place to the next and walk without the torches. If we can get ahead of everyone else, we'll be OK."

"You think we can overtake the other teams?" I pointed at her ankle.

"They're still trying to complete the geocaches. We're not. We just have to get all the coordinates and move on."

"Wearing our cloaks of invisibility?"

"Don't be like that, Ben." Grady stood beside Will and Carmen. "We know how to move quietly, stay low and walk below the horizon."

I rubbed my eyes and felt Somia watching us. "I'm only trying to protect us."

"If we can get two more checkpoints completed tonight, while most of the teams are camped out, we'll be exactly where we planned to be by tomorrow," Grady said hopefully. "If we only sleep for a couple of hours, then we can stay out in front."

"You girls decided yet?" Somia sneered.

"I don't like this." I pulled out of Lizzie's grip and walked past them all.

"Don't have to *like* it, *chico*," Carmen spat. "Just

252

have to *do* it."

▼

We needed to walk back across the river mouth —
we hiked in silence, our torches unlit.

Grady located the north star and we used it to
guide our way. The moonlight cast a faint glow on
the scrubland, helping us to keep our footing. The
wind bit through my jacket, but the midges and bats
were gone. It was too late even for them.

We moved slowly, carefully; once we were over
the river mouth, we stayed away from high ground
and avoided the cliffs.

Will half-carried Carmen and I supported Lizzie.
I could sense unspoken words cutting her lips. She
hated silence, always had to fill it, but I was grateful
for the quiet. I'd said my piece and been overruled.
Now I had to force every step, while my brain
screamed at me to go to ground. However carefully,
we were going towards danger. I hated it.

"Through the trees, or around them?" Grady's
words shattered the quiet. My heart pounded.

"What do you think, Ben?" Lizzie whispered.

"What do you care?" Resentment sharpened my

253

words and she glanced at me, surprised. Then she looked at Will. "There's more likely to be teams camping or waiting in the woods, don't you think?"

Will nodded.

"Then we should go around." She sounded confident, but I could feel her trembling.

We kept the treeline to our left and moved even more slowly. A campfire glimmered among the trees and I held my breath as we passed it. From Grady's direction, a stick snapped and we all froze.

"Don't lift your feet! Push your toecaps along the ground," Lizzie hissed.

We stood still and listened. Muffled laughter rang through the night. There was no pursuit.

We continued with even greater care. Tension wound my muscles to breaking point. What if I fell and drew the other teams to us, like caiman in a swamp?

The campfire faded out of sight. At least there was one team with no night vision. I rubbed my own straining eyes. What had they been thinking?

Slowly we passed the woods and headed back into the open. The sound of water lapping in the night breeze came from the loch on our left and a glow radiated from the broken windows of the building further around the water. *A beacon*, I thought. Perhaps that's where all the hunters will converge.

I realized with a shudder that I had been thinking of us as prey for a while now.

To the right, outlined against the midnight-blue sky, the shape of a cross blotted out pinprick stars. I touched Lizzie's shoulder and pointed. It was the chapel. We were nearly there.

The moorland turned to meadow and long grass tickled our legs, wet in the dampening night. An owl swooped, its wings almost touching my face, then it was gone. I wiped my sweating hands on my trousers.

Finally Lizzie spoke. "I didn't mean to ignore you, Ben."

"I know," I whispered shortly.

"You have to forgive me." Her voice almost broke. "What if we don't—"

"We're not going to die, Lizzie!" I caught her gaze. "Anyway, I'm not angry with you, just afraid we're walking into trouble."

Lizzie shuffled forwards. "We have to reach the end," she said.

"You *still* think there'll be help there? The last box had a *finger* in it."

"I don't know what's going on here," Lizzie said. "But there *will* be someone at checkpoint seven— there *has* to be. We just have to be strong for one more day." She swallowed. "Twenty-four hours. Less."

I forced a smile. "When you put it like that."

She took my hand. "So you're OK?"

"If you are." I looked up; we were getting closer to the chapel. "Lizzie… I remembered what you and Carmen were saying when I was … ill."

"Ah." She tried to pull her hand away, but I didn't let her.

"Why didn't you tell me your dad's sick?"

Her jaw tightened. "I didn't mean to hurt you."

"You haven't," I lied. "But how can I be there for you if I don't know what's going on?"

For a long time the quiet was broken only by our footsteps. Then she spoke.

"Now you know how I've felt our entire lives."

I caught a breath. "You—"

"I've always known there was something going on with you. Even before your dad left, but you never

256

told me. If I tried to ask, you changed the subject until I stopped asking. I figured our relationship just wasn't like that. We don't talk about the big stuff."

"But we do!" I insisted. Then realized my voice had raised. "Don't we?" I whispered.

"Not really." Lizzie shook her head. "When your mum was hospitalized that time, I found out from Matt, who heard it from *his* mum. It's OK. I found a way to be there for you, just by … being normal. And that's how you're there for me. We don't talk about the bad stuff, we keep it light, and that's a good thing."

"Y-you don't trust me?"

"Of course I do." Lizzie shrugged. "But I still don't know what's going on with you. Maybe one day you'll tell me, but what I'm trying to say is … if you don't, that's fine too." She leaned against me. "I love you, Ben. You're my best friend."

I smiled as my chest ached.

We stopped about a hundred metres from the chapel, behind a crumbling drystone wall. The chapel was as broken as the house we'd sheltered in – one whole side of it caved in, like a sandcastle smashed by a spiteful foot. The moonlight picked out gravestones – weathered, leaning or completely shattered. I thought of the number of houses that had been marked on the map. For only three homes, there were a lot of graves. Generations.

"Is there anyone in there?" Grady said under his breath.

"Impossible to tell." Will cocked his head. "I can't hear anything and there's no firelight, but that could just mean they're smarter than the team in the house back there … or they're laying a trap."

"Is the checkpoint inside?" Lizzie asked.

I shook my head. "It's behind the chapel. In the graveyard, most probably."

"A good place for an ambush," Will pointed out.

"We can still head into the hills and find a cave," I said, but Carmen turned, her head wobbling on Will's shoulder like a broken doll. She glared at me and I held up my hand. "All right." I sighed. "Don't freak out." I leaned my axe on the wall. "So, we do what we did last time. Will solves the riddle now, while we're hidden. We only go for the box when we have the answer."

"Agreed." Lizzie pulled out her notebook. "Here, Will." She dug her calculator from her bag.

"I'll need more light."

"It'll wreck your night vision," Lizzie warned.

"The moon's not bright enough for maths," Will whispered.

Grady got out his torch, but didn't switch it on. We looked at one another. Then Lizzie pulled a dirty green T-shirt out of her bag and wrapped it around the torch.

"Everyone except Will, cover one eye," she warned. "You'll keep your night vision that way." Then she dragged us into a circle and aimed the light at the ground.

Our bodies shielded the faint green glow. Will crouched under it and held the notebook in one hand, Lizzie's pencil in the other. He started to write.

"It's algebra," he muttered. "A, B, C, D, E. E plus C equals fourteen. D subtract B equals one." He squinted closer. "Two B minus A equals one. B plus C equals ten." He chewed the pencil. "A plus B plus D equals sixteen. A plus D plus E equals twenty." He stopped again. "This isn't as simple as I'd thought," he grunted. "I can't *think*."

"Forget algebra." Anxious, I looked around; still no movement. "Just work through the numbers, yeah? If B plus C is ten, then B has to be a number between one and ten, right?"

"What if some are fractions?" Grady asked. "Or negative numbers?"

"Say they're not," I said.

"OK, fine." Will muttered, chewed the pencil and stabbed at the calculator. "I think I've got it," he said after a few minutes.

"What?" I couldn't see the paper, it was too dark. Will sat back on his heels. "A, B, C, D, E … seven, four, six, five, eight."

"It does add up to thirty," Grady whispered after a moment.

"But it doesn't give an instruction for the locked box, does it?" Lizzie frowned. "Not like *fully rotate clockwise*, or *wind*."

"Maybe it'll be clear when we get there," Grady offered.

"You want to take that risk?" My head was beginning to ache. "What letters do you get if you change the number sequence into the alphabet?"

"Nothing that makes sense." Lizzie squeezed Carmen's hand as she shifted restlessly.

"Why aren't we moving?" she demanded.

"Soon," Will soothed her.

"Is it an anagram?" I pushed.

"Only one vowel." Lizzie shook her head. "G, D, F, E, H."

We all stared, clueless.

"We're going to have to go and look at the box, aren't we?" Lizzie whispered.

"Are we *all* going?" Grady asked. "Only, if it doesn't need all of us, maybe I should stay here with Carmen." He spoke in a kind of half-apologetic whisper.

I gaped. "You want us to take the risk while you stay here and hide?"

Grady swallowed. "When you put it like that …"

"I do."

"I just thought … if we're spotted by the box, Carmen will slow us down. But if I stay here with her, to keep her safe, then you guys can run away if you have to and … and meet us back here."

"You're serious?" My mouth gaped wider. "You want us to lead trouble away from you?"

"He has a point, Ben," Lizzie said. "It's what's best for Carmen and we're more mobile alone. *I've* got to go because of my thumbprint. I want Will with me... You could stay here, too."

"Are you kidding?"

"You don't even want to go for the checkpoints."

"That doesn't mean I'm going to leave you on your own. I can't believe this." I pushed my fists into my temples as my headache intensified. "Grady is going to stay here, to watch Carmen. You, Will and I are going to the checkpoint. You and Will can open the box while I keep watch." I rose to a crouch. "We're leaving our packs here, with Grady, just in case we have to sprint." I pulled mine from my shoulders with difficulty; it felt welded on, my skin and bone adjusted to the shape of the straps. I dropped it beside Carmen. "Get some more antibiotics in her," I snapped.

Will stood up and took Grady's torch. "We might need this."

Grady nodded. "Good luck."

I grunted, climbed over the wall and held out a hand to help Lizzie. Will landed beside me, catlike. Although we were heading into a graveyard that could contain an ambush, to open a box that could contain a human body part, it felt good for a moment to be just me, Lizzie and Will, almost like we were in Primary again.

We scurried from grave to grave; Will kept the T-shirt over the torch, moving it over the ground in search of the box and Lizzie clenched her notebook in one hand while she traced her fingers over names and lingered over the impressions of dates. "Sad," she murmured.

"I can't see the box," Will growled. We'd looked around every stone; my head pulsed with each movement I made, my knuckles whitened on the axe.

Lizzie gestured and we ducked behind a large stone that looked as if it might collapse at any moment.

"What do you think? Is it somewhere else?"

"It has to be here," I said.

Lizzie frowned. "What if we have to dig for it?"

I shook my head. "There're teams ahead of us. We'd have been tripping over holes all over the place."

Will was shining the light on one of the graves. "Some of these have stone slabs in front of them. One could lift."

"But which one?" An aura flickered around my

vision. The vision in my left eye blinked in and out. An oncoming migraine. Already I was feeling clumsy and thick-fingered. Unlike myself. I pushed the feeling away. "We can't lift every stone here."

Lizzie was staring over my shoulder, reading. "Bessie Tait, Elspeth Tait, Sinnie Tait, Garthe Duncan, Eaner Galdie, Johne Galdie…"

"Say that again?" Will turned like a whip.

"Bessie Tait, Elspeth Tait, Sinnie Tait, Garthe Duncan—"

"That one." Will stopped her. "Where is it?"

Lizzie pointed. "Just behind you."

"Any other Duncans?" Will started to crawl towards the grave.

"I…" Lizzie frowned. "Actually, I haven't seen any. It's dark, so I might be wrong, but all the rest I found are in family groups: the Taits, the Galdies, the Frasers – Garthe's all alone."

Will stopped in front of the grave. There was a stone slab sitting cockeyed on the hard earth.

"*Garthe Duncan: Farmer, Engineer, Husband*," Lizzie read quietly. "*Your love will light my way.*"

Finally, I saw what had caught Will's ear. "G, D, F, E, H," I said. "It's the clue."

Lizzie nodded. "So we try to lift this stone?"

In answer, Will put down the dimmed torch and jammed his fingertips under one corner. I handed the axe to Lizzie and bent to help him. The stone lifted more easily than I had expected.

"We aren't the first to get here," I murmured.

We propped the stone against the grave. Beneath it lay the checkpoint box.

"Open it, Lizzie," Will said.

The clue to the locked-room game had been written on the gravestone: light. Will shone the torch on the screen and the lid popped open. The geocache box inside was wider and shorter than the previous one. "What do you think is in it?" Lizzie whispered, once she had finished copying the engraved coordinates and clue into her notebook.

I swallowed.

"We could open it and find out." Will stroked the lid. "We don't have to tell Carmen."

"I don't know." Lizzie shook her head. "We don't really need to see, do we?"

"Don't we?" Will asked. "What if it's a normal geocache this time?"

Lizzie's eyes brightened as she said, "You think

that's possible?"

Will shrugged. "If the first caches *were* sabotaged, they might have given up changing them by this point."

"We can only be certain if we're first to reach one," I pointed out.

"It's about the right size for a compass again." Lizzie poked the case.

I looked at Will, but said nothing as he picked up the box. He handed the torch to Lizzie and opened the latch. Although I didn't want to, something made me lean close.

Chapter Sixteen

In the sick green light, a human ear nestled on a large piece of cotton wool. Tiny hairs frosted the edge. Blood stained the cotton black.

Lizzie put her hands over her face.

I grabbed the box from Will and closed it, then put it back in the larger box, snapped the list shut, pressed Lizzie's unresisting thumb against the screen to engage the lock and dropped it in the hollow under the stone.

"It's not going to end, is it?" Lizzie whispered. "Either the saboteurs aren't giving up … or it's meant to be like this. Something has gone wrong with the game." She looked at Will. "We're going to die!"

Will patted Lizzie tentatively. "Ben won't let that happen." Then he swiftly withdrew to the other side of the gravestone.

Lizzie watched him retreat and took a deep

breath. "You're right. We'll be fine. Thanks, Will." As Will moved further away and started to scan the graveyard, she put her mouth close to my ear. "I'm sorry – I didn't mean to scare him. I sometimes forget he's younger than we are."

"You didn't frighten Will." I raised my voice to speak to him. "Can you see anyone?"

He shook his head.

I frowned. "Shouldn't someone have found us here by now?"

Will came back, pushed up my sleeve and directed the light on to the face of Grandad's watch. "It's 2 a.m. Everyone must be asleep."

I pulled my arm back. "We can't be the only ones moving at night."

"The moon's going down, the sun isn't rising." Lizzie looked up. "We *could* be the only ones."

"Or maybe instead of staking out the checkpoints, they're looking for camps," Will said. "Fools building fires."

I smiled then, suddenly, and said, "You're telling me we got away with it?"

Lizzie grinned back. Then her smile died. "We'd better get to Carmen and Grady," she said.

We kept low and, despite my throbbing head, I managed to leap soundlessly back over the wall, surprising Grady, who was still sitting with Carmen, leaning back on the stones, his eyes half-closed.

"Great guarding, Grady." Will frowned and touched Carmen's cheek. "She's shivering."

"She's got a fever." Grady got to his knees. "Did you find the next coordinates?"

"Yeah." I checked Lizzie's notebook, then held the torch over the map and my gut twisted. "It's bad news."

"What?" Grady scrambled to see.

"The next box is on the north-west headland." I closed my eyes to banish the flickering aura that had settled into my vision. "There's no cover."

We were determined to get to the moorland below the summit point before dawn. I crunched bitter migraine-relief tablets as I marched into the darkness, grateful that my eyes weren't fighting the sunlight.

"There has to be somewhere to hide," Lizzie repeated. "A cave or something."

I said nothing. I was focusing on putting one foot in front of the other. My belly was nauseatingly empty, my head pounded, my knee ached, my gum was still sore and my vision flickered – tiredness or traces of the migraine battling the tablets, I couldn't tell any more.

When I knocked into Grady, I realized I was weaving from side to side. He pushed me away with a grunt.

"Sorry," I mumbled.

The sky to the east was starting to lighten. The birds weren't calling yet, but I could sense them stirring. Insects were crawling over my boots and I was beginning to see where I was stepping more clearly.

As pre-dawn started to lift the darkness, I felt increasingly exposed. I shivered, dank night air creeping under my jacket and making my skin feel cold and clammy.

Ahead of us the ground was rising more sharply. I stumbled on to the slope and walked on, exhausted.

"Keep a look out for somewhere we can hole up." Lizzie touched my arm. "Ben? Are you listening?"

I lifted my head. "Somewhere we can hide. Yes."

I blinked at the hill in front of me.

My chin dropped again and I kept walking. The others could search. If I stopped concentrating, there was no way I'd be able to put one foot in front of the next, in front of the next, in front of the...

"Ben. Stop!" Grady this time.

I reeled to a stop and looked up. Will had Carmen in a fireman's lift: her head bobbed on his rucksack, both arms dangled down his back.

Lizzie and Grady stood beside them. Behind them, a rockfall. Beyond that, a tree with deep, twisted roots and under the roots...

"Another cave?"

"I only found it by crawling inside the hollow under the roots," Grady said, smug. "It's well camouflaged."

"And defensible." Lizzie clutched her broken spear. "The entrance is narrow."

I nodded. "Let's go then."

Lizzie guided me into the smell of tree roots, damp earth and insect husks. She switched on the torch, still covered with the T-shirt, and helped me take off my rucksack. The cave was more of a fissure; the roof made of snarled roots, the ground stone-pitted earth. In one corner, water trickled between rocks, leaving pockets of thick clay among the mud. The space was just big enough for the five of us and our gear – if we squeezed together. I sighed and Lizzie touched my forehead.

"Your face is all screwed up. You've got a migraine?"

"It's better," I lied.

"You need to sleep."

Will dumped a feverishly protesting Carmen on to my rucksack. I helped her into a more comfortable position and she opened her eyes. "Where are we?"

"Cave," I said. "Sort of."

"Don't worry," Lizzie said, sitting beside her. "We're not staying."

"*You* are," Will said.

"What?" Lizzie looked up.

"You, Carmen and Grady are staying right here. Ben and I are going for the headland."

I rolled my head towards him, too tired to lift it.

Will stretched out his legs beside me, winced and moved a sharp stone. "We can move faster and more quietly alone," he explained. "But we need some sleep. It's half three. Work out that riddle and wake us at four."

"Riddle?" Grady asked.

"It's a good one," I said, fighting my drooping eyes. *What grows when it eats, but dies when it drinks?* My head pounded.

I fell asleep.

▼

"You'll need this." Lizzie pressed a lighter into my hand.

I put it in my top pocket. I'd had just enough sleep so my brain had stopped feeling like it was filled with wasps and I could think again, but I was still light-headed.

Will crawled between the tree roots and I started to follow.

Lizzie caught my arm. "Don't get hurt."

"I'm not sure I can promise that." I smiled weakly.

"Try," she insisted.

We looked at one another, suddenly awkward.

"This *is* best, isn't it?" she said abruptly.

"Yeah. You need to rest your ankle. Carmen needs time for her fever to break. Grady can watch Carmen and guard you while you sleep."

"When do *I* sleep?" Grady cried.

"We'll take it in turns, Grady." Lizzie's voice held an edge. "An hour each."

Grady folded his arms and I turned to go.

Lizzie cleared her throat. "Come back safe, Ben and—"

"Watch Will?" I raised my eyebrows.

She snorted. "Hah, no… If you can't get to the box without being seen, then leave it."

"What about Carmen? What about getting to the end of the route?"

"We'll have to think of another way to find help."

Lizzie's fingers hung in mid-air between us, as if she wanted to touch my face. Did she? What if I was misreading things? Especially after our last conversation.

"Ben?" Will hissed. "Come on."

"I–I'd better go."

"Right."

I crawled out to meet Will.

Outside, the sky was still dark grey, but the stars were fading. It was half past four.

I hoisted my axe on to my shoulder, glad I wasn't carrying my rucksack.

"Can you run?" he whispered.

I nodded and we started towards the headland.

▼

We soon left the moor behind us, but were careful to keep the hill at our back.

"There'll be other teams around," Will huffed as he ran.

Jogging beside him, I silently agreed. Fires would be sleepy embers by now; we'd have no smoke or flame to warn us we were heading for a camp, and there could be teams already moving, trying to get to the checkpoints ahead of everyone else. Our feet crunched on pebble and gravel, unmade sand. Behind us the cliffs cut off as if sliced through.

We ran in step. Will was only a little shorter than me, and he kept his arms pumping in time with mine. His skin was blotchy with exhaustion, but he seemed as calm as ever.

In the far, far distance another island showed pinpricks of lights – streetlights or glowing windows … early rising farmers perhaps. If we set off a flare, someone might come to help. But if they did pay attention to the firework, would they reach us before the hunters did?

The headland was turning into a beach with flat rocks to the left and right. I caught my breath as I saw movement among the rocks, then realized there were seals around us, their dog-like faces curious but unafraid. I saw heads break the surface of the water. Barks warned others of our presence.

We kept going. The sky was lightening further now; pale grey, the stars washed out altogether.

"Ben, look." Will pointed and we stopped. In front of us, picked out on the sand in larger, darker rocks, was a single word, in human-sized capitals: *HELP*. I had almost tripped over the tail end of the letter P.

"Someone was here before us." Will rubbed his chin. "But they weren't going for the checkpoint."

"There're people out there like us," I gasped. "People who don't want to play the game any more."

"Looks like it."

"Well, where are they?" I looked around. "They left their message and then ran away?" I shivered. "Maybe they were chased off."

"Or maybe they realized it was pointless," Will said.

"Pointless?" I stared at him.

"Have *you* seen anything fly by that wasn't a bird?" Will pointed upwards. "I don't think there are any flight paths over the island."

I looked at the sad piles of stones. Will was right. Who was there to see the plea?

"They had to be desperate."

Will shrugged.

"So how many teams are still hunting, do you think?" I kicked a stone, dislodging the top end of the P this time.

Will held up a finger. "The team that almost found us on the moor, that's one. Reece's team, that's two."

"Do you think An's is still out there?" I looked around again, as if they would pop up from behind a rock.

"Could be – that's three. And there was that girl we saw with the machete. That's four. Somia's team are probably still looking for *them*. She said it was a guy called Liam. I reckon that's Liam Jones – team seven. Reece told Carmen he saw someone with a girl on a lead, didn't he? So that team are sorted. Still in the game, but not after anyone else."

"I still think at least one team would've dropped out at the second checkpoint," I said.

"Probably." Will nodded.

"So where does that leave us?" I bit a nail. "Four teams definitely hunting for 'spare parts'." I winced at my own use of the phrase. "One team looking for Somia, but who would probably take anyone they came across. One likely dropped out – they're probably back at the jetty – and one ahead of us with a prisoner. That's seven. So there's just one team out here with us, looking for help. Who do you think it is?"

Will frowned. "You want me to *guess a name*?"

"I suppose not." I started to walk forwards, preparing to break into a jog.

Will moved into step with me.

As we sped up, I glanced back at the word on the beach. I'd made a mess of it. Now it said *HELL*.

Will pressed his fist into his side as he jogged. "Lizzie still thinks there's going to be help at the end," he said.

"I know." I had a stitch, too. It felt as if we were

running so slowly, every step hampered by the sand. "There might be."

Will looked at me. "Really?"

"There has to be someone at the end of this … doesn't there?"

"Someone who intends to help us?"

"Someone from the Gold Foundation," I panted. "They'll deal with the saboteurs."

Will blinked. "You don't still think one of the other teams changed the boxes? You aren't that naive…" He kept pushing forwards.

"Why wouldn't they – for a million pounds?"

"It's not *that much money*!" Will paused and leaned on his knees. "Not these days. You couldn't even live off the interest."

"Other people might not see it that way." I stared at him. "You think the Gold Foundation brought us here to do this on purpose?"

Will nodded. "Why only raise the crossing every three days? Why not build it so it's permanent?"

"Privacy – like they said?"

"A gate would be a lot cheaper. No, it's to make sure we can't leave until they're ready to let us go. I could understand none of our phones having reception here, but Grady's Iridium? They have to be blocking the signal somehow."

"But … why?"

"I don't know yet." Will was irritated; angry that there was a puzzle he couldn't solve. "We'll find out at the end."

I stared at him. "*That's* why you really want to finish the course. *That's* why you're on Carmen's side – so you can find out what's behind this? You're as bad as Grady. Sometimes you don't get to know everything, Will."

"Don't you want to find out?"

"Not that badly." I closed my eyes. "I just want to get us all home safe. That's it."

Will regarded me coldly. "You know you can't guarantee that," he said. "Use your brain. If the Foundation did set this course, will they want anyone going home and talking about it?"

I gasped. "What are you saying?"

Will looked at his pick. "I think someone got us to the island and set this course on purpose. Maybe it was the Gold Foundation, maybe it was some fake—"

"Now you really do sound like Grady."

"I don't know what their reasons are, but I do know that when we find whoever is behind this, they aren't just going to help us. But they might be willing to cut a deal."

"We agree to say nothing about the game and they get us home?"

"Something like that." Will's eyes glittered.

"Then hiding won't help." I sagged.

"If *I* didn't want anyone leaving the island to tell tales, I'd be hunting down all the groups before they leave. I'm not sure the jetty is going to be safe. I wouldn't want to be in the team waiting it out there."

I groaned and turned to start running again, but Will wasn't moving.

"This isn't all your responsibility, Ben," he said eventually.

"I do know that." I met his cool gaze.

"You don't, *Saint Ben*. Not really."

"I'm oldest. I brought you here." I clenched my fists.

"Lizzie brought us," Will said. "Blame her."

"I-I can't."

Will nodded. "Mother made you like this. She

trained you – like a dog."

I stiffened.

"She made sure you'd look out for me," Will continued. "Especially after Dad left. But now you feel like you're answerable for everything."

"I'm not some animal," I cried.

"I know about Cardiff," he sneered. "Mother told me you didn't get in, but it wasn't hard to find your offer letter."

I hesitated as my rage burned away. "In the recycling," I said.

He nodded. "I didn't ask for that."

"Yeah, well, Mum didn't give me much choice."

"You can't be my shadow for ever." He looked out to sea. "I'll speak to her."

"She's right though. I should be there for you. University will be hard."

"Harder than this?" He gestured at the beach. "I can handle it. Look at me. I. Don't. Need. You." The night wind shifted his hair across his face and he pushed it back impatiently. "Give up your life if you must, but I won't feel guilty about it." He turned his gaze back to the distance. "I just don't know what you expect from me."

"You're my brother. I don't expect—"

"Well, don't," Will's voice continued, inflectionless. "Don't expect anything from me. I don't owe you."

"I-I know. I never—"

"All this 'poor Ben, he has to look after Will' stuff has to stop." Will's top lip curled and he faced me again. "I don't know about you, but I've had enough of it. Don't come to Oxford. I don't want you there. You'll hold me back."

"*Hold you back...*" I echoed, but Will was already moving, striding along the shore. "You ungrateful bastard," I called. "My whole life revolves around y—" I stopped.

There *was* a seed of resentment inside me. I tried not to acknowledge it, but oh yes, it was there. And it was growing. How long before I loathed him? Before I demanded the debt be repaid?

A week ago, Will wouldn't have had a problem with me keeping an eye on things in Oxford. But *now* he didn't want me there. Why not?

I thought of the way he had called me 'Saint Ben'. Perhaps there was room for resentment on both sides.

I jogged after him and when I caught him up, we

ran without speaking, our feet thudding in time.

Finally we ground to a halt. We seemed to be alone and at the very edge of the island.

"Where is it?" I turned.

Will frowned.

"We did get the right coordinates, didn't we? Maybe we haven't seen anyone because we're in the wrong place!"

"We haven't seen anyone because it's five o'clock in the morning," Will said mildly.

I gripped his elbow. "Will, what's that?" I pointed out to sea where something was being moved by the waves.

"A seal?" Will said, but he lifted his binoculars.

After staring out for what felt like a long time, he passed me the glasses. I hesitated before I held them to my eyes. For a second I thought I *was* seeing a seal and I started to lower the lens. Then the sea exhaled and something green billowed in the waves. A camo jacket floating around a body. As the waves shifted, a pale forearm twisted up and down. I almost leaped forwards, but Will's arm slammed into me and then I saw what he had seen. The body was face down, moving only with the sea.

"Someone tried to swim for it." I shook as I handed him back the binoculars. "They're ... dead."

Will nodded. "They shouldn't have tried to swim." He turned me to face inland. "Don't look. Focus. We have to find the fifth checkpoint."

I nodded and let Will redirect my attention. Where was the box?

Shells curled in among the sand, and worm casts wound around my feet. When I moved my boots, a crab burrowed quickly away. We rotated. Nothing in view.

"It could be underwater," I said abruptly. "In a rock pool."

Will nodded and we started to look between the rocks, in the puddled water and seaweed.

The box was at the bottom of a dark pool of about an arm's depth. Its chain curled around it like a tentacle and jellyfish floated on either side.

"Stingers?" I asked.

"Probably." Will used his pick to drag the box out of the water.

We looked at it.

"You reckon this'll work then?" I asked him, suddenly nervous.

"It had better."

Will took the clay imprint of Lizzie's thumb out of his pocket.

"Has it dried?" I reached out for the clay. It was flaky around the edges, but had hardened. Will unwrapped the mess of melted gummy bears, which had turned into soft gelatine. Then, while I held the clay, he pressed the gummy bear 'finger' on to the imprint.

"Just hope it's a lo-res scanner," Will said, and he pressed the fake finger on to the screen.

Nothing happened.

"Try again," I breathed.

Will rocked the 'finger' over the scanner; there was an eternal pause and the screen lit up.

WELCOME, ELIZABETH BELLAMY.

"Yes!" I punched the air and Will turned back to the keyboard.

"Fire," I reminded him. "*What grows when it eats, but dies when it drinks?*"

He typed in the answer to the riddle and the locked-room game appeared.

"I hope this is right." I flicked on the lighter and held the flame close to the sensor. "Nothing's happening."

"Give it a chance to warm up." Will blew on his own fingers.

After a few more seconds, there was a click and the box opened.

Just like last time, the riddle and coordinates were engraved on the underside of the lid.

IRON TEEN

Checkpoint 6

22.55: 87.91

Alone I am 24th, with a friend I am 20.
Another friend and I am unclean.

"Where's the pencil, I'll—"

"Got it," Will said.

"What?"

"It's easy." He tilted his head at me. "You haven't worked it out?"

I ground my teeth. "No."

Will sighed. "What's the twenty-fourth letter of the alphabet?"

"X."

"What's X with a friend?"

"Um …"

"XX, dummy – twenty in Roman numerals."

"And XXX is for *dirty* movies. OK, I get it. What about the coordinates?"

Will shook out the creased and dirty map. "There." He pointed and I moaned with relief – the next box wasn't too far away. Back to the others and then another half-mile further. It would be somewhere on the edge of the loch that filled the bowl between the three of the highest points on the island.

Finally, we turned our attention to the geocache box.

"It's a lot bigger than the last one," I whispered. Will reached out and I caught his hand. "Why open it?"

"Don't you want to *know*?" Will shook free and touched the box with his fingertip, almost reverently.

"Not really." But I didn't move. My eyes caught Will's. "What would happen if…"

"If what?"

"If we just threw this box away," I said. "The teams behind us wouldn't know what to put in the cache. They wouldn't have a reason to keep hunting."

Will froze, his eyes flickering as he processed the idea.

I grabbed the box from him, stood and pulled my arm back to throw.

Chapter Seventeen

"Don't do it!" The words were roared from behind us in a familiar deep voice and I dropped the box as if it burned. Roosting birds, disturbed by the shout, burst from the cliffs. We spun round and stared as a team of five guys pounded towards us along the shingle. Dawn had turned the sky red behind them.

There was nowhere for us to run. We were trapped.

Will raised his pick. The team were still a distance away, but there was no route around them.

"Hold this," Will growled. Automatically I closed my hand around the checkpoint box as he thrust it at me. Sparks flew from rock as he used his pick to smash the links of the chain. Separated, the chain slithered back into the pool. Then he snatched the box from me.

"Grab the one you dropped," he yelled as he ran towards the sea.

I obeyed and followed him, trying not to think about exactly what was thumping against the cold metal in my hand.

"Oi! What're you doing?" I looked over my shoulder to see the other team running faster, powering after us.

The headland shattered into rocks. Will leaped on to the furthest. We were at the very end of the island. He balanced there and dangled the box with the coordinates over the water. I stood behind him and did the same, suspending the geocache over the waves.

The other team skidded to a halt.

"Cheats."

Will shook the checkpoint box. "You want this?"

The guy who had spoken was a redhead like me, but his face was so freckled he looked almost tanned. Patches of white skin stood out like islands on his forehead and chin. He grimaced. "You gonna drop it, mate?"

In answer, Will gave the box another shake.

"Stop him, Curtis," one of his mates said. He was the smallest and thinnest of the group. He wore thick glasses over pale eyes that glittered with a familiar sharpness. I glanced at Will.

"All right, what d'you want?" Curtis demanded.

"We want you to let us past, unharmed," I snapped.

Five faces glowered at me.

"What's yer name?" Curtis asked.

"Does it matter?" I licked my lips.

"What's in the box?"

"We haven't looked."

"You put the box down and we'll let you walk past." Curtis glanced at his mates. "Right?"

They all nodded, expressions unreadable.

"Bull." My voice came out higher than I'd have liked. "I don't know what's in here, but I know what was in the last box and none of you have given up an ear." I shook the box and it came open in my hand. I yelped and leaped back as something thudded on to my foot and then rolled towards the sea.

Curtis lunged forwards, his arm outstretched, but froze when Will gave a jerk, as if to throw his box.

Carmen's hand teetered on the edge of the rock. Her delicate fingers were curled into rigor mortis, one of them missing.

I threw up. Sick spattered into the sea.

"I-it's Carmen's hand." I looked at Will. "Look at the tattoo. Do we t-take it back to her? Can they …

sew it back on?"

One of the lads behind Curtis swallowed loudly. "Don't you watch telly, mate? It's gotta be on ice."

"It's too late," Will agreed.

We all stared at the hand. Curtis raised his hatchet; I brandished my axe. "Stay back!"

"What now?" Curtis asked.

"You all go stand over there." I pointed to the rock face beneath the nesting birds. "Or I'm going to kick Car— the hand into the sea."

Curtis jerked his head and his mates backed away.

"This is out of control, Curt, mate," the lad with the bruised face muttered loudly. "A tooth ... even an ear ... not so bad, innit? But this is a *hand*. I mean, there're two more checkpoints left. What's in the last one? A head?"

"Shut up, Kyle." Curtis stared at me. "Now what?"

"We take the box with the clue and the coordinates as far as *that* rock." I pointed to a rock shaped like a curved beak, sticking out from the cliff, further along the beach. "You stay right where you are. When we get there, we'll put the box down. You can pick it up when we've gone."

"How do we know you won't take it with you?"

"You don't." Will raised his eyebrows. "But you have no reason not to trust us."

"You were gonna chuck it," Curtis yelled.

Will looked at me. "Well, *now* we're leaving one box here and the other one over there. Right?"

I carefully put the empty box beside Carmen's hand, trying not to look at it.

"All right." Curtis gestured. "Go on, then."

"You make any sudden moves and I toss the box as far out to sea as I can," Will warned.

"We're staying right here."

My heart pounded as we stepped off the rocks and edged past Curtis and his team. They watched us with hunters' eyes. When we were past, Curtis gave a nod and two of his friends went to retrieve Carmen's hand and the box that had held it.

"I don't like leaving her hand with *them*," I groaned.

"I know." Will's arm was still poised ready to throw. He didn't take his eyes from Curtis. Eventually we reached the rock I'd pointed to. Slowly, as if he was holding a bomb, Will put the box down.

"Run!" he yelled.

Curtis's team started sprinting after us. Shouts chased us down the beach and I could hear the crunching of their pursuit.

Will grunted as a rock bounced off his right shoulder, but he didn't stop. He turned and grinned at me, his eyes alight.

Despite my fear, I grinned back; we were outpacing Curtis. His team were bigger, slower and hadn't taken the time to ditch their rucksacks. We were getting away.

When they were finally out of sight I stopped. "Will, did you hear what that guy said – about the last checkpoint maybe having a head in it?"

Will nodded.

"What do you think?"

Will said nothing.

▼

It was past half past five when we got back to the cave.

"Did it work?" Grady greeted us the second we ducked inside.

"It worked," Will answered and he smirked as he put down his pick.

"You're glad I brought the gummy bears now, huh?"

"I was glad before," I said. "How's Carmen?" There was no way I was telling her about her hand.

"We think the fever's broken." Lizzie stretched as I sat beside her with a sigh. "She seems calmer. We've just dosed her up."

"Hey." Carmen stirred sleepily. "Are we moving out?"

"We need a rest, Car," Will said. "Give us a couple of hours to sleep and then we'll go on. The next checkpoint isn't too far from here. Then only one more and we'll be at the end."

I nodded. "It'll still be early when we set out."

Grady grinned. "We've got a chance, then. We can still *win*."

"Only if we can steal a full set of geocaches," Will reminded him without looking at me.

"And we're only doing that if no one is going to get hurt," Lizzie added.

We crept out of the cave and into a bright day that was just starting to warm up. Carmen was able to walk, but Will hovered beside her, one hand on her elbow and the other on his weapon.

Lizzie's ankle had healed enough for her to put weight on it and she didn't seem to miss her broken crutch. She had removed the knife from the end of the spear and it was now tucked in her belt; her hand hovered close to it.

Grady had left more of his equipment in the cave – he moved faster under the lighter pack, his face grim.

"I still think this could be aliens," he said to Lizzie, apparently continuing a conversation Will and I had missed. "It's the only thing that makes sense. It's a test – to see how humans react to a super-stressful situation. They could be finding out how we work, how we think, how easily we turn on one another."

Carmen stared at him with horror.

"They're finding out how to kill us," Grady concluded.

Lizzie shook her head. "Grady, if *aliens* filled the geocaches, they already know how to kill us."

"They don't know how we think though – not how we work as teams, or react to danger or stress."

Will studied Grady closely. "Do you really believe

this stuff?"

Grady frowned. "I…"

"I get your Kennedy-assassination theory, the Russian infiltration of US politics, your Diana conspiracy, even the faked moon-landing. But you're talking about aliens – that's a whole different kind of thing."

Grady halted. "There's so much we don't know, you guys. Is it such a stretch to believe that there are creatures hiding among us who are more intelligent and powerful? I mean, there must be ancient species out there, evolving on their planets for millions of years, in forms we'd never recognize, and technologically light years ahead of us." He stopped. "I find it just as strange that you *don't* believe in the possibility."

We had reached the loch. Morning mist clung to the water and I pulled out my binoculars. We kneeled behind the cover of a gorse bush as I checked the area.

"Can you s—" Lizzie was cut short by a scream to our left. I spun round. Across the moor, on the other side of the river, a kid was sprinting with his head down, shrieking as he ran. On either side of him, like African hunting dogs, were An's team. They were wholly focused on the running figure. Two of them had found another way around and were waiting for An to drive the boy towards them. He looked up, saw that he was boxed in and hurled himself at the river.

The tall girl came up behind and tackled the boy so that he landed half in the water, half out. He screamed again and tried to drag himself into the river, but they pulled him back.

Will grabbed Carmen and drew her close, covering her ears and eyes as best he could. Lizzie grabbed my hand. Grady gaped. I hadn't seen the boy before and there was no sign of the rest of his team. Had they run and left him, or had they got separated?

An's team held the boy in place as An drew a serrated knife.

"Let me go! Please," the boy begged. "I don't want to die."

"S-should we help him?" Lizzie's voice trembled.

Suddenly the boy howled and thrashed wildly. Lizzie lunged towards the river, but her instinct to protect was too late; the knife flashed.

"What was it?" Carmen whispered, visibly shaking in Will's arms. "What did they do?"

"His ear," Grady whispered. "They've got his ear."

"They're behind us then," Will said with satisfaction.

"Will!" Lizzie gasped. "How can you think about that now?"

We watched in silence as An dragged the sobbing boy to his feet. He was clutching his head and blood ran between his fingers.

They consulted their map and then An turned and looked in our direction. He knew we were there. I stood and we glowered at one another across the moor. An said something I couldn't hear and the rest of his team turned to look. The tall girl waved. Then An jerked his head and they moved off into the trees, dragging the wailing boy with them.

"I want this to be over," Carmen sobbed.

"One more checkpoint after this one." Grady patted her shoulder awkwardly.

"Where *is* this one?" Will looked at the loch.

I pointed. Just on the other side of the water, there was a small wooden jetty. Under it, easily visible from our vantage point, the box was chained to a piling.

"Let's get this over with," Lizzie said.

▼

We hiked slowly, carefully, around the water. There was nowhere to hide, but nowhere for other teams to take us out from either.

"Unless they're underwater," Grady said suddenly.

We all froze.

Then Will laughed. "I doubt anyone's brought scuba gear."

I laughed too, but nervously. Now I was picturing a team lying inside the loch, ready to spring up in a shower of spray as soon as we came within reach.

We reached the jetty. Our boots rang on the wood with hollow booms and Will leaned close to me. "How far behind d'you think Curtis is?"

I licked my lips. "They've got to get someone's hand … or something of equal value." I shuddered. "They have to be ages away."

Will nodded, but he kept his eyes on the hill that hid the headland.

Leaving Will on watch and Grady looking after

Carmen, Lizzie and I took off our boots and waded into the water. I pulled the box up by its chain. It was smaller than the last one. Lizzie pressed her thumb on the scanner and the screen lit up. I typed the letter X and the locked-room game appeared.

"What do we do?" Lizzie looked at the closed door. "Our clue is X."

"Swipe from top left to bottom right and then top right to bottom left," Grady instructed.

Lizzie made an X on the screen and the box opened. The lock clicked and the box gaped slightly.

Lizzie handed it to me. "You do it."

I swallowed and took the box, the chain trailing between my feet.

"Hurry up, *chico*," Carmen hissed, her eyes on the horizon.

I opened the box. Inside, etched on to the lid, were the new coordinates – the *final* coordinates – and the riddle.

I read it out. "*We hurt without moving. We poison without touching. We bear the truth and the lies. We are not to be judged by our size.*"

"Write it down, Grady." Lizzie threw over her notebook and pencil.

"Where's the final checkpoint?" Carmen looked at us.

Will held the map so I could see it.

"Of course." I snorted. "It couldn't be anywhere else."

"Where?" Grady frowned.

"The highest point on the island." I gestured south. "The most difficult place to reach and not that far from where we started. It's … poetic."

"And the geocache?" Grady asked. "What's in the box?"

"I don't want to know." Lizzie shook her head.

"I don't either." I stared at the lid, picturing Carmen's hand, ragged on that rock, a finger missing. "It's small. It'll be something gross."

Will didn't turn round. "It's an eye."

"What?"

"It's small. What else is left?"

I opened my mouth and shut it again. He was right. There was nothing else it could be. Stomach churning, I began to put the boxes back.

"Throw it away," Will said suddenly. "Like you were going to with the last one. We can't destroy the coordinates, they're etched into the lid, but without

303

the geocache the next teams will be stuck. They can follow us, but they won't have a full geocache collection either."

Grady grinned. "If nobody has a full set of geocaches, then they might take the team with the best time."

Will raised an eyebrow. "There're teams ahead of us," he reminded him.

"Just get rid of it," Carmen snapped.

I pulled back my arm and threw the little box as far out into the loch as I could. It plunged through the mist, splashed into the water and sank. Ripples circled my thighs, one after the other.

Lizzie locked the outer box and pushed it back under the jetty, then we climbed out of the water and put our boots back on while Will and Grady kept watch. Carmen leaned against the piling, cradling her arm. She had black circles under her eyes.

I stood up. "Still no sign of them?" I asked Will.

He shook his head. "Once they find the geocache box gone, they'll be after us fast."

I nodded.

Lizzie gasped and I turned. She was pointing. "There's the group ahead of us!"

I looked through my binoculars. She was right, a team had just come into view on the distant hill.

"Wait," she frowned. "They're not going up, they're heading west."

"Then they're going in the wrong direction," Grady whooped.

"Are they, chico?" Carmen asked. "Or are *we* wrong?" She glared at me. "Did you check the coordinates properly, Ben? Or did you just assume, because the location made sense to you?"

"I…" I closed my mouth. Was I sure I'd read the map correctly?

"You didn't ask me to write the coordinates, Lizzie," Grady said, with worry in his voice.

"I'll climb back in and double-check." I bent to undo my laces.

Will raised his hand. "No time! There's Curtis."

Curtis's team raced over the hill; they had a direct line of sight to us. Shouts smashed the morning calm.

"Run!" Lizzie leaped to her feet.

"We have to check the coordinates," Grady cried.

"No!" Lizzie spun him round by his pack and shoved him towards the path. "If we're still here when they arrive, they'll *make* us tell them what was in that box. Then they'll use one of *our* eyes. We've got to keep ahead of them."

"Where do we go?" Grady wailed as he stumbled forwards. "South or south-west?"

"Trust Ben." Lizzie was pushing Carmen now. "South."

Chapter Eighteen

We ran, again. Lizzie and Carmen set the pace so they wouldn't get left behind. As we ran, the axe that was tucked in my belt kept knocking against my thigh, but I left it there. It was easy to get to if I needed it. I dashed the sweat out of my eyes and looked behind us. Curtis would have to find and open the checkpoint box in the loch, but that wouldn't delay him for long. I tensed, expecting furious shouting at any moment. But we made it to the slope without pursuit.

A short climb in front of us, the cliff turned into a sheer wall.

"Lizzie, are you ... sure ... about this?" Grady panted, staring upwards.

"I trust Ben." Lizzie shaded her eyes as she looked at the cliff. "We'll take the most direct route. Get your climbing equipment." She twisted her rucksack off her shoulders.

I looked at Carmen. "I-I left Car's behind, remember?"

"Can't climb anyway, *chico*." She made a small gesture with her arm and winced.

"Make a sling." Lizzie tossed me some of the webbing from her pack. "Can you pull her up behind you?"

"I'll do it," Will said, taking the webbing.

I dug through my pack, tossing anything that got in my way: my bedroll, bivvy, washbag, medical kit, spare trousers and tops. I yanked out my climbing gear – trainers, helmet and belay gloves, ropes and harness.

Lizzie added carabiners, quickdraws, harnesses, belays, ascenders, wires, hexes and a couple of spring-loaded cams.

Heaps of discarded clothing grew around us. I found Lizzie's cap and tugged it on to her head.

She adjusted the angle and smiled bravely. "I'll go first." She slipped on her climbing shoes.

"No." I shook my head. "We don't know what's waiting at the top. I'll go in front." I yanked off my boots and my aching feet breathed a sigh of relief. "If you use the cams and wires I set up, we'll go faster." I laced my trainers and Lizzie pulled on her gloves.

She stood next to me looking at the wall.

"Can you see the route?" she asked.

I pointed at a handhold just above my head and she took my hand, moving it across my eyeline. "Not that way – see that crack?" It ran about halfway up the cliff. "You can hand jam up it."

I nodded and tucked my gloves into my belt.

"I'll be coming up right behind you," Lizzie said. "If you get stuck, I'll be your guide."

"Sounds good."

Will came to stand beside me. "If you spike a cam in up there, I can use it to pull Carmen up."

Lizzie touched my hand. "Remember how excited we were about all this?" Her voice was sad. "I thought we'd be coming home rich, maybe a little sunburned." She glanced at Carmen. "I never thought…"

"How could we have known?" I took a deep breath and looked back.

"They're coming," Grady whispered.

Leaving my pack lying on the ground, I leaped at the wall. The crack started about a body-length up.

I caught a foothold and, with my thumb pointing straight up, jammed my right hand into the crack. I pulled myself upwards. Once I was high enough, I started to foot jam too. I turned my knee and slid my left foot into the crack, just a few centimetres, then twisted my leg back in line with my body. I used the grip to push and reached up for another handhold. Staying balanced along the narrow line was the hardest part. My shoulders were tense, my neck aching.

I rammed in a spring-loaded cam and attached a rope, letting it drop behind me.

"Well done, Ben. I'm coming up," Lizzie called.

Beside me the rope tensed and twitched. I climbed swiftly past and kept going upwards.

As I climbed, I couldn't help questioning myself. Had I really read the coordinates properly? Or did I just see what I expected to? What if we *were* going the wrong way?

"Why've you stopped?" Will yelled. "What's the problem?"

"N-nothing." I shook my head like a dog spraying water and kept climbing. The crack was thinning – I was almost at its end. I stuck in another cam and attached the rope. Then I searched for handholds.

I risked a glance upwards. Maybe another eight metres still to go. My lungs were tight and my hands were sweating.

Thankfully the cliff was a good one for climbing – there were plenty of footholds. I held the rope with one hand and pulled on my belay gloves with the other. Then I glanced down to see Lizzie was looking up at me, her face pale.

"That way, right?" I gestured and she leaned back slightly, then gave me a thumbs-up.

I stepped sideways out of the crack. My feet and hands were bruised, throbbing, but I pushed the discomfort from my mind. The rope beside me shuddered as Lizzie reached it and I heard Will boost Grady up on to the first one.

Only Carmen and my brother on the ground now.

I slotted wires into cracks as I went; I needed to attach my own rope. I wasn't sure how high I had come, but if I fell… I set up the harness and made sure I was firmly attached to the wall. If I slipped now, I'd be caught.

Eight metres.

Five.

Three.

Finally, I was able to hear Will climbing. That only left Carmen, all alone at the bottom.

Everything in me wanted to look back, but I resisted. From here I'd be able to see Curtis and his team. But what if they were almost on us? The wind kept whipping the sound of furious yelling into my ears and then out again.

"Get to the top, Ben," I muttered. "Then you can check on them."

I reached up for a protruding rock, white with droppings, but perfectly palm-shaped. I had just settled my fingers over the edge when there was a cry below me and my rope jerked hard. I lost my grip and was almost dragged backwards off the cliff, but I managed to jam my left hand into a horizontal crack. Someone was dangling from my safety rope. My left shoulder screamed. Focusing everything I had on keeping my grip, I couldn't even yell. I groaned.

"Grady!" Lizzie screamed. "Get off Ben's rope."

"I was going to fall," Grady squealed.

"Your own harness would've caught you." Even Will sounded angry. "Let go of Ben!"

"I didn't mean to. It was instinct," Grady argued, even as his weight began to pull me backwards.

You can let go. My shoulder pleaded. *You're wearing a harness.*

But with Grady hanging off me, that would put both our weights on a single cam and I wasn't sure it would hold. In fact, I was almost certain it wouldn't. I closed my eyes and kept my hand locked in the crack.

"Get off Ben's rope!" Lizzie yelled.

"I'm trying."

I felt it swing as Grady reached for the cliff and I gritted my teeth, fingers slipping. Belay gloves weren't meant for hand jamming.

Then his weight was gone and I let out a shuddering breath.

I looked up – I was almost there. I leaned my helmet on the wall and took a deep breath. My blue T-shirt was black with sweat.

"You all right, Ben?" Lizzie called.

"Yeah." I pushed upwards as the sun beat down.

Instead of pulling myself to safety, the first thing

I did when my fingers gripped the top of the cliff was look back. I saw Curtis immediately, his red hair easy to spot. His team was racing alongside the riverbank, about to enter the treeline. I exhaled shakily; we had a little time.

I looked down. Lizzie wasn't far below me. Grady was just above my cam and Will was climbing with Carmen attached to his back, dangling from him like an apple from a branch. She swung about two metres below him, using her feet and her good hand to help as much as she could.

"I thought you were going to pull Carmen up behind you?" I yelled.

Will glanced up. "I decided not to leave her by herself."

"We've got time," I called. "Curtis is only just at the grove. Go back and start again. I can pull Carmen up from the top if I have to."

"Don't leave me down there on my own," Carmen cried. She gripped the rope tightly.

"I'm fine, Ben. Stop hassling me." Will reached for another handhold, using the ropes I had left to help him climb.

"Your harness won't hold both of you if you fall."

I ground my teeth.

"Stop mothering me," Will snapped. "I won't fall."

My pulse pounded as I watched them climb higher; a slip could kill them both. But as Lizzie came up behind me, I realized I had to get out of her way. It was time for me to climb over the clifftop.

Could there be another team up there, waiting for us? There was only one way to find out. I unhooked my rope and propelled myself up and over.

I rolled and came to my knees, fists held in front of me, looking frantically around.

I was on a wide, flat plateau. There was nothing to see but a few scrubby bushes and some kind of beacon in the middle – the kind that would have been lit in the old days to spread news of an attack. Could it be the checkpoint? A gust of wind slammed into me, almost knocking me back over the cliff and I hunched lower, shaded my eyes and looked around one more time to be sure. We were alone.

I shuddered in relief and turned to help Lizzie over the edge. She clambered over the top and gripped my shoulder, gasping.

Grady was close behind. I let him pull himself to safety, ignoring him as he crawled to my side; I was

315

watching Will.

Carmen was doing her best to take some of her own weight, but still Will's face was strained.

I held my breath. As soon as he was within reach, I stretched out my hand. He caught it, and Lizzie and Grady helped to pull him over the top. Immediately, he turned to pull Carmen the rest of the way.

Once we'd untangled her from the harness, we looked at each other wide-eyed.

"We made it," Lizzie gasped.

Grady snorted a shocked laugh and I wrapped my arms around them all.

After a long moment, we pulled apart and Grady got to his feet. The wind almost knocked him flying over the drop. Lizzie shrieked and Will tackled him back to the ground.

Grady swore and pressed himself flat.

"We need to get away from the edge." Lizzie raised her voice over the wind.

We all crawled closer to the beacon before attempting to stand once more.

When I was on my feet, I sheltered my eyes from the biting wind and looked out. The whole island was laid out below us. I could see the yellow-green moorland, the lochs and rivers, the chapel, the cottage where we'd sheltered. To my right was the jetty where we had started and to my left...

I swore.

"What is it?" Lizzie turned.

"It's a *plane*."

"It can't be." Grady followed my gaze.

"It is."

Carmen's face lit with hope. "Someone's come to help?"

But Lizzie took my hand. She'd seen the same thing I had. The plane below us was a small passenger craft, just a little bigger than the one we'd arrived in. It was hunched on a narrow strip of beach, broken.

"It's crashed," Lizzie said. "The right wing is damaged. Who knows how long it's been there."

"Those poor people," Carmen whispered.

I raised my binoculars. "I can't see anyone." I glanced at Will. "But you know what *will* be in that plane?" I smiled. "A radio."

"You mean ... we could call someone?" Lizzie straightened.

Grady looked sceptical. "My satphone wouldn't

work. What makes you think a radio will?"

"Actually, it is possible," Will said. "It seems like someone is blocking phone and satellite, but would they have thought to block radio? I mean, how many teens would bring a *radio*? One hundred and twenty-one point five is the emergency frequency, isn't it?"

I shrugged.

Will folded his arms. "I'm pretty sure it is."

"You think we should climb *back down there*?" Grady stared at him. "That radio might not have survived the crash."

Carmen gave a slight smile. "We've got Ben. He can fix *anything* – remember?"

Lizzie hummed thoughtfully and again it struck me how long it was since I'd heard her singing. She was like a broken radio herself. Finally, she shook her head. "We know the plane's there. There's a chance it'll have a working radio. But we're up here now and we haven't found the last checkpoint. There could still be someone waiting to help us."

Will avoided my eyes and looked instead at Carmen.

She nodded. "If we *can* find that last checkpoint,

I want to. If it's not up here, *then* we can talk about going to the plane."

"Grady?" I said.

"Hey, I'm still hoping for the win." He grinned suddenly and then turned serious. "We've got a chance, right? We're here first?"

"It does look that way." I frowned.

"We don't have any geocaches," Lizzie pointed out.

"There's still a chance if we're fastest," Grady said stubbornly and crossed his arms.

"Will?"

"You know what I think." The wind dragged his hair across his face and he held it out of his eyes. "Finding the last checkpoint could be our only chance to get off the island."

The others started towards the beacon at the centre of the plateau, but I stayed, staring down at the plane.

"Come on, Ben," Lizzie called.

I jogged over to join them. That radio wasn't going anywhere.

The beacon was ancient – an eroded granite monolith with a giant fire-stained metal basket

319

attached to the top with rusted bolts. Completely exposed, the only living things I could see were a few weeds clinging to the base. There was no box anywhere to be seen.

Lizzie wrapped her arms around her chest. "We could light a fire. It might bring help from one of the other islands."

"What're we going to burn?" Grady asked. "Have you felt the wind up here? To make a blaze big enough to stay alight *and* be seen from Fetlar or Unst, we'd need a ton of fuel."

Will crouched by the beacon. Then he frowned, leaned close and rapped it with his knuckles. He put his ear to the rock and tapped it again.

He pulled me to my knees at his side. "Listen."

"It's hollow?"

"Is *this* the last checkpoint?" Lizzie got to her knees beside us. "But … if it is, then where is everyone? Where's the Foundation?" I put an arm around her.

Carmen slumped to the floor.

Grady pulled half a packet of gummy bears from his trouser pocket and offered them around, but no one wanted any. He took a handful for himself, tipping their colourful little bodies into his mouth.

"Maybe this isn't the end," he said as he chewed. "If it's hollow, there could be more instructions inside – one final place to go." He touched Lizzie's back. "You're right. There has to be *someone* waiting at the end – otherwise how will they know who's finished first and how many of the geocaches they collected?"

Lizzie smiled up at Grady. "OK, then how do we open it?"

Will was running his fingers along the base of the beacon. Eventually he shook his head. "I haven't a clue."

Chapter Nineteen

Grady, Will and I explored every inch of the beacon. Lizzie even pressed her thumb against any spots on the rock that looked smooth, but nothing happened.

Carmen rose and started to walk slowly around the concrete base, looking at the ground. Then she widened her circle. She stopped about ten metres out, the wind whipping her hair like dark flames. She called something, but the wind stole her words.

I stood, holding on to the beacon. "What was that?"

"Behind this stone," Carmen croaked as she clutched her arm against her chest. "There's a plaque."

We raced to join her, fighting the dragging wind.

When we reached her, Carmen crouched and pointed. There was a low stone with a commemorative plate attached. It told us the beacon had been erected during the Napoleonic Wars.

"If the beacon *is* that old," Grady said, "are you sure it's hollow?"

"It's hollow." Will touched the screws on the plaque. "And *these* seem new. Anyone got a screwdriver?"

I passed over my Swiss army knife and he got to work. The rest of us stood shivering around him, the wind tearing at us angrily.

Finally the screws dropped out and Will lifted the plaque. Beneath it was a familiar screen.

Lizzie looked at us.

"Do it," I said.

She kneeled and pressed her thumb to the sensor. The screen lit up.

WELCOME, ELIZABETH BELLAMY

Her fingers hovered over the keypad. "All right, you guys, what was the answer to the riddle?"

I looked at Will and he blinked. "I haven't even thought about it." He looked shocked. "I completely forgot."

Lizzie looked up. "How much time do we have before *they* catch up?" She gestured back towards the grove.

"Not long now." I shifted from foot to foot. "What *was* the riddle?"

"I wrote it down." Grady licked his lips.

Lizzie stared. "Tell me we didn't leave the book in the rucksacks … down there."

Grady nodded, his face pale.

"OK." I swallowed. "OK … we just have to try and remember what it was." I looked at Will and Grady. "Between us, we should be able to. Didn't it start with something about being hurt?"

"*We hurt without moving,*" Will said faintly.

"Yes," Grady brightened. "Now I remember. Then it was, *We poison without touching.*"

"Didn't it finish, *We are not to be judged by our size?*" I asked. "I remember because it made me think about the girls."

"Yes, but something's missing." Will frowned. "It doesn't scan. It needs something that rhymes with *size.*"

"Eyes," Lizzie suggested. "Cries. Dies?"

I rubbed my temples. "I don't know, I can't—"

"Thanks for leaving the ropes for us!" The yell shuddered up the cliff.

I jerked and met Lizzie's eyes.

"How did we forget to cut the ropes?" she cried.

"You're in tro-o-o-uble," came a higher male voice, singing.

Grady pressed his palms against his eyes. "I didn't think!"

"Neither did we." Will had caught hold of Carmen, whose face had turned phantom-white.

"We're co-o-o-oming!"

"What do we *do*?" Sweat had broken out on Grady's forehead. "There's nowhere to hide up here! We're trapped."

Will's eyes were flickering, considering scenarios and rejecting them.

I closed my fingers around my axe.

"We can't take them on." Lizzie's wild eyes met mine. "Car can't fight – we're outnumbered."

"We could climb down the other side and head for the plane."

"We haven't got the *ropes*," Lizzie said.

"But we're so *close*," Grady wailed. "There's no one else even *here*. We started last and we've beaten everyone to the final checkpoint. It's not *fair*!"

Grady slumped. I put my arm around Lizzie and leaned my face against her hair.

Suddenly Grady straightened. "Hey!" He looked at the cliff and his eyes hardened. "We've been so scared, we forgot something."

"What?" Carmen turned her tear-stained face towards him.

"That team is dangling about fifteen metres above the ground." Grady showed his teeth. "Right now, *they're* the vulnerable ones."

Carmen's eyes widened. "He's right."

"I'm not dropping *anyone* off a cliff." Lizzie shoved her glasses higher up her nose. "It would be murder."

"And what would they do to *us* if they could?" Carmen raised her arm.

"You aren't *dead*, Car," Lizzie said. "Even that bastard Reece didn't kill you."

"He might as well have done," she snarled.

"But he didn't. Anyway, we're better than they are … aren't we?"

"I know what to do." Will stalked towards the cliff edge. "Follow me."

Will lay on the clifftop and leaned his body over the edge. I copied him. Grady, Lizzie and Carmen stayed back, holding our legs.

Curtis was about six metres below us. The skinny boy with the sharp eyes was just behind him.

Spread out below were his remaining three teammates – one was climbing properly, wearing real climbing gear, like Lizzie's, carefully picking out handholds. He was quite a way to the left of the others and higher. The final two were stuck further below, using the ropes secured in the vertical crack, unable to move up further until the next ropes had been freed by Curtis and his skinny mate.

"Hey," Curtis yelled. "We're gonna tear you apart!" He narrowed his eyes at me. "You better run."

"Or not," Will said calmly.

Curtis stared at Will and then back at the skinny boy climbing below him. He saw what I had seen. Although the two boys looked nothing alike, there was something there, some appalling similarity between the two.

"You see, *we're* at the top." Will smiled horribly. "And you're not. In fact, it wouldn't take much effort to push you off that cliff. All we have to do is wait till you're in reach." He pointed at me. "See

Ben's axe?"

I pulled it from my belt and brandished it over the edge.

"That's for your fingers."

"You're bluffing!" But Curtis had stopped climbing.

"Curtis, whatcha doin'? Get up there and sort 'em out!"

"Shut up, Ryan." Curtis didn't even turn his head. He kept his eyes fixed on Will. His Adam's apple moved up and down. "Maybe we can make a deal."

"Maybe." Will shrugged. "But we've got all the cards here – right, Ben?"

I nodded.

Curtis winced. "What was in the box you tossed?" He licked his lips. "Tell us. We'll go back and finish that geocache. When we get back here, you'll be done, right? And we could still finish the course in a faster time than you."

"That means you'll hurt someone else!" Carmen shrieked. "We're not telling you *anything*."

Curtis frowned.

"Yeah, as you can hear..." Will spread his hands helplessly. "*We* aren't the ones in charge, so there's no point in arguing."

"You want us to just … back off?" Curtis was red-faced now, his shoulders trembling with his own weight.

Will leaned further out. "We've got rocks here to drop on you," he lied. "But we haven't. Not yet."

"Why not? What do you want?" It wasn't Curtis who spoke this time, but the boy behind him.

"We haven't been completing the geocaches – not since another team stole our first one."

Was it me, or did Curtis flinch a little at that? I frowned. Will went on.

"So here we are at the end of the course, but we're going to need your stash to win."

Grady's hands tightened on my legs.

"Ain't gonna happen, you chancer," the big lad called from below. "Just eff off."

"Sticks and stones may break my bones," Grady yelled. "You want a rock dropped on your head?" He was almost breathless with glee.

"Just hang on a minute." Curtis called quickly. "We were only joking before, right?" He gave a shaky laugh. "I mean, we're all on this island together. Maybe we could … team up? I mean, you've got there first, obviously. I get it. But we've got the geocaches. You know what we need for the one in the loch. *We* don't. We could work together. Get the money, divvy it up fairly. Fifty–fifty. Half a mil each – that ain't so bad."

"That—"

"Shut up, Ben." Will didn't even look at me. He shouted down to Curtis again. "What's to stop you from going back on the deal once we've told you what the geochache was? And which of us gives up the body part? You? I don't think you'd be up for that, *mate*."

"We could set up an ambush – there'll be other teams coming," the skinny boy murmured.

"You already heard the boss's view on that one," Will called with a sigh. "We're helpless, really. I do think the best way is for you to climb up here, pass us your geocaches and then be on your way – back down, obviously."

I looked up as a great skua cried out and wheeled overhead.

Abruptly the wind changed and brought with it the sounds of waves smashing on rocks. I looked back down. Curtis was flushed with fury and frustration.

"The thing is," he called finally, "I'm not carrying our geocaches. Max has them."

"That true?" Will asked.

"Show 'em," Curtis shouted.

"It's a bad idea, Curt."

"Show 'em, Max."

Max rolled, so that he was holding on to the rope with one hand, then he reached behind him and opened the top of his rucksack. On the top, I could clearly see bloody T-shirts wrapped around misshapen lumps and, tucked to one side, Lizzie's familiar floral glasses cloth.

"Pass the rucksack up the line," Will said calmly as blood beat in my ears.

"Ain't happenin'," Max shouted. "Bloody cheats."

The skinny boy looked down. He spoke in such a quiet voice that I could barely hear it, but Max paled and did as he was told. Contorting himself as he dangled from the rope, he pulled off his rucksack.

"Good," the boy said. "Now drop it."

"No!" Grady almost lurched off the cliff.

I watched, throat tight, as the pack dropped like a boulder and then bounced at the bottom, its grisly contents spilling out on to the slope.

Carmen's hand lay half in and half out of the bag, fingers curled up to the sky.

The great skua cawed and dived, heading for the unexpected bounty.

"Get away!" Max started to abseil, waving his arms frantically.

The skinny boy looked back up at us, his eyes sparkling. "Your move," he said to Will.

Behind me Carmen was whispering over and over again, "Sticks and stones may break my bones, break my bones, break my bones…" until her words were one with the wind and a chill ran down my spine.

Then I saw her out of the corner of my eye as she stood up.

"Where are you going, Car?" Lizzie called.

Carmen looked back at us, her dark eyes almost black. "…but words will never hurt me," was all she said. Then she lurched away.

I couldn't worry about Carmen right now. She was safe enough up here on top of the world.

"So, what's it gonna be?" Curtis tried to sound nonchalant. "You aren't getting our cache."

"We can see that." Will ground his teeth. "And

you aren't getting up here."

"But you'll let us climb back down, no dropping rocks?"

Will nodded. Curtis made a gesture and his other teammates started moving down towards the dropped rucksack and the safety of the ground, escaping Will's make-believe rocks and my ready axe.

Then I stiffened. "Words will never hurt me," I hissed. "*Words*. Lizzie – Carmen worked out the riddle! She's gone to open the last checkpoint box."

As I rolled to sit up, shifting her from my legs, there was a blood-chilling scream from beyond the beacon. I jolted to my feet with ice in my veins.

Will rolled sideways and got up in one swift movement. Then we were running for Carmen, sprinting against the wind.

She wasn't alone. Carmen was standing just in front of the checkpoint, with her arms behind her back. Stalking towards her with a twisted expression of joy on his face was an enormous lad wearing full army camouflage, complete with stripes across his face – green, red and brown.

He grinned. His teeth were big and yellow –

smoker's teeth. His eyes, also yellow-tinged and slightly bloodshot, were pale blue and humourless, despite his wide smile. Behind him four other big lads were rising from the other side of the cliff.

They hadn't been going *west* when we'd seen them, they'd been going *around*.

"Spare Parts!" he exclaimed. "So glad we found you."

Chapter Twenty

Carmen just stood there, screaming. Apart from her hair, which was being whipped into a frenzy by the rising wind, she was completely still.

Will reached her first and shoved her back at me. Boosted by the wind, she stumbled in my direction. I grabbed her and pulled her close. She wilted against me, clinging to my shirt with her hand. Her screaming faded into small shrieks that came on each outward breath. Her heart hammered against my chest.

Reece started laughing. "Boys, you've got something that belongs to me. Hand it over." He sounded almost friendly – a good bloke to meet on a night out.

"He's insane," Grady muttered.

Lizzie gripped my arm. "Oh no!" She pointed back the way we had come. Curtis was climbing over the cliff edge, triumph lighting his face. He fought the wind and rose to his knees, reaching back to pull the skinny boy after him.

I looked at Will. An air of eerie calm had dropped over him. But even with Will fighting like a maniac, we were trapped: us versus ten of them.

"I'll take the five on the left, you take the five on the right," Lizzie said into my ear, her voice shaking.

"No, no, no..." I was on a mental loop. All I could do was plant my feet against the wind and look from Curtis to Reece and back again.

Lizzie took her knife from her belt with a trembling hand. I had my axe. Will's pick was dangling from his left hand, as if he barely knew it was there. Grady had his fists raised and he was trembling almost as hard as Carmen.

I pushed Carmen into Lizzie's arms.

"All right, then," she whispered. "I'll deal with the ones you leave!"

This fight was going to be over in seconds. Then Curtis would force us to tell them what was in the previous geocache and he'd take someone's eye.

And after that ... my eyes flickered to the final geocache box: the hollow beacon. I still had no idea how it opened – perhaps automatically, once the checkpoint box behind the plaque was solved, but it was huge. For the first time, I really began to consider what was in it.

It was big enough for a body … wasn't it?

I grew aware that Lizzie was hissing at Carmen. "*You* wanted to stop them from winning – so stop them. Stop behaving like a princess in a tower and stand up for yourself."

"Lizzie!" I was shocked. But Carmen started to straighten.

"You're not alone, Car," I murmured. "We won't let them hurt you."

"Be quiet, Ben," Lizzie snapped. "Come on, Car, where's the bitch I know? Where's the freaking *warrior*? Will, give back her knife."

Will grinned and shoved the knife into Carmen's hand, and as the wind intensified to a wail, Carmen raised her head.

"It's still five against ten." My voice was shaking.

"No," Lizzie hissed. "Right now it's only Curtis and the little guy up the cliff. The rest went back down, remember? That makes seven. Five against seven. We can do it." Her voice was high-pitched.

"That's enough of that." Reece started to stride

forwards, flanked by his team. "I want my Spare Parts back." He raised his hand, revealing a narrow red line on the meat of his palm. "She owes me. This has been stinging."

I gasped. He'd taken her beautiful hand. He'd destroyed her life – Carmen, the one person who had always been full of life. And *he* was complaining because she'd made his hand *sting*.

Rage burned the fear out of my bones and a howl ripped from my throat... I bounded forwards, my mind gone.

Lizzie screamed my name and I heard Grady yelling something at her. Something about leverage. But I didn't care. I leaped at Reece, axe raised.

Something thwacked into the side of my head, knocking me sideways. I flew into a hard body, but didn't stop to think. I punched with one hand and rammed the handle of the axe upwards with the other. There was a grunt and the pressure against me fell away.

Arms came around me from behind and I roared and jerked back, trying to slam the back of my head into the bridge of a nose, but I couldn't reach. I struggled blindly for a second, then I scraped the heel of my trainer down my captor's shin, reverse-punched him in the nuts, and when he leaned forwards in pain, *then* I headbutted him.

I immediately swung back to Reece. Will was there. He fought with vicious precision, but two others were closing in on him. I didn't stop to wonder where Grady was or whether Curtis had reached us. I hollered into the wind and jumped.

A fist smashed into my face and my nose cracked. For a moment, pain really did blind me. An explosion of warm blood covered my chin and neck, and I swung the axe wildly, felt it stick and heard a scream.

Were we the only ones who were armed? Could we be that lucky?

I staggered sideways as a gust of wind hit us. Someone was bowled off their feet, there was a yell of surprise and another person thudded into my leg, not quite knocking me over.

A burning line of pain drew across my right bicep and blood splashed in the edge of my vision.

I kicked out wildly and the boy who had stabbed me buckled. My eyes refocused on Will, just as the skinny lad from Curtis's team reached him and aimed a karate chop at the back of his neck. Will jerked.

I had to get to him. But before I could move, Curtis appeared. He punched Reece's teammate to the ground, then grabbed me one-handed by the throat. With his other arm, he easily held my axe away.

"What was in that geocache box?"

I struggled, but he was bigger and stronger. Beside me Reece had Will locked in a sleeper hold. Somewhere Will had lost his pick.

And where was Grady?

It was Lizzie who came to the rescue. She sprinted in, low and fast, leaping over a lad who was rolling on the ground. She ran past me and, to Reece's surprise, rammed her knife into his forearm. He yelled and released his hold on Will. Lizzie released the knife, jumped out of reach and raced for the beacon. Reece followed her, crimson-faced.

Curtis shook me and spat in my ear. "What was in it? Tell me!" His grip tightened and I had to fight for breath. The world started to fade and I lolled.

Will bashed Curtis over the head with doubled fists until he let me go, and shoved him at the cliff edge. Then he took my arm and ran after Lizzie.

I stumbled after him. "There's nowhere to run to," I gasped through my flattened nose.

"Here." Grady's voice was faint over the still-rising gale. "This way." He was gripping the beacon with one hand and Lizzie was backing towards him.

Reece was striding forward, smiling and cracking his knuckles. "I'm going to enjoy this." He wasn't running; there was no hurry. He knew there was no escape.

I tried to shake Will off and go for Lizzie, but my legs collapsed.

I struggled against my brother's hold. "Help Lizzie."

Will shook his head.

"Grady!" I choked. I realized I was still dragging my axe, the head bouncing on the ground as we stumbled nearer.

Reece pulled the knife out of his arm and flourished the blade at Lizzie. "Do you know where I'm going to put this?"

Lizzie tripped, falling over the edge of the beacon and landing on her elbows. As Reece finally leaped for her, she scrambled desperately backwards.

Then Carmen appeared. She rose like a demon from behind Grady, clutching her knife.

Lizzie gasped. "No, Car!" But there was no halting her.

Taken by surprise, Reece staggered back, far enough for Will to grab hold of him with one arm.

I dropped my axe and grabbed on to Reece's shirt, helping Will to hold him. If I let go, he would hurt Carmen and Lizzie.

Reece kicked backwards, but in a second Carmen was on top of him, screaming. He tried to use the knife in his hand, but Will kept a tight hold of his elbow.

"Get off me," he growled.

Carmen wailed in his ear, her hair lashing in the gale, her eyes wild. Then she stabbed him in the right cheek. She yanked the knife free as he yelled and a fold of skin dangled over his face, revealing gum and tooth.

I stared in horror.

Reece howled, then shouted for help. "Boys!"

But one of them was trying to pull his mate back on to the clifftop. Curtis and the skinny boy had another cornered, and the fourth was too far away, fighting the wind.

Carmen stabbed again; this time she took off half of his ear. Blood stained his collar.

He screamed his shock and rage. "I'm gonna kill you!"

Carmen thrust her stump into his face and stabbed again, this time sticking the blade between his collarbone and throat. A great spurt of blood gurgled up when she pulled the blade. It was hot where it splashed against my bare skin.

Stunned, I let go and fell to the ground, but Will held on. Carmen stabbed again, into Reece's shoulder, then again up under his jaw.

"Carmen," I whispered. "Stop! Please!"

Reece fell to his knees. Even though Will let him go, he didn't rise again. Carmen's breath was a rasp now and tiredness slowed her arm, but she kept on stabbing. It was hard for her to pull the knife out each time, but Reece wasn't even trying to push her off him any more. He collapsed full length and lay still. His eyes bored into mine, a tear ran down one of his cheeks and suddenly, as his life ebbed away, I saw that he really wasn't any older than I was after all.

"Enough!" Lizzie hauled Carmen to her feet, holding her tightly in a hug from behind. Carmen panted and shook as she stared at the dying boy.

Then she spat at him.

"You *killed* him!" Reece's mates were running to get to us. Curtis too.

"This way, hurry." It was Grady. I looked up. Will yanked me to my feet. Instinctively, I grabbed the haft of the axe as I was hauled past.

"Come on, Ben – I've got to close it!"

Close what? My head was pounding, blood was streaming from my nose, my eyes were swollen – definitely blackened – and the wind was screaming. Carmen and Lizzie reached Grady first. I closed my eyes, and when I opened them, they'd gone. Was I hallucinating again?

Will spun me round and shoved the small of my back. I rammed into the side of the beacon, then Grady grabbed me and pulled me round, past the stone base. I gaped. The stone beacon, the last geocache box, had been opened.

Will was on my heels and then … I was lurching downwards.

I blinked, trying to clear my eyes of Reece's blood.

Will propelled me from behind and I stumbled further down – disoriented, confused – the wind cutting out as I dropped below ground level.

"Lizzie!" Grady was screaming. "Lock it!"

Lizzie pushed past me and I could hear furious yelling from above, a booming sound and the whirring of a lock engaging. Then total darkness.

Two ticks of my heart, two seconds, then lights came on.

The wind had gone, but my ears rang. I could hear the detonation of each heartbeat, feel the blood pounding in my nose, my face, my arm, my legs. I was bruised, hurt, bleeding. Slowly I raised a hand, but Lizzie was there first, gently wiping the blood out of my eyes.

I looked at her. Her glasses were cracked.

Then I looked at Carmen and Grady, and finally at Will. We were all dazed and shaking.

I looked down.

"It's a staircase." I blinked.

"Carmen and I – we solved the last checkpoint box," Grady said. "When we finished the puzzle, the beacon opened automatically. I guess we have to go downwards."

"And quickly." Lizzie looked up at the door closed above us. "Before Curtis and the others work out how to get in, too."

Chapter Twenty-one

The staircase seemed to descend for ever. Darkness pooled at the bottom and I couldn't see what lay beyond.

"Where are we?" I whispered. My mouth tasted coppery with blood from my broken nose.

Will was ahead of me. He looked back and up, eyebrows raised. His hair was slick, as I assumed mine was, with Reece's blood. There were smears of mud and blood on his cheeks, and he had a bruise already emerging on his forehead.

My arm was slung over Grady's shoulders. Without him, I'd have fallen down the stairs on the first step. I reached up to touch my nose and Grady caught my hand.

"Don't, Ben."

"Right."

Lizzie had her arm around Carmen and was whispering in her ear, keeping her moving.

The stairwell was cold, the air slightly stale and there was a faint hum, like an office building – computers and air conditioning.

"It's like we've stepped into an alternative universe," Grady muttered.

"Yes." I winced. Speaking made my nose throb and sent a jagged pain up into my temples.

The sound of Lizzie and Carmen coming down the stairs behind us stopped. I looked back to see them halted on a step, four above me.

"You OK?" I tugged at Grady, who was trying to get us on to the next step.

Lizzie shook her head. "I can't get her to go any further."

Carmen was as stiff as an ice sculpture and almost as pale.

"She's in shock," Grady said and he helped me lean against a wall.

"What do we do?" I looked up at the top of the stairs. They ended in what looked like an airlock from a science-fiction film. Right now it was closed tight, but soon one of them would work out how to get inside. We had to get further ahead.

"Car?" Lizzie said, shaking her.

"I killed him," Carmen said eventually, her lips barely forming the words. Slowly she raised her hand and stared at the blood that coated her hand and arm. "*Asesino. Me voy al infierno* … I'm going to hell."

"No, you're not." Lizzie tried to hug her closer, but Carmen was unyielding.

Finally, Carmen looked at me. She laughed suddenly, bitterly, a gunshot of sound. "He took my hand *and* my soul."

My eyes slid away from the pain in her gaze. "That's not true. You're still *you*. You just need to … to speak to your priest or something."

She nodded, slowly.

"Come on," Lizzie said. "We have to get to the bottom of the stairs. If Reece's mates get in…"

They started moving again and I let them go past. I leaned on Grady once more and looked back to the top of the stairs.

"It's too quiet," Grady whispered.

I nodded. There was no way to know if they were still fighting up on the plateau or working together to open the checkpoint. Were they seconds away or hours?

I turned my face to the stairs again and we started back down.

"I'm sorry I didn't help you fight." Grady was babbling. "I wanted to, but I figured if I could get to the geocache, I could hold it to ransom or something. Like you did before."

"Instead we managed to get inside," Lizzie said. "Well done, Grady."

My calves were burning; maybe another twenty or thirty steps to go. Will was already at the bottom, waiting for us in the gloom. "You did the right thing," I said.

"I'm still sorry." Grady caught me as I missed a step and almost fell. "You look terrible, Ben."

I tried to smile, but it pulled my face painfully. I let it drop. "Could've been worse."

"Yeah." Grady fell silent. Then he spoke again. "Can you believe what Carmen did?"

I shook my head slowly. The last of the adrenalin was draining from my body and I was craving sleep.

"Maybe we never really know anyone," Grady added.

"You might've done the same." I looked at him.

"Maybe."

Will looked up at me. "We have a problem. There's a door here, but it's locked, and there's a chute in it." For the first time he sounded genuinely worried. "This is bad."

"Huh?" My head was hurting too much to allow me to think. Grady helped me down the last step and I leaned on the wall beside the door.

Will pointed at the hatch. "I can only assume that this is where we have to deliver our geocaches."

"You mean the door won't open until we put *body parts* inside the chute?" Grady gaped.

"We're trapped?" Lizzie said faintly.

Grady started to hammer on the door. "Hey! Let us in."

Lizzie joined him. "We need help. Please, let us in!" She put her whole body into it. Bashing, not just with her fists but her whole arms. "We have injured!"

Carmen just stood still. Grief rolled from her.

Will and I looked at one another.

"The door's not going to open like that," Will said, and I nodded.

Finally, Lizzie turned, defeated. "W-what body parts did we need?"

"Tooth, finger, ear, hand, probably eye." I listed them tonelessly, barely noticing that my nose was clearing and I was managing to speak more easily.

"Or equivalent," Will reminded me.

"Yeah." I scratched at the blood dried on my hands, only then noticing I was still holding the axe. I let the weapon thud to the floor.

"Do you think there's someone on the other side?" Grady asked. "To check what goes through?"

Will shrugged. "It's possible. Maybe they have a scanner, like an airport X-ray scanner. Or it could be done by weight."

"There can't be a person there," Lizzie said confidently, "or they'd have let us in. So we just need to match the weight or … the shape of … things."

"We don't have anything we can use, Lizzie." I groaned. "We left our bags behind."

"We still have the fake finger, don't we?" Lizzie looked at Grady. "You didn't eat it, did you?"

"Don't be disgusting." Grady felt in his pocket. "It's still there."

"What else have we got?" Lizzie was moving now. "Empty your pockets."

"This isn't going to work," Will warned.

"It might," Lizzie insisted. "It's worth a try. If it's only a machine back there, we can fool it. We did before, when you opened the fifth checkpoint without me."

We collected together a sad pile of detritus and laid it on the stairs: penknives, a bag of gummy bears, string, a tissue, a hairgrip, two chapsticks, a dead iPhone, a flat stone with a vein of quartz that had attracted Lizzie's eye, a box of matches and a random credit card.

"What's that?" Grady pointed to Carmen's jacket pocket.

"Magic mushrooms," I replied awkwardly, remembering how happy Car had been on them.

"Let's see." Lizzie took the package from Carmen's pocket. She grinned and held up a curled mushroom cap. "Eyeball."

Will bent and lifted Carmen's foot; she was the only one still wearing her walking boots. "Knew it." He poked the tread. I couldn't see what he meant, but he picked up my axe and levered something out with the corner of the blade. Then he held up a piece of stone. "Tooth."

"What's left?" Lizzie asked.

I frowned. "Ear."

Grady cleared his throat and held up a piece of beef jerky.

"I was saving it…"

"Perfect." Lizzie took it from him and tore it into a rough semicircle.

As one we looked at Carmen, then let our eyes slide away.

"Hand," she whispered.

My eyes went to my axe. There was a long silence.

Lizzie broke the silence. "Or equivalent."

"Yeah, but what's equivalent to a hand?" Grady frowned.

"A foot?" Lizzie shrugged.

"Forget it," I snapped.

Will snorted. "If we're hoping this is a scanner or a set of scales, we just have to *make* one." He pointed to the belay gloves still stuck in my belt. "We can stuff one of those."

"What with?" Lizzie took it from me. "Socks?"

"It should be heavier than that." I poked my toe at the pile of stuff in front of us, shifting it about.

"We can use the two penknives for fingers." Lizzie demonstrated by pulling the blade of each

354

knife halfway out, so that she had made a V-shape, then sticking both sides into the fingers of the glove.

"Socks should work for the palm." Will pulled off his climbing shoes and then his socks, rolled them up, took the glove and tucked them in.

The thumb hung limply.

"It doesn't look right." Grady sniffed.

"It'll have to do." I looked at Will. "Right?"

He nodded.

"Ready?" Lizzie picked up our collection.

There was a loud knocking from the airlock at the top of the stairs and I held my breath, but nothing followed. They weren't in yet.

"Quick!" Carmen urged.

We opened the chute and put our fake caches inside. Lizzie closed the chute.

"Please," she whispered. "Please, please, pl—"

There was more knocking from above us.

"It didn't work." Grady groaned. "I knew it—"

Suddenly there was a slight whirr and the hatch in the door slid back to reveal a thumb scanner. Grady cheered.

"Go on, Lizzie." Will pushed her. She wiped her sweating hand on her trousers, then pressed her thumb against the pad. My heart hammered.

The door shuddered and then swung slightly open.

My eyes widened, but I seemed to be rooted to the spot.

"Breathe, Ben." Will pushed the door the rest of the way.

The first thing we did once we were inside was secure the door. It clicked closed with a final-sounding thud. Then we turned round to see where we had ended up.

The fluorescent light was blinding after the dim stairwell. I rubbed my eyes, slowly becoming accustomed to the glare. Lizzie's optimism must have infected me, because I did somehow expect to see a human figure melting out of the brightness.

Her noise of disappointment was enough warning. When my vision adjusted and I saw the room was empty of anything living, I wasn't surprised.

The room itself wasn't particularly big, perhaps three metres square, and it was totally white – white tiles beneath our feet, walls painted white. Even the ceiling was white – tiled like the floor, with lights set into the surface.

On one wall, though, there were ten screens in two rows of five. Blank.

I stared at them, expecting … something … but the only sound in the room was the buzz of the lighting, the rasp of our breathing and the *tick-tick* as blood dripped from my bleeding nose on to the tiled floor.

"Easy clean," Will murmured, his gaze drawn to the crimson splatters.

I nodded and glanced behind him. Our pile of fake parts lay on top of a metal plate, below the end of the chute we had put them through. Will pressed his hand against the plate and it gave slightly.

"Weight," he said.

"There was no need for anyone to get hurt," Carmen whispered.

I wasn't sure if that made the whole thing more horrific, or less.

Carmen sat down and then let her feet flop out in front of her as she leaned against the door, her eyes half-shut.

Suddenly Grady whooped. "We got in, you guys. Don't you get it?"

I blinked at him.

He spun round in a happy circle. "We're first here, and our geocaches have been accepted. We've *won*."

"We *have*?" I looked at Will. "I guess we have."

"A million pounds each!" Grady punched the air. "We're millionaires. Those guys outside can *suck* it. It doesn't matter about Carmen's hand any more."

"Grady!" Lizzie snapped, horrified, as Carmen stared at him.

"I mean … she'll be fine. She doesn't need to work if she doesn't want to. She'll be ok."

Lizzie licked her lips. "A million pounds! I can do it – pay off the mortgage. Mum can look after Dad without working. Dad won't have to worry about us." Her smile slowly died. "But … now what?" Lizzie walked towards the monitors. "We're under the last checkpoint, so what do we do now? How do we get the money?"

A tile depressed under her foot and with an explosion of colour, but no sound, the monitors flickered to life.

"What is this?" Grady ran to her side. "Is it another puzzle?"

I grabbed Will's arm as he started forwards.

"There isn't going to be any money, is there?" I whispered.

Will shrugged free and glided towards the screens, fascinated.

"It's the island." Lizzie touched a screen with a trembling finger. "Look – there's the chapel."

I staggered closer. She was right – the screen showed the graveyard. A team was moving among the stones – more girls than boys in the group – and one of them was being led by a rope. I felt vomit rising.

Electronic text appeared on the bottom of the screen. **Team 2: Lancett.**

I looked at another screen, then another. All seven checkpoints were represented. The other three screens were cycling through different points on the island. They seemed to activate when a team appeared: motion-sensitive.

The first screen gave a view of the jetty. A team lounged around a campfire. I could almost hear their laughter. My hand drifted up towards the writing: **Team 1: Sadana.**

"That could've been us," I muttered.

Wordlessly Grady pointed at the eighth screen,

which revealed a rowan grove. At the bottom, the scrolling text said: **Team 5: McCarthy. Team 6: Chase.**

The girl we had seen before, with a buzz cut and machete, was lying on a branch. Beneath her, creeping, with terror in his every movement, was a younger boy.

"I can't watch." I covered the screen with my hand, grateful that there was no sound. I turned to see Will leaning close to screen seven, his nose almost touching the glass.

"Will!"

"It's the beacon." He poked the screen. "They've found the checkpoint box behind the panel, but they seem to be arguing. Maybe over the answer to the riddle? Or which team gets to use the thumb scanner, I don't know."

"But ... Curtis *has* to use the scanner. Reece is dead." Lizzie nudged him to one side, so she could see.

"They've dragged his body over there," Will said matter-of-factly. "He still has his thumbs."

The writing beneath the image read **Team 4: Wellington. Team 8: Armstrong.**

I turned from the screens and walked over to the opposite wall. I touched the seamless paintwork with a groan, then leaned against the cold plaster. "There's no other way out of here. Just one door. End of the line. So now what? We just wait here for the other teams?"

Carmen flinched.

Will's eyes narrowed at the tenth monitor. Then he went to the pile of fake parts and picked up the glove.

"What are you doing?" Lizzie asked.

"I need the Swiss army knife." Will pulled the fake hand apart. Then he opened out the tin opener. "I want to get behind there." He started to lever the monitor out of the wall. "If I can hack the feed, maybe we can send a message."

I jolted. "You can do that?"

"I don't know." Will got his fingers behind one edge of the screen and pulled hard. It came free. He leaned it carefully on the floor to reveal a tangle of wires in the hole. "Watch me try."

After a while, Lizzie came to sit beside me. I took her hand and she curled her fingers around mine. I leaned my head on her shoulder.

Grady remained by Will, looking over his shoulder and making the occasional comment.

We watched as Will grew increasingly red-faced. The fifth monitor flickered and went blank, the picture on the second dissolved into hissing static. Will's hands started to shake and eventually he threw the knife with a yell. It cracked the seventh screen, where Curtis's and Reece's teams were now shoving one another, a new fight beginning, and then thudded to the ground.

"No luck at all?" I asked.

"There's a thicker wire." Will gestured at a black cable that he had partly pulled out so that it protruded from the wall like a tongue. "But I don't know what it does. It could be the main power source. If I cut it, we could lose the monitors, maybe the lights. It could open the main door and let the others in. I daren't touch it."

"That's it, then." Lizzie's hand twitched in mine and a tear slid down her cheek. "We're at the end. No final puzzle to solve. No last clue. No one to help us ... or t-tell us *why*." She hesitated. "No prize money."

Will leaned against the wall next to me. Grady

362

paced the room, frustration in his clenched fists. Finally, he too curled up with his head on his knees. "I thought we'd won," he said.

As Grady's shoulders dropped, the monitors flickered and I looked up. They flickered again, then suddenly the remaining views of the island were replaced by a single huge face, looking down on us. There were two holes, one on the forehead and one on the cheek, where the screens Will had blanked showed nothing.

I nudged Will.

"It's Gold." Lizzie pulled her hand away from mine and got back up to her knees.

"Congratulations, Elizabeth Bellamy and team. You have reached the final checkpoint and done so in the fastest time." The accent was strong American, brash and loud.

Grady leaped to his feet. "We get the money then, right?"

"Shut up, Grady." Lizzie rasped. She was shaking with rage. "Did you know?" She jabbed a finger at the screens. "Was it you?"

The face frowned.

"The checkpoints – did you *know*?" She surged to

her feet. "Was it you who put ... body parts in them? *Was it?*" She was flushed and her eyes flashed.

Carmen looked up at this. She pushed her hair out of her face. Gold seemed to look only at her and then he cast his eyes over the rest of us before coming to rest on Lizzie once more.

"Of course it wasn't me." The face smiled. "But ... I did arrange to have it done."

Chapter Twenty-two

Lizzie gasped and then there was silence. Even though Will had warned me, even though I had known deep down, I hadn't *believed*. I had still been hoping for a happy ending: grown-ups who would pale in horror at our story, put foil blankets around our shoulders, tend our wounds and hand us hot chocolate before helping us to call home. I had been picturing a large, friendly nurse, or a pilot, impressed by our bravery. Not this matter-of-fact confession.

My chest felt hollow. I got to my feet and pulled Lizzie back to my side, needing her warmth. She came unresistingly. Will still stood off by himself, scrutinizing the big screen.

"But what was the point?" It was Grady. He clutched his hands to his chest. "*Why do this?*"

"People died," I said.

Gold smiled. "I have a new hiring policy. I want ruthless — this way I get it."

I stared. Then I looked back at our fake geocache collection. "Joke's on you," I muttered.

"Not at all," Gold said with aching benevolence. "But you are right, Torben. As your team managed to circumvent the first part of the selection process, these interviews will require an additional element. So here it is: there is a considerable sum of money available – five million pounds to be exact – and, in addition, an internship in the Gold Foundation, directly under me, matched with a top-flight education and, before you are twenty-five, a directorship of one of my businesses." He winked. "This package will be available to the first of you to indicate you'd like to take me up on my offer by showing exactly how ruthless you are."

"What do you mean?" Lizzie asked faintly.

"You know what I mean, young lady." Gold tutted. "I would like one of you to kill another. Do this and the world will be yours. A guaranteed future and a lifestyle you could only dream of."

"B-but," Grady stammered, "*why?*"

Gold sighed and his eyes focused on the middle distance, perhaps on something at his end of the screen. "My hiring policy has always been to seek

366

high achievers with low self-esteem – you can get a lot of work out of those people. But I don't want to have those idiots running my businesses. I need leaders." He looked back at us. "What I am seeking is the psychopathic personality. Intelligence, drive, ruthlessness, remorselessness, an ability to charm, to manipulate: all essential in today's business environment. I want to get you young so I can mould you, and of course I want something *on* you, so you remain under my influence. A video of a murder committed when you were old enough to face trial as an adult – that would be most effective.

'In a decade or two, I'll be in control of global business enterprises run by the most intelligent and pitiless business people in the world. This isn't the only Iron Teen contest running." He grinned. "A new global power based on money and manipulation, with me at its head. I'll be the one shaping the world."

Grady shuddered. "Whichever of us does it would be in the centre of every global conspiracy, like the Illuminati or the Freemasons."

"That's right. Imagine the possibilities, talk it through. But don't take too long." He licked his lips.

"Your team got through the assessments for one reason only." He laughed.

"What reason?" Lizzie yelled.

Gold was silent.

Lizzie ran from me and banged her fists on the monitors. "Tell us!"

"Can't you guess?" I asked quietly. Lizzie turned to look at me. "That assessment form with all the questions on it. Gold was looking for kids who fit his criteria." I rubbed my eyes and flinched as my palm caught my swollen nose. "The competition wouldn't be any good if there weren't people on the island with psychopathic personalities, would it? I mean, look how fast the teams out there started cutting each other up!"

"You're telling me that one of us…"

"It's the only reason we got into the lottery in the first place." I closed my arms around my waist and looked at my brother. "Isn't it, Will?"

Lizzie put a shaking hand to her mouth. Then she faced Carmen. "Car, it's you. You're the one he's after. You killed that guy."

"His name was Reece." Carmen hung her head.

Lizzie retreated further from her. "A psychopath

doesn't feel anything – isn't that right?" Tears ran freely down her face. "It's all empty charm and, what did Gold say – manipulation?" Lizzie sobbed. "Was our whole friendship a lie?"

"No!" For a second Carmen looked as if she was going to get up and go to Lizzie, but then she slumped back down. "*Dios*. Maybe it *is* me. Would I know if it *was* me?" She looked at the giant, grinning face still frozen on the monitors.

"You'd know." I was still watching Will. I didn't dare take my eyes from him. "Lizzie, it isn't Carmen."

"It has to be," Lizzie insisted.

"It's not."

"Ben," Will said, warning in his voice.

"They deserve to know." I bit my thumb.

"Know what?" Grady had been watching Lizzie and Carmen, now he turned to me. "What do *you* know that we don't?"

"Carmen doesn't have a psychopathic personality. Of course, she doesn't. She was just pushed to breaking. Any one of us could've done what she did."

"I don't think—" Lizzie began.

"Well, you're just so perfect, *chica*," Carmen spat.

"It's not Carmen," I said again. "I know which of us passed Gold's test."

It was Grady who first turned to face Will. "Will?"

Will folded his arms. "Yes?"

"You're … a psycho?"

"I prefer to think of it as *emotionally advantaged*, Grady." Will gave his odd half-smile.

"You can't be serious." Lizzie returned to my side and put her hand on my arm. "Will's your *brother*, Ben! Why would you say that about him? I thought you looked after him."

I snorted bitterly. "I'm not *only* looking after Will. I've never been only looking after Will." I put my head in my hands. "I've been looking out for everyone around him."

Lizzie froze. "I don't get it."

I looked at Will. "I'm sorry."

"They deserve to know, I suppose." Will spread his hands. "Ben's my … cultural canary." He flicked his hair out of his eyes. "I copy his behaviour to seem 'normal'. With him around, I *fit in*." He snorted. "I reckon I've learned all I need to now though,

370

Ben. I don't need you any more. And if Gold comes through, I won't need you ever again."

"But you're my *friend*," Grady cried.

"I'll be honest, Grady." Will exhaled. "I don't think I feel any more for you than I do for the guy who runs the corner shop."

"Or me, or Mum." I dropped my hands to my sides. "He likes having us around, I think. We're convenient and useful." I blinked. "I've never asked though, Will. Do you ... love us at all?"

Will shrugged.

"When your dad left..." Lizzie took my hand. "Will's the reason?"

I blinked my eyes clear and nodded. "Dad wanted to get help for the family, but Mum wouldn't even consider it. I think ... maybe she's the same as Will. She knew he'd get good at hiding who he is the older he got – after all, *she* did. Plus, if he saw a professional, how would it make *her* look? The woman who gave birth to the next Fred West."

"You exaggerate," Will groaned theatrically. "I've never killed anybody or even tried to. Most psychopaths don't go that far, you know."

I smiled at him, a weak twitch of my lips. "But

you've thought about it," I said. "How many times have you ended one of *us* in your head. Or Mum?"

Lizzie wrapped her arms around me. "How could you have lived like that?"

"He's my brother. There've been a few ... incidents, but mostly I'm pretty sure he'd rather manipulate me than hurt me."

"That's true." Will folded his arms. "Also, prison doesn't have much appeal."

"A-and you aren't planning on killing one of us now?" Lizzie clung on to me.

Will wrinkled his nose. "I'm still thinking about it."

Lizzie spun back to Gold. "We're not *stupid*, you know." She wiped her tears from her cheeks. "Say Will does kill one of us – you're not going to let the rest of the team go. You've been monologuing like a Bond villain. We know what that means." She choked on a sob. "You're not going to let any of us go home." She turned to Will. "Ben's been helping you all these years. You *owe* him."

"I'm not sure what you're getting at." Will's grey eyes pinned her.

Lizzie was almost hysterical. "We have to work

together to get out of here, not kill each other for his amusement." She gestured wildly at the monitors. "Even if Gold's offer is real, there'll only be one survivor – whatever you choose, *who*ever you pick on, Ben dies. Isn't that right, Mr Gold?" She panted, drained.

Gold's eyes crinkled. "That seems obvious."

"Win or die…" Grady murmured.

I caught Will's eye. "I was wrong before. There has to be another way out of here – a way for the winner to leave safely without going past the other teams."

"Another way out." Will nodded. "Yes. But how does that help us?"

"There's still the plane," I whispered. "The radio. If we can find a way out of here, I can—"

Gold laughed. "You saw that, did you, Torben? Did you like my stage setting?"

"Stage setting?" Lizzie stepped back into the circle of my arms. She was cold against my chest.

"Yes, of course. Once I have my winner, the rest of you will be gassed, your deaths staged. I'm already taking out the team at the jetty. Losers. Any-hoo, your plane crashed on its way off the island. It's very tragic. Tell you what, I'll even donate money to a charity in your names. What do you think?" He leaned closer to the camera on his end and his nostrils loomed. "You seem like a Cancer Research kind of girl."

"You can't do this," Grady pleaded. "There has to be another way – some sort of deal we could make. What if we *all* come and work for you? OK, we're not all psychos, but surely you need more employees, good ones."

Gold sighed, as if he was genuinely sad. "Grady, Grady, Grady. I'm sorry – but what guarantee would I have that one of you wouldn't talk?"

"Who'd believe us?" Grady was animated now. "I mean, you've got the money and power to cover this up, right? We'd just be more conspiracy nuts."

"I'm sorry." Gold shook his head. "It doesn't seem financially viable and the risk–reward ratio doesn't work for me."

"Pay us off! We'll sign anything."

"Not going to work, I'm afraid." Gold sighed.

I sensed Will drawing nearer and I tightened my arms around Lizzie.

"She brought us here." Will pointed. "This is

Lizzie's fault."

"What are you saying?" I tried to straighten; I felt like one enormous bruise.

"Give her to me."

Lizzie tensed as I flinched. "No. I don't think so."

"Ben." Will was at my side now. "Without her, we wouldn't be here. Carmen would have her hand, so it's her responsibility to get us out, don't you agree?"

"I don't—"

"You know all about responsibility, Ben. This is hers. Just let go."

Lizzie squirmed, but I held her close.

Will lowered his voice to a whisper. "Once I've won, I'll tell Gold I won't work without you – that I need you and Carmen to function. We'll get out of here, all three of us."

"Hey!" Grady snapped.

Will didn't even look at him. "What do you say, Ben? Brother?" He was smiling now, charming. Disarming. Leaning close. "You have to protect me. It's how Mother brought you up."

"You said you didn't need me any more," I rasped.

"I was wrong. I need you to do this one small thing. That's all."

"*Small?*" Lizzie struggled, but my hands had locked around her and she couldn't escape.

"I love her," I said in a small voice.

"And me?" I was mesmerized by Will's eyes. "I'm your brother. I'm more important."

Will was right. It didn't matter that I loved Lizzie, he *was* more important. I'd been trained to think so since the day he was born. Mum's voice filled my ears.

Watch the baby.

Take care of your brother.

Look after Will.

Bring him back safely.

It'll be your fault if something happens.

I was so tired and it was so hard to think, to argue. If Will said this was our only way out, then it was.

But … I didn't want to lose Lizzie. My fists clenched and she whimpered; her voice sounded very far away.

"It's genetic, Ben," Will whispered. "If it's in Mother and me, it has to be in *you*, too." He was so close now that his breath touched my ear, warm against my skin. "It's easy. It'll be like she's falling asleep. She's tired. Don't you think she's had enough of fighting?" His hands were across me now, reaching for Lizzie's throat. "Just don't think about what's happening. It's my turn to look after you."

His biceps tensed as he touched her neck. I stood still, frozen by indecision. Should I stop him? *Could* I stop him?

Lizzie had started to fight. She was kicking my shins and shouting my name. I hardly felt her, barely heard her. I kept my eyes on Will's.

"Remember how good it felt up there, Ben?" He squeezed, and Lizzie started to make choking noises. "Remember how good it felt to fight *together*?"

This wasn't real. I was dreaming, floating.

"B-Ben." Lizzie's voice was reedy, gasping. I didn't look at her, couldn't think about what Will was doing. What *we* were doing.

"*Too late!*" There was a crowing screech from behind us. "You thought you could cut me out, but it's *too late!*"

Will spun round, his eyes released mine and I gasped. His hands fell from Lizzie's neck.

Suddenly the world rushed back. Lizzie punched me and struggled free, her face pale, her blue eyes unfocused. Her knees folded and she fell to the floor, her hands around her throat.

"Oh no, Lizzie, I didn't mean..." What had I done? She would never forgive me. I'd never forgive myself.

I reached for her, but she looked past me and screamed.

I turned as if I was in treacle, the whole world slow and thick and strange.

Will was already on the floor, his arms around Carmen; her head was lolling back and she was staring at the ceiling. Like a broken doll, she didn't blink.

"What happened to Car?" My voice was a little boy's.

"You were *too slow*," Grady crowed. "*I'm* the winner, right, Mr Gold? You have to give the prize to *me*. *I'll* be in your Illuminati organization. *I'll* be the one with all the answers. Those guys are the losers – right?"

"What have you *done*?" Will howled. His tears were falling on to Carmen's hair. It was almost more shocking than anything else I'd seen.

"She was done for, anyway." Grady retreated to the back of the room, the bloody penknife dropping from his hand. "What was her life going to be like after this? And she was a killer anyway. She *deserved* it."

"*How could you?*" Lizzie lurched after him, swinging.

I swayed in the centre of the room and addressed the monitors. "But … you didn't *want* Grady," I whispered. "You wanted Will."

"Oh really, Ben." Gold's smile was as wide as his face. "You didn't think there was just *one* psychopath in each team, did you?"

Chapter Twenty-three

Will's wail shivered through the room. I'd never heard him make a sound like it. Lizzie stopped hitting Grady and tried to get to Carmen, but Will blocked her with an outstretched arm and shoved her sprawling.

He raised his face to the monitors. "You must have a medical team on standby – send them in. Fix her!"

Gold ignored him.

My mind kept flicking back over the past three days, trying to understand. How was *Grady* anything like Will? Slowly, scenes gained clarity. No, I realized, Grady wasn't *like* Will. He was *better*. Somehow, he'd got me to carry his rucksack for him. He was the one who stayed safely with Carmen while Will and I took the risks. He'd got out of every fight, avoided every difficulty. We hadn't known Grady in Primary – he'd learned how to act long before he met us. Now he bumbled his way along, faking ineptitude, handing around those bags of sweets. All he cared about were his precious conspiracies.

Conspiracies… I kept staring at Carmen. I couldn't see any blood. Where was she hurt? I blinked. This didn't feel real. I caught my breath and took care to hide my face from the monitors. Of course – this *wasn't* real! Will was faking his grief.

We'd fooled the door with the fake body parts, now Grady had fooled Gold with a fake murder. Will must have seen it instantly. Grady had come up with a solution. All we had to do was wait until someone came to take the winner to safety and we could rush them.

Will cried out again and pulled Carmen's right hand to his cheek. When he released her fingers, it dropped to the floor with a thud.

Her acting was amazing. Maybe Carmen couldn't be a vet any more, but she could get on TV. Will was laying it on a bit thick though. Gold wouldn't believe this outpouring of emotion any more than I did.

I limped over to Will and put my hand on his shoulder, but Will shrugged it off violently.

"Ease off a bit," I whispered, hoping the microphones in the room weren't too sensitive. "He won't buy it if you go over the top."

Slowly Will lifted his eyes to mine, confusion in his expression. "Buy what?"

"This." I gestured at Carmen and put my lips to his ear. "You're hamming it up too much." I pulled back and gave Will a tug. "Come on, bro, leave her be."

Will said nothing. Instead he lifted his left hand and showed me the palm. It was covered in blood.

I frowned. "Where's that coming from?"

I looked down and saw where he had been pressing on her chest. I jerked backwards as if I'd been stung. There was blood on her shirt – fresh blood. Without Will's hand applying pressure, it was spreading, like an oil stain, over her chest and stomach.

"C-Car?" I started to tremble.

Lizzie glared poison at Grady. "You killed Carmen."

"She *deserved* it."

"You've killed *us*," Lizzie choked.

"Yeah, well, it's not like you ever did anything for me. Ben and Will were going to leave me out of their plan. *They* were trying to kill *you* a minute ago!"

"I wouldn't have…" My hands were on Carmen's chest now, helping Will as he tried to staunch the blood. I couldn't feel a heartbeat. She was already gone, but neither of us could stop.

"Yes, you would," Grady snapped. "You *were*."

"What about me?" Lizzie clutched her elbows. "I was your friend."

"Not one of you was my friend," Grady yelled. "You only let me join you for Duke of Edinburgh because my dad *made* you. You *laugh* at me." He calmed suddenly, as if a switch had been flicked and he was the same old Grady. "You never thought anything of me. Stupid conspiracy theorist. You never thought I'd be the winner." He shrugged. "Well, here I am. I'm going to be rich and powerful and I'll know *everything*."

Lizzie closed her eyes. "I liked you, Grady. We all did."

"Liar." Grady's voice was mild.

Finally, Will abandoned his efforts to save Carmen and got to his feet.

"I had *plans* for Carmen," he said. And for the

second time I heard true emotion in his voice – cold fury. "She was *mine*. You don't mess with *what's mine*. She was in my future."

"Well, now you don't have a future." Grady looked at the monitors. "Mr Gold, I've done what you asked." Sweat burst on to his upper lip. "Aren't you going to come and get me?"

The monitor remained quiet.

"He's still letting this play out," Will said. "Aren't you, Mr Gold? After all, there's more than one psychopath in the room." He offered his odd half-smile. Then he looked at me and Lizzie. "I've thought of a way we can get out of here."

"What?" Grady held up his hands. "Now listen – I did what you asked." He was still appealing to the monitors. "You offered a deal and *I* took it."

Will was looking at the two of us. "Right now, Gold has Grady. But if he doesn't have him…"

"Then we'll be back where we were a minute ago," Lizzie croaked. "Your hands around my neck. Don't think I've forgotten!"

Will shook his head firmly. "No. If we all kill Grady *together*, then we all win. He has to take the three of us."

384

"I'm not sure he *has* to do anything," I muttered. I was exhausted.

Will focused on Lizzie. "If anyone deserves to die, it's Grady. You know what he is now. See what he did to my Carmen? He's just standing there, waiting for Gold to take him away and kill the rest of us. Are you OK with that?"

Grady was backing away now, edging to the corner of the room. "*Mr Gold!*"

"You think there's an afterlife, Grady? You think you'll find the answers you want there?" Will stalked him, kicking the bloody penknife into the far corner as he passed it.

Lizzie dragged herself to her feet, her hands curled into claws. "Do you still feel like a winner?"

I stared at my own bloody hands. If I didn't join in, didn't help them kill Grady, I'd be next. Will was right, there was only one way out. I looked at Carmen. She lay facing the wall, her back to the rest of us, as if in death, she chose not to see us.

Gold, however, was watching the spectacle avidly, his eyes sparkling.

"*Mr Gold!*" Grady squeaked.

Will reached out and grabbed the front of his

shirt. There was a ripping sound as Grady twisted away.

Then another noise shattered the air – a high-pitched ding. We all jumped and I shook my arm to reveal Grandad's watch. It was shuddering on my wrist as the alarm sounded.

"The estuary," Lizzie said, with wonder in her voice. "The tide's going out, the crossing is rising." She grabbed Will's arm. "If we can get out, we can go home."

Will punched Grady as hard as he could in the forehead. Grady's head smacked back, cracked against the wall and he slid to the floor.

I lurched to my feet and staggered to the knife lying on the floor. It was slick in my hands, wet with Carmen's blood.

I picked it up.

Lizzie froze. "Ben, what are you doing?"

I staggered to the monitors and took the black wire in my fingers. The plastic surrounding it was almost tacky, organic.

"Worst case, it kills the lights and opens the door to the other teams," I said tiredly. "We can tell them what Gold really wants – that he intends for most of us to die in that plane crash."

"They'll *have* to be on our side." Lizzie's fingers went to her hair, twisting.

"It could kill the power and trap us here for ever," Will muttered.

I shrugged and placed the blade under the wire.

"Ben!" Lizzie cried out and I looked round. A yellowish gas was spreading into the room from the edges of the floor.

"Hurry, Ben!" Will pulled his T-shirt over his face and I saw Lizzie's pale belly as she did the same thing.

The gas rose faster than I could have imagined and I took a deep breath, trying to hold it as it started to fill the air.

I began to saw.

The blade was slippery, the wire strong, and my hands shaking.

Lizzie and Will met in the centre of the room, standing back to back.

My eyes watered.

Will collapsed to his knees.

With a final heave of my shoulders, I jerked hard and felt the knife bite into the sheath. Then I yanked my arm backwards and sliced through.

Instantly the bright lights flooding the room went out.

I could no longer see Lizzie or Will – or the gas. What would happen if I took a tiny breath? Flashes of red light burst inside my eyes as my body fought for air, and then a blue glow. It took me a moment to realize that the blue was some kind of emergency lighting.

I squinted into the dimness and heard, as much as saw, the click and shush of an opening door. Immediately fresher air started to dissipate the gas being piped into the room.

The monitors flickered and revealed Gold's face again.

Will was coughing. I could hear him over the hiss of the gas and realized he had fallen on his face. I pulled my T-shirt over my broken nose and stumbled across to him. I was running on empty; my adrenalin had gone; my body was on its last reserves. All I wanted to do was sleep. I found Will's arm and hoisted him up with a grunt.

There was a thud, a yell and footsteps on the stairs. Will was right, cutting the wire had opened the main door. The other teams were on their way.

Then Lizzie's face was next to mine. It seemed distorted – stretched out of all proportion, like a distended balloon. She was pointing frantically.

I turned to see her gesture at a second doorway, a rectangle that opened into darkness – one I hadn't seen before.

"A secret door," I said. "Secret door. Se-cret-door. See-crit—" The words tasted like insects scuttling across my tongue.

"It's the gas," Lizzie shouted. She caught my shoulder and shoved me towards the opening.

"Stop!" Gold ordered. "There's nothing for you that way. If you leave, I'll destroy you. I'll ruin your families – everyone you've ever cared about."

I showed him a middle finger and felt Will trying to regain his feet. "Come on, bro, we're going home."

I used the door frame to pull us into another corridor. The emergency lights turned everything blue, so that it was almost like swimming. Will coughed in my ear. Lizzie was ahead, holding on to the wall. The echoing corridor seemed endless, but we were definitely heading downhill; the clean air swept the gas from my lungs and I began to think more clearly.

Will took his own weight and I let him go. He looked back. "Can you hear them?"

"Yeah."

We weren't the only ones in the corridor.

I broke into a shambling run, pushing Lizzie to speed up. Behind us came an wailing howl: some jerk pretending to be a wolf. The sound was taken up by others and, despite myself, I trembled. Perhaps it was the gas, but it was all too easy to picture slavering beasts behind us, rather than kids our own age.

Not just kids. I shook my head. *Psychopaths.* More than one in each team.

Lizzie gave an exhausted sob, but I couldn't help her; I could barely keep moving myself. It felt as if I was falling – my body was numb from the waist down, my feet only moving because it was the last command I'd given them. I wasn't sure I even knew how to stop any more; only that if I did, I wouldn't get up again.

Abruptly the corridor ended. Somehow, I'd ended up in front. When had I overtaken Lizzie? I stared stupidly at the door in front of me.

"It's another door," I said.

Will came up behind me, then Lizzie.

"No! It's not *fair*." Lizzie collapsed against the door with a wail … and fell forwards into the light.

"It opened." I looked at Will. "It just … opened."

Will nodded and we stepped out into rain – where had the sun gone?

The door shut behind us and I looked back. Then I blinked. The door had vanished; in its place, nothing but a crack in a rock wall.

I looked down. I was standing on soaking shingle. I lifted my head, then I started to laugh. We had emerged on the edge of a beach, surrounded by cliffs. In front of us, sharp, tooth-like rocks were ranged in a half-circle and, still caught on a stone spur, tangled in the shrinking pools, I could see Grady's paracord belt.

"What is it?" Will frowned.

I could only point.

"You mean … we're back where we started?" Lizzie rasped.

I sniggered, then laughed. My sides ached and I held them tight, but I couldn't stop. I was hysterical.

Raindrops pattered hard on my forehead and ran down my face – cooling, refreshing. Ahead of us, the crossing was rising, straight edges appearing in the sand. In the far distance, a splash of red – a phone box, civilization.

Lizzie dragged a hand through her short hair and her eyes were haunted. I saw with shame that silenced me that her throat was bruised. "We have to get back to the first checkpoint if we want to use Gold's crossing. The tide isn't all the way out either."

She was right. Although patches of wet sand were dotting the distance, the water near us was still at least neck-high; the currents would be too dangerous if we tried to leave now. I nodded. "The only way off this beach was up that cliff, remember?" I swallowed. "I'm not sure I can climb it right now."

"We don't have a choice," Will said.

Lizzie nodded. I looked behind me. The door had closed on Curtis's howls, but he had to be right behind us.

Chapter Twenty-four

Lizzie propelled herself into movement; small, jerky actions as she started to make her way across the rocks. With no alternative, my feet doing as they always had, I followed her, slipping and sliding on the barbed crags. Will was right behind me. We just had to stay far enough ahead to get to the crossing in front of our pursuers.

The noise as Curtis and his team tumbled out of the door was sudden and brutal. Yipping and yowling, they broke into the rain.

Lizzie twitched as if she was going to clutch my arm, then she wrapped her arms around herself instead. I looked back at Will, who tiredly raised a hand. For the first time, I noticed how pale he was; his grey eyes almost colourless, his hair hanging in wet and greasy hanks.

Curtis was first out. His blue eyes bulged and his freckles stood out like scars. He raised both fists and grinned, his howl cutting off mid-bellow.

"The crossing is raised," Lizzie called. "We can *all* get out of here."

"Yeah?" Curtis stepped nearer. The rain slicked his wiry hair to his head and streamed down his face. Behind him the skinny lad showed his teeth.

"Yes! There's no one here to stop us leaving. We can go home. It's over."

Curtis kept moving towards Will.

"Will," I called. "Careful."

Will cleared his throat. "Before we leave, we should make a pact of silence. We don't tell anyone what happened here. No one has to pay. We leave, then go our separate ways. We never have to see each other again."

"That so?" Curtis said.

Lizzie started to retreat towards the sea. Spray splashed my calves as waves were pushed against the rocks, only to be pulled free with the sound of a toddler with a straw. The clouds overhead were so grey that the day seemed later than it was, colour bleeding into the chattering rain.

Will headed for me, but kept his eyes on Curtis. "What do you think?"

Curtis sniffed. "Here's the thing, *mate*. Gold's made a pretty good offer. We bring you back in and we get a million pounds each, no question. No need to look at our time through the checkpoints – we just win."

"He's lying," Lizzie called. "There's only one winner – Gold already told us so. The rest of us get gassed."

"Yeah, right!" Curtis laughed.

"There was gas in the room with the monitors. Didn't it affect you? Couldn't you smell it?" I was at the edge of the rocks now with Lizzie and we had nowhere left to go. The tide was going out but we couldn't risk walking across the sand without using the crossing; it was too dangerous. The sea looked like it was chest-high now, but if we tried to swim for it, we'd be swept away.

Curtis snorted. "You think I'm stupid? You're coming with us." There were six of them now. I don't know what had happened to the others. The groups had naturally split into two, the remains of Reece's team and that of Curtis's. And now they were closing in on us from two directions. Only two choices: go back with Curtis or into the sea.

I met Will's eyes. He gave a slight nod, then he raced towards me and together the three of us leaped into the waves.

The wind lifted me forwards and then bitter cold slammed into me as I hit the water. My ankle jarred as I landed half on a submerged rock and slipped sideways. Will grabbed my shoulder and steadied me, but the current was already pulling.

Lizzie turned her pale face to mine and I grabbed her elbow; if we stuck close, forged forwards together, we might prove stronger than the current. We had to be lucky, but if we aimed for the bobbing buoys, we would intercept the crossing.

We started out, away from the rocks, Will in front. Seaweed dragged against my legs and the further from the rock we waded, the more strongly the invisible hands grasping at my knees hauled me sideways.

"Come back!" Curtis yelled. He spotted Grady's forgotten belt, grabbed it and swung it over his head. "Catch this and I'll pull you in."

We ignored him.

"*Take it!*" Curtis roared. Then he wrapped the cord around his own waist and chucked it back to the skinny lad. "Hold this, Elliot."

He followed us into the sea. Lizzie's shoulders heaved and I realized that she was crying silently.

My feet went out from under me and I gasped, inhaling water. I spluttered and waved madly, but there was nothing to catch hold of. I was yanked sideways, then Lizzie's hand was on mine, pulling at me, but who was holding on to her?

I slammed into a rock beneath the water and then scrambled back to my feet. Lizzie crashed into my chest and I wrapped my arms around her while I looked frantically for Will. He was still standing where I had been, Curtis approaching.

"This way," I waved furiously. "I'll catch you."

Will offered me his odd half-smile. "I can't."

"Yes, you can," Lizzie yelled. "Let the current take you."

"I can't," Will repeated.

"What do you mean you *can't*?" My gut twisted.

"I'm not going anywhere." Will spread his hands and I saw that he was lower in the water than he had been. Quicksand.

Curtis staggered to a stop, holding tightly to the paracord, frowning.

397

"No!" I tried to push off from the rock holding us in place, but Lizzie shoved me back down.

"Don't struggle, Will," she yelled.

Will rolled his eyes.

Curtis folded his arms. "We just have to wait for the tide to go out and there you'll be – trapped in the sand."

Elliot giggled at the end of the rope.

"I'm coming!" I tried to push off again and Lizzie punched me in the nose. An explosion of agony and I was blind. I tasted blood.

When I could see again, Lizzie was glaring at me. "You *can't* get him out."

"She's right." Will was shivering, his lips almost blue with cold. "You can't. But you *can* go for help." He looked at Curtis. "They can't touch me until the water's gone down. At least I'm marking the quicksand for you. Get to the crossing. Run to Fetlar, tell someone what's happened and bring them here."

"Will…"

"He's right." Lizzie's voice was soft.

Curtis sneered. "You two can't go any further until the tide's out. You're *all* coming back to Gold."

I looked at Lizzie and she looked at me. All I could see were her blue eyes, rimmed with black lashes, her short dark hair plastered to her pale face. It could be my last chance to speak to her.

"What happened back there, that wasn't *me*," I insisted.

"I—"

"Listen." I closed my eyes and the words fell out of me. "Here's the truth." I caught my breath. "I love you. Not just because you're beautiful," I opened my eyes and touched her cold cheek, "but because you get angry with me when I skateboard without you, and because you hum old songs when you're concentrating, and you fiddle with your hair when you're worried. I love you so much it hurts to breathe. When you're happy, I am, too, because I love your smile. And you're smarter than me, which is hot. And you make me laugh, and I need that."

It was her turn to close her eyes.

"We're going to die, Lizzie. Please – tell me you feel something for me."

She was silent and my heart broke a little.

"If you don't … it's OK. I'll always be your best friend. But throw me a line here. Say … *some*thing."

"We're *not* going to die." Lizzie opened her eyes again. "I love you, Ben, and we're not going to die."

She twisted out of my grip and started to swim.

For a few heartbeats, I clung on to the rock and watched her, gaping. The rain pounded mercilessly on her head, and she kicked and pulled determinedly towards the floating buoys.

Curtis and his team started to yell again and I looked back at Will.

He tilted his head. "Stop mothering me, Ben. Go!"

"I'll come back for you – do you hear me?"

Will nodded, then I launched from the rock and started after Lizzie.

The rain lashed into my eyes, but all I had to do was keep myself pointed towards that crossing.

I focused on Lizzie's kicking legs, unable to see how far we had travelled. The current tugged and pulled, heaving me sideways, and my shoulders ached. I decided to put my feet down, to wade for a while.

I dropped my legs, and water went into my mouth. There was no seabed. My eyes widened and I propelled myself back to a swimming position, trying to see. The current had taken us and I could barely locate the crossing now.

And where was Lizzie? I looked around frantically. While I had been submerged, she had disappeared. "Lizzie!" I yelled. There was no answer.

I had to keep swimming. I kicked and pulled. A bigger island was in view, a grey hump through the rain. I had to get there, to save Will. To expose Gold.

Suddenly, through a weary haze, it struck me – if I didn't expose him, Gold would win. In a decade or so, he would be at the head of a global power run by business people with no conscience, all completely under his control. He'd be king of the world.

I set my jaw and swam harder. The sea clutched me with icy black hands, trying to drag me out to its depths. I couldn't let it defeat me. I kicked and pulled, kicked and pulled. Where was Lizzie?

My whole world shrank to just my arms and legs, stroking and kicking; I had a future with Lizzie and I would not let Gold win.

End

Mum's voice, calling at me to get up. I had to watch Will while she ran to the corner shop.

I groaned and rolled. Or tried to. My limbs were not receiving messages. It felt as though I were made of sand: soggy and crumbling. "He's almost seventeen," I wanted to say, but I couldn't speak.

My eyes were glued together. I tried to blink and couldn't make them move. My right cheek was crushed into my pillow, my left was wet.

I didn't remember getting home, but I must have done. Mum was insistent.

Was Lizzie OK? I tried to sit up, but my battered body ignored me. Was I sick? That would explain why I couldn't remember. *I should be in hospital, shouldn't I?* I twitched – it was all the movement I could make.

Mum's voice again, angrier now. I tried to respond; my throat was closed. I coughed. Spasms went through my chest. I spat and twitched again. *Yes, I should be in a hospital.*

Finally, I managed to open one eye. Bright sunlight was streaming in through my curtains. I winced and closed it again.

Slowly I reopened my eye. Something was nagging at my attention, something … not quite right.

The brightness faded slightly as I got used to the stabbing light. A gull sat on a stone in front of me, cawing angrily.

A gull?

Now I moved. I managed to get on to my elbows.

I wasn't home.

I rubbed sand and grit out of my eyes, and rose painfully to my knees. I ached everywhere. How long had I been out? Where was I?

Slowly my mind caught up with my body. Gold! That's right. I had to get help. The current had taken me to a shore. Now all I had to do was find someone. I swayed on to my feet and turned round, seeking some kind of clue to show me which direction to go.

Then I fell back to my knees.

On the beach in front of me was a plane. A small passenger plane with one broken wing. There was a burning smell and the wreckage was blackened.

Some of the seats had been torn from the plane in the crash. Carmen lay on one. There was a spur of metal sticking out of her chest and the whole of one of her arms was missing. Her pink-tipped hair was splayed over her face. I began to retch.

Others lay around the plane. Some in seats, some out. Wang An was lying on top of one wing, his body spattered in sand. The girls, Somia and Pasha, were curled up together as if they were asleep. Curtis was there, his red hair splashed with blood, his freckles pale. There was no sign of his friend, Elliot.

Finally, I located Will. He was inside the plane. I tottered towards him, hands outstretched, whispering his name.

His hair was hanging over his face and there was a large bloody bruise on his forehead. He wasn't moving or breathing. His usually mobile hands were utterly still.

I looked for a reaction, but I was empty – as if my soul had been hollowed out with a spoon. I staggered backwards, then turned to the beach.

"Lizzie!" I screamed her name. Where was she?

I found her in the water. Tangled in a seatbelt, her

legs were trapped beneath the fuselage and her face was half-submerged. Her blue eyes were closed, her lips slightly parted.

I fought to pull her free and then dragged her into my arms. I kissed her, gently, on the lips, half-thinking it would wake her. She was rigid and chill.

"Lizzie?" I pleaded.

They were all dead. All of them. It was so real, so unquestionable that I started to wonder – had we actually been in a plane crash? Had the last three days been a … nightmare?

Then I realized that someone else was missing.

Grady.

"Hello, Ben."

I turned. He stood there, clean and showered.

"I've been waiting for you to wake up. Guess who's been given his first job?" And he walked towards me, smiling.

Acknowledgements

There are many people whose hard work goes into making a book, too many to thank, but special mention must go to my father-in-law, Charles Pearce, who, by telling me all about geocaching one day, sparked off the idea for *Savage Island*. *What if you were geocaching*, I thought, as he explained it all, *and you found a finger in the box?*

Writing inspiration comes from a hundred different places, but this time, it came from Charles.

Thanks also to all the schools that I visited with this very idea – "What do you think would be in the boxes?" I asked them, "and what would you do, if it meant winning a million pounds?"

And thanks to my nephew, Ben, who gave me information about his time doing the Duke of Edinburgh's Award and who told me that at the first geocache, he would have given up a tooth.

Thanks to my editor, Ruth Bennett, and the wonderful design team at Stripes, and to my agent, Catherine Pellegrino, whose help and support is beyond price.

Thanks also to friends and family, who have tolerated me along the way. Particularly to my husband, Andy, and children, Maisie and Riley. Always filling my heart.

And to the other authors who have been shoulders to cry on, voices of sanity and cheerleaders. You're all amazing!

Thank you.

ISBN: 978-1-84715-722-0

At least £1 from every copy sold
will go directly to Crisis.

BRAND
NEW
STORIES
&
POETRY
ABOUT
CHANGE

A CHANGE IS GONNA COME

MARY BELLO • AISHA BUSHBY • TANYA BYRNE
INUA ELLAMS • CATHERINE JOHNSON
PATRICE LAWRENCE • AYISHA MALIK • IRFAN MASTER
MUSA OKWONGA • YASMIN RAHMAN
PHOEBE ROY • NIKESH SHUKLA

ISBN: 978-1-84715-839-0

"One of the best anthologies for young adults."
Wei Ming Kam

FROZEN CHARLOTTE
ALEX BELL

ISBN: 978-1-84715-453-8

SLEEPLESS
LOU MORGAN

ISBN: 978-1-84715-455-2

DARK ROOM
TOM BECKER

ISBN: 978-1-84715-457-6

BAD BONES
GRAHAM MARKS

ISBN: 978-1-84715-454-5

FLESH and BLOOD
SIMON CHESHIRE

ISBN: 978-1-84715-456-9

THE HAUNTING
ALEX BELL

ISBN: 978-1-84715-458-3

FIR
SHARON GOSLING

ISBN: 978-1-84715-823-9

CHARLOTTE SAYS
ALEX BELL

ISBN: 978-1-84715-840-6

RED EYE
Do you dare?